D0039882

## Praise for *Welcome to Last Chance*

"A wonderful debut novel. . . . Readers will enjoy the simplicity of *Welcome to Last Chance* and the complexity of Lainie's character."

—***New York Journal of Books***

"Cathleen Armstrong's debut novel is a warm-hearted look at ordinary people living out genuine faith."

—**Crosswalk.com**

"With equal parts hope, charm, and tender faith, Cathleen Armstrong spins a tale as warm and welcoming as a roadside cafe on a dusty highway. Exit from the fast lane and visit Last Chance. It's a place you won't soon forget."

—**Lisa Wingate**, bestselling and award-winning author of *Firefly Island* and *Blue Moon Bay*

## Praise for *One More Last Chance*

WITHDRAWN

"Armstrong continues her A Place to Call Home series with this sweet romance that features vivid descriptions of the Southwestern landscape, colorful supporting characters, and engaging relationships subtly shaped by Christian faith."

—***Booklist***

"A gentle love story with a cozy feel. . . . It boasts well-crafted characters who feel like old friends, and its theme of hope leaves readers with the knowledge that for everyone, there really can be one more last chance. This tale is recommended for all fans of sweet and light romances."

—***Library Journal***

## Praise for *At Home in Last Chance*

"Armstrong breathes fresh life into the familiar faces and places of Last Chance as she introduces new characters with their own compelling problems and continues, with satisfying results, ongoing plotlines. Once again, Armstrong demonstrates her gift for capturing tiny details and creating moments of descriptive magic that will captivate new and returning readers."

—***Booklist***

"Devotees of Armstrong's series will be thrilled to return to this small town. First-time readers will be delightfully entertained as the author carefully weaves plot threads with details of each character's backstory so that one can jump easily in with this installment. Fans of Melody Carlson will be quick to snatch up this entry that is full of adventure, romance, and fun."

—***Library Journal***

# Last Chance Hero

## Books by Cathleen Armstrong

A Place to Call Home Series

*Welcome to Last Chance*

*One More Last Chance*

*At Home in Last Chance*

*Last Chance Hero*

A Place to Call Home #4

# Last Chance Hero

A Novel

Cathleen Armstrong

Revell
a division of Baker Publishing Group
Grand Rapids, Michigan

© 2015 by Cathleen Armstrong

Published by Revell
a division of Baker Publishing Group
P.O. Box 6287, Grand Rapids, MI 49516-6287
www.revellbooks.com

Printed in the United States of America

All rights reserved. No part of this publication may be reproduced, stored in a retrieval system, or transmitted in any form or by any means—for example, electronic, photocopy, recording—without the prior written permission of the publisher. The only exception is brief quotations in printed reviews.

Library of Congress Cataloging-in-Publication Data
Armstrong, Cathleen.
Last chance hero : a novel / Cathleen Armstrong.
pages ; cm. — (A place to call home ; 4)
ISBN 978-0-8007-2647-8 (softcover)
1. Self-realization—Fiction. I. Title.
PS3601.R5747L38 2015
813′.6—dc23 2015020132

This book is a work of fiction. Names, characters, places, and incidents are the product of the author's imagination or are used fictitiously. Any resemblance to actual events, locales, or persons, living or dead, is coincidental.

15 16 17 18 19 20 21 7 6 5 4 3 2 1

For my mother,
Elizabeth

# 1

Good morning, and welcome to Last Chance." Rita Sandoval, owner and manager of the Last Chance Motel as well as the town's mayor and chief booster, tucked her pencil back behind her ear and smiled up at Dr. Jessica MacLeod. "I know you're going to love it here."

"I hope so. I'm counting on it." Jess found the big urn of coffee in the corner of the motel lobby and filled a Styrofoam cup to the brim. Cradling it between her hands, she gazed out the front window. The sky had just begun to lighten an hour ago when she began her run, but now the sun was fully up, spilling its light over the desert, shading the distant mountains in blue and purple and the nearby desert floor in sage green and gold. Over it all arched a sky of such brilliant turquoise that it almost hurt to look at it, so different from the gray and foggy mornings she knew in San Francisco. She took a sip of her coffee. *Oh, I do hope so, because there's no turning back now.*

"Well, I wish I had time today to take you around and introduce you to everyone." Rita picked up a clipboard from her desk and stood up. "Ordinarily, that's just what I'd do, but I'm afraid I've got to get right over to the Dip 'n' Dine and start getting set up for our fiesta tonight."

"That's okay. I'll meet everybody eventually. It's not like I'm just passing through."

"You should come with me." Rita slung her purse over her shoulder. "It's only a couple blocks from here, and you're going to want some breakfast anyway. Have you eaten at the Dip 'n' Dine yet? Well, I'm here to tell you that you are about to eat some of the best food you'll ever put in your mouth. Carlos, the cook, has been famous in these parts for years, and he and Chris Reed, the new owner, are doing some great things. Chris was a big chef up in Albuquerque before he bought the place, you know, and it took him a little while to find his footing here, but now there's just no holding 'em back. This fiesta tonight is just one of a series of food and live music events we've been having all summer. This one's called Red Chile and Bluegrass."

Still talking, Rita put the "Back Soon" placard in the window, ushered Jess outside, locked the front door, and headed across the parking lot at a brisk pace. Jess's choices were either calling after Rita that she was staying behind or going along. Going along with Rita seemed the easier course of action, and as Jess hurried to catch up, she wondered if most people didn't find going along with Rita the easier route.

"Oh, there's Manny Baca opening up Otero Gas and Oil. You'll want to meet him. He's got three little kids, twin girls and a boy. He bought Otero's from his father-in-law last spring, so by rights, it should be called Baca's now, but once something takes hold in Last Chance, it's hard to change it." She waved her hand over her head as she led Jess across the road. "Manny, I want you to meet our new doctor. This is Dr. Jessica MacLeod. She's opening an office right here in Last Chance. What do you think about that?"

"I think it sounds great." Manny grinned and offered his hand. "We've been wearing a groove in the Last Chance highway getting our kids back and forth to the pediatrician in San Ramon for one thing and another. I'm not sure what Patsy would think about changing doctors, though. He's been taking care of us for years."

"I'm not here to raid anyone's practice." Jess liked the wide smile and firm handshake of the proprietor of Otero Gas and Oil, although he did seem way too young to be a business owner and father of three. "I've joined the family practice at San Ramon Medical Center, and I'll have a satellite office here in Last Chance."

"Well, we've got places to go and things to do." Rita's stated purpose in crossing the road had been to introduce Manny, and clearly, since that objective had been met, it was time to move along. "We'll see you all this evening at Red Chile and Bluegrass, right?"

"Wouldn't miss it. Nice meeting you, Doc." He lifted his hand in a wave and turned back toward his office as Rita led Jess back across the road.

"Now, up ahead across the road is Last Chance's newest business establishment, Desert Sage. It's a beauty salon, and I'm here to tell you that Kaitlyn Reed, who owns it, can do anything. Don't think for a minute that just because ninety percent of the people who come out of there have wash-and-set perms, she doesn't know what's what. She just knows how to give her customers what they want, that's all. She's from Scottsdale and only moved here because her brother's here. I told you about him; he's the one who bought the Dip 'n' Dine. Oh, good. It looks like the place is full."

They had reached the parking lot of the Dip 'n' Dine, and Jess found herself wondering how someone could walk so fast and talk so much and not be out of breath. Rita had to be at least sixty.

"Hey, everybody, I want you to meet our new doctor. This is Dr. Jessica MacLeod." Rita's voice carried well, even through the buzz of conversation and clatter of dishes. Silence fell as everyone stopped eating and looked toward the door Rita had just blown through with Jess in tow. "I know. You all think she doesn't look old enough to be a doctor, but she is, and a good one too from everything I hear. She'll have an office right here on Main Street, and for starters she'll be here three days a week and in San Ramon for two. Right, Doctor?"

"That's right." Jess tried to smile but was suddenly extremely aware that this was not how she had planned to meet the people of Last Chance and her future patients. All she had wanted when she stopped in the office of the Last Chance Motel after her run was a cup of coffee. She was wearing shorts, running shoes, and a Beat Stanford T-shirt. Her strawberry blonde hair was pulled off her face in a stubby ponytail, and she could almost feel every last freckle beaming from her scrubbed face. What had she been thinking to follow Rita down the street looking like that?

Everyone smiled, some called "Welcome," and all went back to their breakfasts. Jess felt a tap on her arm.

"I need to talk to Chris about the fiesta tonight, so I'm going to set you right here at the counter, if that's all right. You'll want to meet Andy anyway. He's our new high school football coach. Andy, this is our new doctor, Jessica MacLeod."

"Morning." Andy put down his fork and extended his hand. "Welcome to Last Chance. I hope you'll be happy here."

"Thanks. I'm pretty sure I will be."

A woman wearing a name tag that read "Juanita" appeared on the other side of the counter and beamed a wide smile as she poured coffee Jess had not yet asked for into the cup sitting in front her. "Mornin', I'm Juanita Sheppard. Welcome to Last Chance. It's about time we got our own doctor. Of course, Russ and I have had the same doctor in San Ramon since our kids were little, so you probably won't be seeing much of us. At least not professionally."

"Well then, I hope we'll be seeing each other on a nonprofessional level." Jess returned the smile, but she did notice that Juanita was the second person she had met in the last twenty minutes who expressed delight that Last Chance was finally getting its own doctor and told her she could look for patients elsewhere in the same breath.

"Oh, I don't doubt that for a minute. The Dip 'n' Dine is the heart and soul of this town, and I'm here just about every day. Just come on in and I'll be happy to introduce you to folks." She slid a menu across the counter toward Jess. "Although I'm sure you've already heard of Andy, here. This is Andrew Ryan. Quarterback for the Denver Broncos?"

"Um, I'm afraid I don't follow football very closely." Jess looked back at Andy and shrugged. "Sorry. I know I should know who you are."

"Not necessarily. I spent a whole lot more time on the bench than on the field." Andy's grin was rueful. "And as of the end of last season, it looks like I'm out of football for good. At least out of professional football."

"Well, their loss is our gain, that's all I can say." Juanita pulled out her order pad and cocked her head as she looked at Jess. "You say you don't follow football? Huh. What'll you have for breakfast?"

Jessica hadn't had time to even open the menu, but she had been in diners before and knew from experience that there wouldn't be a whole lot on the menu that she wanted to eat. "I guess I'll just have a single poached egg and some dry wheat toast."

"Alrighty. Red or green?"

"Red or green?"

"You want red or green chile with that egg?" Juanita didn't look up from her order pad.

"Neither. Just the egg and toast, please."

This time Juanita did look up. "Neither? Huh." She tore off the order and put it on the rack in the window to the kitchen. Tucking the pad back in her apron pocket, she headed back to the dining room with the coffeepot, but not before giving Jessica one last curious look.

"Well, that was a little awkward. I feel like I made a giant misstep somewhere, but I'm not sure where."

Andy swiveled his stool around and leaned his elbow on the counter. "Well, I'll tell you. Football's pretty big around here, my short lusterless career notwithstanding. Same with chile. It's not whether you want chile that's the question. It's what color. Juanita probably never met anyone who doesn't care about either."

"Oh." Jess shrugged again and took a sip of her coffee. "Well, now she has."

Andy raised one eyebrow. "You are a brave woman." He gestured at Jess's T-shirt with his chin. "You must have been at least a little interested in football at some point. That's some rivalry you're sporting."

Jess looked down at her faded blue Beat Stanford shirt. "Oh, this? I think it was one of my roommate's when I was an undergrad. I don't know how I wound up with it. I know I didn't buy it. In fact, I didn't make it to a single game the entire time I went to Cal."

"You're kidding." Andy leaned back for a better look. "Not one game in four years?"

"No." Jess was starting to feel a little warm. "Is there something wrong with that? I'm beginning to feel like I have a horn growing out of my forehead or something."

"Oh, no. You might run into someone around here with a horn growing out of their forehead, but someone who doesn't like football? Now, that's weird."

Jess looked closely at Andy. He did not appear to be kidding. A little flare of anger shot up between her shoulder blades and made her neck prickle. For one thing, she didn't believe him. Sure, you could expect the high school football coach, and a former pro no less, to think football was the be-all and end-all of life. Juanita probably wasn't his only fan either. But surely grown-ups in Last Chance—Manny Baca, for example, with his three kids and his service station, and Rita Sandoval, who was mayor as well as the owner of the motel—had other things to think about than a bunch of high school kids and their football game.

"Well, I suppose I should get used to being a curiosity then." She cradled her coffee cup in her hands, wondering how rude it would be if she got up and moved a stool or two down the counter.

"Here you go." Juanita set her toast and egg in front of her. "And I went ahead and brought you a little green chile anyway. You don't have to eat it, of course, but honey, if you're going to live in Last Chance, you really need to learn to eat chile. It's who we are and what we do around here."

"So I hear." Jess's smile felt stiff. She lifted the egg to the toast with her spoon while Juanita watched, and when she realized what Juanita must be waiting for, added just a touch of the chile. No need to alienate every single person she met today.

The chile was hotter than she expected, but the creamy yolk quickly soothed the heat. It was the chile's flavor, though, that really took her by surprise. Rich and sharp, it bore no resemblance whatsoever to the pallid, tasteless green stuff she had spooned from cans.

"This is really good!" She looked up at Juanita with a real smile.

"Thought you'd like it." Juanita gave a brisk nod as she picked up a couple more plates off the shelf to take to a booth by the window. "You just need to learn to try new things, that's all."

Jess turned to her breakfast as Juanita disappeared. Actually, she had been under the impression that leaving Marin County in California and heading out to a tiny town in southwestern New Mexico to begin her practice was pretty darned adventurous, although some of her friends and relatives used other terms ranging from ill-advised to downright crazy. But hey, what was pulling up stakes and moving a thousand miles from home compared to eating green chile with your eggs?

"I'm sorry. Didn't mean to make you mad." Andy's voice interrupted her thoughts. "I've known lots of people who didn't like football."

"Really." Jess barely glanced at him. All she wanted was to finish her breakfast and get back to her room.

"Well, actually, not a lot, but I've known some. A few. Three, maybe. No, not that many, but there was this one girl . . . Nope, now that I think about it, she was just mad at her boyfriend and he was on the team. I guess when you get right down to it, there's just you. You're the only one."

Jess's fork stopped halfway to her mouth as she turned to stare. Seriously? What was his problem? Was he really expecting everyone he met to fall at his feet in admiration because he knew how to throw a football, or kick one, or whatever quarterbacks did with footballs?

Andy met her gaze with a look both grave and sorrowful. She shook her head and was about to dismiss him for good and turn back to her breakfast when she noticed the little crinkles around his brown eyes and the tiny twitch at the corner of his mouth. She narrowed her eyes, and Andy's grin broke through.

"I am sorry. Truly." He laughed. "I'm not being very neighborly, am I? Truth is, you're welcome here in Last Chance. We are glad you came. Honest."

Andy's grin was infectious, and as annoyed as Jess had been with him a minute before, she found herself returning it.

"Friends?" Andy stuck out his hand.

Jess slipped her hand in his. "Friends, I think."

"Are you about done?" Rita came up behind Jess and put her

hand on her shoulder. "They're fixing to bring the tables and chairs over from the church, and I need to get over there and see about that. You can come if you want."

"I think I'll walk on back to the motel, but thanks."

"Got your key?"

Jess patted her pocket. "Right here."

"All right then. See you after a while." Rita headed out the door, and Jess could see her waving her hand over her head and calling to someone as she strode across the parking lot.

"Rita is a dynamo, isn't she?" Jess turned to Andy with a smile.

"Wait till you get to know her better. Dynamos come to sit at her feet and learn."

"I'll just bet."

Jess forked in the last bite of eggs and toast as Juanita appeared on the other side of the counter.

"Here, let me give you these checks." She placed one ticket on the counter in front of Jess and another in front of Andy. "You don't need to rush, but we'll be closing here in a minute to get ready for the big shindig tonight, so if you don't mind, I'll just run these for you now."

Jess had a panicked second or two as she looked around for her purse before she remembered where it was—safely tucked in the top drawer of the dresser in Room 3 of the Last Chance Motel. Her hand flew to her mouth.

"Oh my goodness, Juanita, I don't have any money. I went for a run this morning and then stopped by the motel office for some coffee, and before I could think to grab my purse, Rita brought me here. If you can give me twenty minutes, I'll run back and get my wallet. I am so, so embarrassed!"

Juanita flapped a hand. "Don't worry about it. I'll just catch you next time. It's not a big deal."

"Let me." Andy picked up Jess's check, added his own, and

handed them both to Juanita with a couple bills he pulled from his wallet. "Don't need any change."

"No, I can't let you do that." Jess made a grab for the ticket, but Juanita had already whisked it away. She turned back to Andy with a resigned sigh. "Well, thank you, although I'd have been happy to go get my purse."

"I know, but this'll save you a trip. It's getting hot out there." He stood up as Jess slid from her stool and followed her to the door. "Can I give you a ride? Truck's air-conditioned."

Jess's first inclination was to say thanks but no thanks. She had already taken enough from Andy for one day, from the hard time he gave her about football to the price of breakfast, but he was right about one thing. It was hot, and getting hotter. And hot in Last Chance was nothing like hot in San Francisco. She hesitated just a second. "Thanks, I'd appreciate that."

It was only a couple minutes' drive before Andy's truck pulled into the driveway of the Last Chance Motel, and he used the entire time talking about the Red Chile and Bluegrass fiesta that night at the Dip 'n' Dine.

"Everyone for miles around comes. Tickets sell out as soon as they go on sale. They set up tables outside and there's live music and the best food you'll ever eat. And every one of these fiestas has a different kind of music. Tonight is bluegrass, of course, but they've had jazz, and classic rock 'n' roll, and I think they're planning one to coincide with the chile harvest called 'It's Chile Country.'"

Jess had a feeling she knew where this was heading and tried to forestall it by opening the pickup door and starting to get out. "Sounds like you'll have a lot of fun. Thanks for the ride."

"So, can I pick you up? About 7:00?"

"I don't have a ticket, and if they're sold out . . ." Jess finished her thought with a shrug. "But thanks anyway."

"But I do." Andy leaned across the seat with a grin. "The town council gave me two tickets when I got here. Sort of a welcome home. And one of them will just go to waste if you don't use it."

"I don't think so, Andy." Jess wanted to make her own place in Last Chance, and she had no intention of turning up tonight on the arm of the local football hero. "But thanks again."

She started to swing the door shut, but Andy stopped her. "Wait."

Jess stopped. She was really beginning to get annoyed. Andy may have still been in the cool cab of his truck, but she was standing in the heat of a gravel parking lot. The hum of her window air conditioner six feet away called her, and she longed for a shower.

"Here." Andy opened his glove box and pulled out a slip of card stock. "It's my extra ticket. It will just go to waste if you don't use it. If I see you there, I can introduce you to a few people. Or not. But if you go, I'm pretty sure you won't be sorry."

He lifted his hand in a little salute as he leaned back behind the wheel before shifting into Drive. Jess heard the tires take hold in the gravel as she pulled her key from her pocket and fitted it into the lock. What had she gotten herself into? Since a family vacation through the Southwest when she was in middle school, she had dreamed of practicing medicine in a place like Last Chance. The research she had done on rural medicine, southwestern New Mexico, and the San Ramon Medical Center before she made her final choice was detailed and exhaustive. That's how she did things. How then had she failed to consider that there were people involved, with their own thoughts and ideas about her work? The answer came to her, and she winced as the door opened and a blast of overchilled and slightly stale air engulfed her. Because all too often, the one element she left out when making her minutely detailed plans was other people.

# 2

Except for the fact that it stood empty and deserted, Last Chance High looked exactly as it had ten years earlier when Andy and the rest of his class filed onto the football field in caps and gowns while the marching band played "Pomp and Circumstance." It was the same long, low, series of windowless brick buildings, built at a time in the mid-twentieth century when it was considered prudent to have a school that could also serve as a bomb shelter, should the need arise. Still guarding the front courtyard, a bronze puma, ears back and teeth bared, snarled from a brick pedestal.

Andy drove around to the back of the school and parked by the gym under the freshly painted "Reserved for Coach Ryan" sign. For a moment he just sat and watched the water from the sprinklers shoot back and forth across the field. In country where only sage and cactus grew unless coaxed, the football field lay like an emerald, closely trimmed and pampered as any hothouse orchid.

"Well, might as well see what we've got." Andy got out of his truck and let himself into the athletic complex. Newer than the rest of the school, it had been built in what had come to be known as the Glory Days, those eighty-four games without a loss, spanning nine years, when the team could do no wrong and the town stood ready to give them everything they could possibly want or need. Andy had been right in the middle of that, leading a team so invincible that each of them knew in their hearts that no obstacle life could ever throw in their path could stand before them.

Trophy cases ran along one wall of the main lobby, and Andy stopped in front of them. A row of trophies filled one shelf, and behind each trophy hung a team picture. He leaned in for a better look. Who told them not to smile? Someone must have, because each boy stood or knelt, team jersey stretched over shoulder pads and helmet tucked under his arm, wearing the fierce scowl of a warrior. A small smile tugged at the corner of Andy's mouth, and he shook his head.

"Oh, man, we were so young. What in the world did we know?"

Behind him, the door opened and he turned to find Russ Sheppard, president of the Boosters, coming in.

"Hey, Coach. I thought that was your truck turning off the road up ahead of me." He gestured toward the trophy case with his chin. "So, what do you think? Are we going to get any of that back?"

"Those were some days, weren't they?" Andy turned back to the case. "Something like that happens once in a lifetime, if that. Sometimes I can't believe I got to be part of it."

"You were a lot more than part of it, son." Russ clapped him on the shoulder. "You made a whole bunch of it happen. And I'll tell you what, we're looking for big things to happen again now that you're here."

"Wait a minute, Russ." Andy held up a hand and stepped back. "I think your expectations might be just a tad high there. I can promise you my best, but right now, that's all I can promise."

"And that's all we ask." Russ smiled and clapped Andy's shoulder one more time. "You're right. That win streak was a once in a lifetime thing, and we're all mighty proud it took place right here in Last Chance. Just give us what you've got. That's all you've ever done, but it's been enough to get the job done."

"So what do we have to work with this year?" Andy began to move toward his office, and Russ fell in alongside him. "I saw film, of course, but I don't know any of these guys. They were, what, first and second graders when I left Last Chance?"

"You've got some good boys. Some of them show a lot of promise. Of course, it's nothing like when you were here, but maybe they just need some good coaching."

"Russ, you need to listen to me." Andy stopped with his hand on the door. "With one breath you're telling me that you know the Glory Days were a once in a lifetime thing and all you want from me is my best—which you know you'll have—and with the next you're talking like you can see it all unfolding like it did back then. I'm telling you right now, this is a different time and a different team. It's not fair to them to saddle them with a lot of expectations."

"I know that." Russ followed when Andy walked into his office. "And I know it's not fair to you either. But you've got to remember, these boys cut their teeth on the Glory Days. They may not remember much about that time, but they've heard about it, and you, all their lives. I realize things have changed. The town's a lot smaller than it was back then. Heck, we're not even in the same division we were in when you were here, but these boys are hungry. They're going to give you a hundred and fifty percent. You wait and see."

Andy looked around the spare office without answering. How many times could he caution Russ against saddling the team with a lot of ten-year-old dreams, and how many times could Russ assure him one minute he wouldn't and then in the next let his longing for the return of the Glory Days spill all over the place? Russ wasn't alone in that either. Nearly everyone he had seen since coming back to Last Chance had found some way to work it into the conversation.

"Looks like someone did a little decorating." Andy gestured

toward the wall behind the bare metal desk in the middle of the room, which was festooned with framed pictures and yellowed newspaper clippings.

"That was Rita, wouldn't you know." Russ rolled his eyes. "She started a subscription to the *Arizona Daily Star* the day you got your scholarship to University of Arizona, and then when you got drafted by the Broncos, she added the *Denver Post*. I don't think she's missed an article you were mentioned in since you left Last Chance. And those on the wall are just a few of them. Most of them are pasted in that scrapbook there on top of the file cabinet."

"Think she'd mind if I took a few of them down? I appreciate the thought, and I won't forget to tell her so, but having the athletic office look like a shrine to the coach just seems a little off to me."

"Well, good luck with that. I've been trying to talk sense into that woman since she was elected mayor the same year I was elected town treasurer. I think it'd be easier to teach my dog to play dominos. But you've got the key now and she doesn't. I'd say fix this place up like you want it. And while you're at it, take a look around and see what you need. I can't promise we can do everything, at least not at first, but we'll sure do our best for you." He held out his hard, calloused farmer's hand and Andy shook it. "Well, I need to get going. I was on my way into town to talk to Chris Reed about the Booster breakfast next Saturday. You got that on your calendar, right?"

"I'll be there." Andy walked Russ to the door. "But I'd really appreciate if you'd help me temper this Glory Days talk. This year's team is the important one. Help me get that across, will you?"

"You bet."

Russ's footsteps reverberated in the empty hall, and when they stopped, Andy stuck his head out to see what was going on. Russ stood, hands in his pockets, in front of the trophy case gazing at pictures of teams long grown, now men with jobs and families, successes and failures, all of whom would always carry with them the knowledge that they had been part of the Glory Days.

Vehicles lined both sides of the road and filled the parking lot of the Desert Sage Salon across the street from the Dip 'n' Dine when Andy pulled his truck onto the shoulder just at the City Limit sign and switched off the engine. Stepping from the cab, he could hear in the distance the sound of banjo and bass and the low rumble of the crowd gathered to enjoy a night of music and food. He smiled as he shoved one hand in his pocket and headed back down the road. It was good to be home.

"Well, here's our hero now." Rita, sitting at the ticket table, smiled up at him. "Where's your date? We gave you two tickets so you could bring someone, you know. We don't have a whole lot of single women in Last Chance, I know, but any one of them would have jumped at the chance to turn up on the arm of Andy Ryan."

"I sincerely doubt that, Rita, but thanks for the vote of confidence anyway." Andy grinned down at her as he surrendered his ticket. Jess had obviously not mentioned that he had given her one of his tickets, and if she didn't say anything, Andy certainly saw no reason to. Rita was far too eager to make him out to be more than he knew he was. Of course, most of that was Rita's unwavering mission to put Last Chance on the map, but still, he was mighty uncomfortable with it. He looked over her head, trying to find a face in the crowd who might want to talk about something other than high school football, past and future.

"Ray Braden was asking if you were coming tonight." Rita took his ticket and crossed his name off a list attached to the clipboard in front of her. "He's sitting over yonder in that third row of tables.

He may have saved a couple seats for you. I told him you were probably bringing someone."

*Perfect*. Andy scanned the crowd until he found Ray sitting next to an attractive blonde woman Andy hadn't seen before, and he began making his way over. He and Ray had been good friends in high school but had sort of lost touch during college when Ray had gone to the University of New Mexico to study art and Andy got his scholarship to U of A.

It took a few minutes to get through the welcoming crowd, but when he finally made it, Ray looked up with a wide smile and got to his feet.

"Hey, look who turned up." He shook Andy's hand while giving him a one-armed hug. "I was sure hoping to see you but figured I was only going to be able to hold these chairs for about five more minutes. Glad you made it."

"Wouldn't miss it." Andy looked down at the woman smiling up at him from the chair next to Ray's. "Hi, I'm Andy Ryan."

"Oh, this is my wife, Lainie." Ray dropped a hand to her shoulder. "Lainie, this is Andy. He and I grew up together. Andy was the big football hero in high school while I warmed the bench."

Lainie held out her hand, and Andy took it in his. "It's nice to finally meet you, Andy. The town's been really looking forward to your coming home. I think Rita's even talking about a parade."

"Nope. No parade." Andy sat down in the chair next to Ray. "As far as I'm concerned, I'm the new coach. Period. I've got a job to do, and that's why I'm here."

"Good luck with convincing Rita." Ray grinned as he slid back into his own chair. "At the very least, she'll have you as the grand marshal of the Christmas parade."

"Yeah, well . . ." It was time to change the subject. "Where's the rest of the family? Don't you guys usually travel in a pack?"

"Usually, yeah, I guess we do. But Gran stayed home tonight. Big crowds are a little much for her these days. And Steven is still at the Law Enforcement Academy. Should be home soon. And everybody else is working this clam dig. You knew Sarah got married, right? She married the owner of the Dip 'n' Dine, so she's around here somewhere."

"I did not know that." When Andy thought of Sarah Cooley, he thought of a skinny little kid barrel racing and roping goats at local rodeos. Hard to imagine her all grown up and married.

"This is her niece, Olivia." Lainie put her hand around the shoulders of a little blonde girl of about seven or eight sitting on the other side of her. "Olivia, say hello to Coach Ryan."

Olivia glanced over before returning her attention to her meal. "Hello."

"Wow, here I thought I'd find Last Chance frozen in time, and nothing's the same. Steven at the Law Enforcement Academy? Now that I think about it, he'd be great in law enforcement, but to tell the truth, it's not something I'd have predicted."

"He's surprised a lot of us." Ray looked up as a tall, slender woman with a shock of pink hair over one eye approached them. "And if you ask me, here's a major reason for that. This is Kaitlyn, owner of the beauty shop across the street, sister of Chris Reed, the owner of this place, Sarah's sister-in-law, Olivia's mother, and the one who seems to have brought out the best in Steven. Kaitlyn, this is an old friend, Andy Ryan."

If Kaitlyn had ever heard of him, she was not awestruck. In fact, if anything, she just seem harried. Her smile was brief. "Hi. Do you know if you'd like the combination plate or the rellenos?"

Andy looked at Ray and shrugged. "The combination plate, I guess."

"Take the rellenos." Lainie leaned across Ray. "These chiles are stuffed with meat and spices and walnuts and raisins. So different! You can get the combo plate tomorrow. Kaitlyn's brother is an amazing chef and he only gets into the kitchen when they have these fiestas. You won't be sorry."

"Okay then." Andy looked up at Kaitlyn and smiled. "The rellenos it is then, thanks."

Kaitlyn nodded as she left. "Be right back with that."

"Excuse me, do you need this chair?"

Andy looked up at the man standing next to him with his hand on the back of the empty folding chair. He was about to tell him to take it when he caught sight of the ticket table on the edge of the parking lot.

"I'm sorry, but it's taken. The party I was holding it for just got here." He pushed back from the table. "Be right back."

Jess was standing next to the ticket table scanning the tables with a bright I'm-going-to-look-confident smile on her face when Andy reached her.

"Hey, you made it. I'm sitting with some friends and there's an empty chair if you'd like to join us."

Jess actually looked glad to see him, and with her coppery hair fluffed around her face and just a little makeup, Andy had to admit that she cleaned up real good. "I'd like that," she said. "Goodness. You said everybody in town would be here, but I had no idea that Last Chance was so . . . big."

"Spread out, it seems pretty small. Bunched up like this, well, there's a lot of us. Plus, from what Rita tells me, people come from all around. Anyway, we do have a place over here. I'm sitting with an old friend I grew up with and his wife, who I just met. I think you'll like them."

He led the way back to Ray and Lainie and began the introductions. The trouble with introductions in Last Chance was that they never stopped with just names. Lineage, relationships, and connections all had to be explained. Jess's smile began to look a little fixed and her nod a little automatic.

Lainie laughed and reached across Ray to touch Jess's arm. "Don't worry about getting everything straight. It'll take weeks, months. I'm not sure I've got it all, and it's been two years since I came to Last Chance."

"Wow, practically a native." Jess grinned, and as she and Lainie went on talking, Andy sat back and watched.

Jess smiled a lot, and her eyes crinkled at the corners when she did. There was an eagerness about her when she met folks that seemed to say she had been looking forward to the pleasure and was delighted that it was finally taking place. When Andy thought about her introduction to the town earlier that day, he felt kind of bad. Oh, they had been friendly enough, and Last Chance was probably a lot more welcoming than a lot of small towns, when you got down to it, but they did have to look you over a bit first, bide their time before they made up their minds about you. Clearly, Jess hadn't been quite ready for that, and Andy was glad that Lainie, a newcomer herself by Last Chance standards, had cut right through all that reticence and was making Jess feel right at home—at least he hoped Jess was beginning to feel at home. He certainly wanted her to.

"So, what do you do, Lainie?"

Andy winced a little. The question, the first one asked in so many places, was not so common in Last Chance. In the first place, everybody pretty much knew what everybody else did, and in the second, what you did just wasn't the most interesting thing about you. But Lainie seemed to take it in stride.

"I work here, actually. The woman who owned the Dip 'n' Dine before Chris gave me a job when I first got here, and I just love the place. If Times Square is the crossroads of the world, the Dip 'n' Dine is the crossroads of this whole area. Take a booth in the corner, and you'll see everyone from miles around pass through."

"Here you go." Kaitlyn was back and placed the plate she was carrying in front of Andy. "And what can I bring you?"

She smiled down at Jess, who looked around and shrugged. "Menu?"

"Combination plate or rellenos?" Lainie, Ray, and Andy spoke in unison with Kaitlyn.

"But the word is that rellenos is the dish to order," Andy finished up.

Jess eyed the dish in front of him and nodded. "Looks good. I'll have that too."

"Here, take mine." Andy set the plate in front of her and looked up at Kaitlyn. "Just bring me another like it."

"No, no. This is yours." Jess began to protest.

"It's fine. It won't take Kaitlyn a minute to bring me one, will it, Kaitlyn?"

"I wouldn't dream of taking your dinner." Jess set the plate back in front of him with a little thump and turned her crinkly-eyed smile back up at Kaitlyn. "And take your time. No need to rush."

Andy sat back, not knowing quite what to do. He had been raised with "ladies first" and "don't eat until everyone is served." Now here he sat with a plate of cooling food in front of him while the lady sitting next to him had just told the server to take her time.

"You eat that while it's hot." Jess jabbed a finger at his plate. She sounded awful bossy, but her eyes still smiled. "My dinner will be here soon enough."

"If I were you, I'd do what she said." Ray nudged him with his elbow. "Times are a-changing, even here in Last Chance."

Andy shrugged and picked up his fork as Jess picked up the conversation that had been interrupted by the arrival of his dinner.

"So, I have to ask. If you love working here and everyone connected to the place or the family is working this fiesta, how come you're not?"

Lainie slid a glare toward Ray. "Because Ray and his grandmother, who we live with, ganged up on me, that's why. They say if I'm on my feet during working hours, I need to be off my feet when my shift is over."

"Well, congratulations!" Jess's face lit up, and Andy noticed that when she really smiled, her eyes almost crinkled shut. But he still had no idea what they were talking about. "But you know, they've got a point. First trimester?"

Lainie nodded. "Ten weeks."

*Ooooh*. Andy got it. And fervently hoped this wasn't going to be *that* kind of conversation.

"All the more reason to get as much rest as you can. You've got a big job ahead of you."

Andy was of two minds. As Jess leaned to give advice to Lainie, who was sitting two seats away, her arm and shoulder pressed against his, and he liked that. But he sure wished she were talking about something else.

# 3

*Well, you win some. You lose some.* Jess smiled to herself as she locked the dead bolt in her room at the Last Chance Motel and shut the blinds. She didn't know if it was her or if Andy Ryan liked taking care of everyone, but he sure had his knight-in-shining-armor helmet on, even if it did resemble a battered cowboy hat. It wasn't that Jess went around with a chip on her shoulder; she knew how to ask for help when she needed it. But when people wanted to rush in and take care of things for her, her back went up, and her independence became a battle to be won. Again.

In the win column: her refusal to be his date at that Red Chile and Bluegrass thing, her insistence that he eat his own dinner while she waited for hers to arrive, and her rejection of his insistent offer of a ride back to the motel when the evening was over. In the lose column, if you could call it that, was the fact that she wound up sitting with him all evening anyway and his announcement that it was a free country and he could walk beside her all the way back to the motel if he wanted to, even if it did mean walking all the way back to get his truck.

Funny, it was all the things in her "lose" column that made her smile. Sitting with Andy and his friends had been fun, and there had been no hint that he thought of her as his date. In fact, they had wound up switching seats around so she could talk to Lainie while Andy caught up with Ray. When it was time to leave, she refused offers of a ride from both the Bradens and Andy, claiming the walk was both short and necessary after her huge meal. It was Andy, of course, who fell in beside her as she headed back to the motel. The walk and the conversation had been so easy that it didn't even occur to her to wonder what he had in mind until he stopped back a few feet from her door and stood, hands in pockets, while she fitted her key in the lock before lifting his hand in a wave and ambling back across the parking lot.

Jess winced as her mother's voice and her litany of warnings sounded in her head. She was pretty sure there was something in there about watching out for strange men. But truthfully? Even though eighteen short hours ago she didn't even know he existed, Andy didn't seem like a stranger at all. Neither did his friends the Bradens. And even though within the week she expected to be so immersed in her work that she wouldn't have time for anything, it was good to have friends.

The phone on the bedside table startled her with its old-fashioned jangle as she headed to the bathroom to run a bath.

"Dr. MacLeod, it's Rita. I didn't wake you, did I? I saw your light as I came in." How did she manage to sound as brisk and energetic at 11:00 at night as she did first thing in the morning? Especially after the day Jess knew she had put in.

"No, I'm still up. And please, it's Jess."

"Just wanted to make sure you got back okay. I noticed you didn't drive over this evening."

"I made it just fine, thanks. It was a nice night for a walk. Where I'm from it can get cold and damp after dark. The warm air felt good." Jess saw no need to mention she hadn't made the walk alone, but then, she had the feeling that Rita probably already knew that. She had to have passed Andy as she drove back.

"Get plenty to eat? Meet some folks?"

"Yes and yes." Jess was about to elaborate, but Rita had apparently found out what she needed to know.

"Well, good. If you need anything, the number's right there on the phone. Good night, now."

Jess looked at the receiver, connection gone dead, for a moment before replacing it in its cradle. Egalitarian to her soul, she had always maintained that people were the same everywhere, but maybe that was restricted to basic wants and needs. Because the people she'd met in Last Chance were different from the people back home; there was no other way to put it.

Jess stepped out the door of her motel room and lifted her face to the predawn breeze. Only a little more than a week had passed since her arrival and her feet-first leap into Last Chance society at the Red Chile and Bluegrass fiesta, but Last Chance was beginning to feel like home. Something about these early mornings in the desert reached deep inside Jess and filled her with well-being. Maybe it was the coolness of the air or the vivid colors of mountains, sage, and sky, all of which would soon be sucked up by the sun just cresting the peaks to the east of town. She leaned against the post just outside her door with one hand and pulled her leg up behind her with the other, holding it a few seconds before repeating the action with the other leg. After a few more stretches, she headed across the parking lot for the side of the road at an easy pace. This was going to be a big day, and she couldn't wait to get started.

Despite the lack of running trails in Last Chance—despite, in fact, the lack of anything but a few paved and dirt roads—running was easy. Traffic was light, almost nonexistent once she turned off the highway that ran through town, and she fell into an easy rhythm as she pounded past small, flat-roofed houses still silent except for the occasional sprinkler sparkling in the early sunlight as it watered a small patch of lawn. On days like this, she felt as if she could run forever.

"To your left."

Jess heard the voice behind her about the same time she heard the approaching steps, and she moved to the right.

"Mornin'." Andy appeared at her left elbow and matched his pace to her own. "You're out early."

Jess glanced at him before turning her attention back to the road in front of her with a little smile. "Yep. Every morning if I can possibly make it."

"Really? I'm surprised I haven't run into you before this." From the looks of him, Andy had to have been running quite a while, but his voice came clear and easy. "You sure you didn't hear from someone that I go for a run every morning and decided to try to run into me? 'Course, I'm used to stuff like that, being a big football star and all, but I just hadn't expected it from you."

"What?" Jess may have been getting a little winded, because her protest came as more of a squawk than she intended, and she slowed down to stare at him.

Andy didn't slow his pace, and Jess had to quicken hers to catch up. "You sure think a lot of yourself, don't you?"

"Me? Nah. I'm just a local boy who caught a few breaks. But you fans just won't leave me alone."

"Fans? Leave you alone?" No doubt about it, talking and running was leaving Jess puffing a bit. Or maybe it was talking, running, and indignation. "Give me a break."

"Save your breath. We still have two miles to go." Andy's eyes were on the road ahead. His pace hadn't changed since he caught up with her.

Three things kept Jess running along at his side. In the first place, even though she hadn't known Andy very long, she had seen him say the most outrageous things with an absolutely bland expression, and she was beginning to believe this was one of those times. Second, in case he really did think she was stalking him, she wanted to set him straight in no uncertain terms at the end of this run. Finally, she had no idea where to go, and clearly Andy did. He led her through the awakening streets of Last Chance and down a dirt path that ran along the top of the irrigation ditch.

Everything had appeared so barren at first look, but as she ran, Jess became aware that there was life everywhere. White blossoms bloomed on trailing gray-green vines at her feet, and a lizard skittered across the path just ahead. She turned her head to find the source of the trilling birdsong, and Andy pointed at a bird perched on a fencepost singing his heart out.

"Red-winged blackbird. Sounds like he's having a good time too."

Jess just nodded. The sun was well up, and the day was beginning to warm up. Even Andy's breath was coming in short puffs now, and Jess was glad when he led the way through an empty lot on a cul-de-sac and onto a paved road again. A battered pickup was backing out of a driveway, and they moved to the side of the road to let it pass.

"Whatever's chasing you, I think you done outrun it." The truck crawled by, and an older man with a grizzled mustache leaned out the window. "Nothin' back there as far as I can see."

"Thanks, Les. I appreciate you watching out for me." Andy slowed to a slow jog and then to a walk, and Jess gratefully matched his pace.

"Looking to see some good football this year." The truck began to pick up speed. "You take care now."

"You too. Tell Evelyn hi for me." Andy returned Les's wave as he drove away and turned to Jess. "Les Watson. Makes the same joke every day."

Jess didn't answer. She was concentrating on getting her breathing back to normal. The run had been amazing. Walking was even better.

"But I guess when you've worked outside with your hands every day of your life, working up a sweat for fun just seems plain crazy." He grinned and swung his arms in circles to stretch them out.

"If it gets this hot, I think I might agree with him. How much farther?"

"Not much." They were walking down the middle of a quiet residential street now. "Turn left at the corner down there, and you're almost to Main Street. The motel is in the next block beyond that."

As she walked, and her breath returned to normal, and the air, warm as it was, began to cool her a little, Jess felt her spirits rising. This was why she ran—this sense of strength and well-being that followed all but the longest of her runs.

"Morning, Miss Elizabeth. Here, let me do that for you." Andy opened the gate of a small brown house they were passing and took the sprinkler a white-haired lady was trying to drag across the lawn. "Where do you want it?"

"Thank you, Andy. I appreciate it." She lifted a cane she had been leaning on and gave it a shake. "Now that I have to take this thing everywhere I go, it's a lot harder to do what I want to. I forget that sometimes."

"Here you go." Andy put the sprinkler where she indicated and extended his arm to include Jess in the conversation. "Miss Elizabeth, have you met our new doctor? This is Jess MacLeod."

A warm and delighted smile filled the lined face. "I have not, although of course, I've heard all about you. Please come in. Lainie's over at the diner working, and Ray's already left for his studio, but I've got some coffee cake left, and it won't take a jiffy to make another pot of coffee."

"Ray and Lainie live here too, Jess." Andy stooped to run a finger under the chin of a huge gray-and-white tabby that had been rubbing against his leg. He looked up at Elizabeth. "Ray was saying you had quite a fall last winter, Miss Elizabeth. Glad to see you on your feet."

Elizabeth flapped her free hand. "Oh, pshaw. The way my family fusses, you'd think I already had one foot out the door. I'm fine, just a little inconvenienced, that's all. You're sure you won't change your mind and come in for coffee?"

Jess had started shaking her head when Elizabeth first mentioned the coffee and was a little surprised to find that Elizabeth had noticed. "I'd love to some other time, but I really need a shower before I'm going to be very good company at all."

"Then come to dinner. Lainie and Ray will be home, and I know they'd like to see you again. Lainie was telling me this morning how much she liked visiting with you last weekend and how much she'd love to get to know you better."

Dinner? Jess didn't know quite how to respond. Who invites a sweaty stranger to dinner? Who, in fact, invites anyone to dinner these days? But Miss Elizabeth, smiling at her with expectation, clearly meant what she said.

"I do thank you, Miss Elizabeth." Jess could only imagine what Lainie might say coming home after being on her feet all day to find out a dinner party was in the offing. "But my movers will be here soon, and I'll be busy with that all day. I'd love to stop by for that cup of coffee some day soon, though."

"If you're moving in today, that's all the more reason to come for dinner. You probably won't have a thing in the house to eat, and the Dip ’n’ Dine closes early, you know. Shall we say about 7:00? You come too, Andy.”

Something in Miss Elizabeth’s tone, warm as it was, said she wasn’t used to being told no. Jess looked to Andy for support, but he just gave the cat one last scratch behind the ears and stood up.

“Sounds great. I wouldn’t miss it.”

Jess felt a wave of frustration. Leave it to Andy not to get that someone was going to have to fix that dinner, and it probably wasn’t going to be the elderly lady leaning on the cane. But it appeared now that the dinner was going to take place whether Jess came or not. She tried to will her annoyance from both her expression and her voice.

“Well, then, thank you, Miss Elizabeth, and 7:00 it is. What can I bring?”

“Just your own sweet self. Oh, and just call me Elizabeth, honey. Most folks do. You too, Andy. You’re all grown up now. It’s okay.”

“All right then, Elizabeth.” Andy stopped and considered, as if he were tasting his words. “Nope. Doesn’t sound right. Sorry, Miss Elizabeth.”

“I’ll see you at 7:00 then. And thanks again.” Jess glanced at her watch. The movers weren’t due till about 10:00, but still, she had a lot she needed to get done before she met them.

“I can’t tell you how much I’ll be looking forward to it.” Elizabeth smiled and turned to go back inside. “Are you coming, Sam?”

As if he understood her, the cat stopped rolling on the sidewalk, jumped to his feet, and led the way. Jess watched Elizabeth ignore the ramp leading to her front door and carefully make her way up her front steps. Jess gave her one last wave and headed down the road, Andy beside her.

“What were you thinking, saying you’d love to come to dinner with almost no notice at all?” She gave Andy’s shoulder a little shove.

"What? You said you'd come too."

"Only after you did. Did you give any thought to the fact either Lainie or Ray is going to have to come home and fix dinner for us?"

"Ray or Lainie? Why?"

"Well, who else? Elizabeth can hardly walk. You don't think she's going to cook, do you?"

Andy grinned as he broke into a slow jog. "Here's your first bit of really useful Last Chance advice: never make the mistake of underestimating Elizabeth Cooley."

Jess basked in a sense of accomplishment as she brought her car to a stop outside Elizabeth Cooley's gate just before 7:00. Not only was all her furniture in place and her bedroom nearly unpacked, but she had found her way back to Elizabeth's without having to ask directions. Okay, considering the size of Last Chance, maybe that wasn't all that much of an achievement, but she felt good about it nevertheless. And fresh from a shower and wearing clean clothes, she was feeling pretty darn good and actually looking forward to the evening.

Andy's pickup pulled up behind her car as she got out, and she waited for him on the sidewalk.

"I'd have been happy to come pick you up." He joined her on the walk and held the gate open for her. "I drove right by your house on the way over here."

"How'd you know where I live?" She hadn't seen him since he left her at the motel and jogged off somewhere. Maybe *he* was the stalker.

"Could be the moving truck with California plates parked outside your house most of the day. Did I mention I drive by on the way to and from my house? We're practically neighbors."

"Oh." Jess was beginning to feel a little foolish and more than a little full of herself.

"Hey! Glad you made it." Ray came out the front door and stood on the porch with his hands in his pockets. "Come on in. Gran has dinner just about ready."

The small living room Jess stepped into was neat and full of wonderful aromas. Sam, looking like a gray-and-white loaf, observed their arrival with gravity from the back of the sofa. Lainie greeted them from a recliner where she was stretched out with her feet up.

"Hey, welcome! I'd get up, but someone would probably start yelling at me if I did."

"You stay right where you are." Elizabeth, a little pink-cheeked, emerged from the kitchen and crossed the room to greet them with a hug. She walked with a slight limp, but the cane was nowhere in sight. "So glad you came. And don't you look pretty. I'd never dream you'd spent the day moving."

"How about me? Do I look pretty too?" Andy bent to kiss Elizabeth's cheek.

"You're a mess. That's what you are." Elizabeth laughed. "But then you always were. The way you and Ray could get around me should make you ashamed."

"Yeah, right. No one easier to fool than you, Gran." Ray perched on the arm of the recliner, and Lainie smiled up at him.

"Well, I'm glad you're back home, Andy. And I'm glad you're here too, Jess. It's about time Last Chance got its own doctor. Now, you just sit right here on the sofa and I'll bring you some iced tea. Dinner will be ready in a minute."

"Let me help." Jess moved toward the kitchen.

"No, I'm all but done." Elizabeth waved her to the sofa. "You just sit right there and rest a bit. Ray, honey, come get the tea for me, will you?"

Ray followed her into the kitchen as Jess and Andy sat down. Lainie grinned from the recliner.

"Ray and I came down to take care of Gran when she fell last winter, but you can see who's taking care of who. When we told her she had another great-grandbaby on the way, she just told me I had worked my last day at the Dip 'n' Dine. This was our compromise." She held out her hands. "I can work for at least a while as long as I spend an hour or so here with my feet up when I get home every day. And this recliner is Gran's personal throne, so when she turns it over to me, you know she means business."

"But if your pregnancy is going well, there's no reason why you shouldn't be able to work as long as you're comfortable."

"Tell that to Gran." Lainie laughed. "Better yet, don't. Believe me, an argument with Gran is not to be entered into lightly. But I may call you in for reinforcements next time Gran decides it's time for me to quit."

"Just let me know so I can get out of here in time." Ray came back in carrying two glasses of tea, which he handed to Jess and Andy. "No one listens to me anyway."

"Awww. Poor thing." Lainie stroked her husband's arm when he came to sit on the arm of her recliner again.

Jess took a sip of her tea and leaned back against the sofa cushions. She was glad she had been more or less forced to accept Elizabeth's invitation. If the evening so far was a harbinger of her life here in Last Chance, she was going to be very happy.

# 4

Jess never thought of herself as a food fanatic, particularly. She just ate sensibly, as she saw it—whole grains, plenty of steamed vegetables, lean meats and fish, and fresh fruit. She would never express it, but secretly, she wondered how anyone could eat any other way. Now she knew. Elizabeth's table held some of the best-tasting food she had ever eaten in her life.

"Have some more chicken." Elizabeth passed her the platter of golden fried pieces. "One little piece of white meat can't have filled you up."

"Oh, but it did." Jess held up a hand to ward off the platter. "With the mashed potatoes and gravy, and all those vegetables, and the biscuits, I'm completely stuffed."

Elizabeth passed the chicken on to Andy, who speared a drumstick before passing it on to Ray. Undeterred, she picked up the basket of bread. "Then at least have another biscuit while they're warm and some of this plum jam. It was my mother-in-law's recipe, and I've made it every year for about as long as I can remember."

Jess eyed the biscuits. She really did feel as if she were about to pop, and she had eaten more bread tonight than she usually ate in a week, but those biscuits were beyond anything she had ever tasted. The battle she fought with her conscience was short, brutal, and over in the amount of time it took her to smile and accept the basket offered her. "Thanks. Maybe just a half."

"Tell us more about this office you're opening here in Last Chance." Elizabeth tried to pass the nearly empty bowl of mashed potatoes to Lainie and then to Ray. Both declined. "We had a doctor here years ago when my children were small, but when he passed on, no one took over his practice and everyone just got used to going on up to San Ramon."

"So I hear." Jess shrugged. "In fact, just about everybody I've met has told me how happy they are that Last Chance has its own doctor, and then in the same breath told me that they already have a doctor in San Ramon who's been looking after them for years. Not that I'm trolling other doctors' practices."

"Well, I'll be your first patient." Lainie smiled at Jess. "I don't have a long history with some other doctor. And I'd love it if I didn't have to run up to San Ramon to see a doctor."

Jess couldn't miss the quick glance Ray and Elizabeth exchanged before Ray cleared his throat. "Um, Lainie, you don't have a long history, but you have already seen a doctor. Do you think it's a good idea to switch now? I mean, he already knows you and everything."

"I've had one appointment, and I saw a nurse practitioner. She just confirmed what we already knew, gave me a bunch of vitamins, and told me I should come back in about six weeks to see the doctor." Lainie reached for the last biscuit and broke it open on her plate. "Pass me that gravy, would you, please?"

When the gravy was passed in silence and no other conversation was forthcoming, she looked up. "What? I'm eating for two now, you know."

It was Jess who broke the uncomfortable silence. "Well, as you say, you have about six more weeks before you need to see a doctor. I'm sure you and Ray will be able to decide the best course for you to take." She watched Lainie ladle the cream gravy, rich with chicken cracklings, over the split biscuit. "Although I'd like to send over some information on prenatal nutrition, if you wouldn't mind. He may be little right now, but he's growing at a rate you wouldn't believe, and I know you want to make sure he's getting everything he needs."

Lainie's fork stopped midway to her mouth. "What are you saying?"

"Nothing, nothing at all." Jess laughed. "Just thinking a little nutritional information might not hurt, that's all."

"Well, that may be, but all I can say is there is a whole valley of folks around here whose mamas ate pretty much what's on this table, and they're all doing just fine." Elizabeth braced her hands on the edge of the table to help herself to her feet. "Now, who's ready for some peach cobbler? The peaches came from the tree just this afternoon."

"Let me help." Jess started to get up. She had the uneasy feeling she had just stepped on some toes, but Elizabeth waved her back into her chair.

"No, you just stay where you are. Ray's going to give me a hand, aren't you, honey?"

"Sure." Ray still hadn't said much since Lainie announced that Jess would be her doctor, and it may have been Jess's imagination, but he did seem awfully eager to jump up from the table and help Elizabeth.

Jess could have kicked herself for introducing so much awkwardness into what had been the most pleasurable evening she had spent in a long time. Trying again, she turned to Lainie with a smile. "So, how have you been feeling?"

"I'm feeling great." Lainie planted her elbows where her plate had been as Ray took it to the kitchen. "I felt a little queasy a couple of mornings last week, but other than that I've been just fine. And as you noticed, there's nothing wrong with my appetite."

Jess cringed a little. She had always struggled with this tendency to call things as she saw them, and she had wound up regretting it more times than she'd like to remember.

"Well, if you sit down to meals like this every day, I can see why." Jess tried again, hoping her smile was a little more confident than she felt. "Have you been taking your vitamins?"

Lainie nodded, and Andy pushed back his chair and jumped to his feet. "Hey, I'm just sitting around like third base. Let me help." He grabbed the nearly empty fried chicken platter and carried it to the kitchen.

Jess sighed. For the last eight years, she had been eating, breathing, and sleeping medicine—with not a whole lot of sleeping, now that she thought about it. Would there ever come a time when she could have a simple conversation without clearing the room in the process? She took a deep breath and tried again.

"So, Lainie." She pasted what she hoped was a friendly smile on her face. "I hear you're from California too. What part? I'm from Mill Valley, just north of San Francisco."

"LA. Long Beach area, mostly."

By the time the table had been cleared and Ray and Andy had placed dishes of warm peach cobbler in front of them, Jess had discerned that other than starting out in California and winding up in Last Chance, New Mexico, she and Lainie had little they could claim in common. Lainie had been tossed out to fend for herself at fourteen, and she had not only survived but through God's grace found her way to Last Chance and to him. The tiny house she shared with her husband and his grandmother was the first real home she had ever had, and it would always be a palace to her.

Jess, on the other hand, had never wanted for anything—except maybe time and sleep. She wasn't even saddled with the monstrous burden of student loans that most new doctors labored under. Her parents, both physicians themselves, had seen to it that she had whatever she needed. Where Lainie's parents could only be called criminal in their negligence and neglect, Jess's family had been and still was close, using what little free time they did have to enjoy and nurture each other. Her parents had always supported her childhood ambition of practicing rural medicine, and even if, as the years passed and the dream never wavered, they did occasionally turn the conversation to more lucrative disciplines of medicine, they never seriously tried to talk her out of it.

She looked across the table at Lainie, who was laughing up at Ray, and found herself wishing two things. First, she would love it if Lainie did decide to come to her for her obstetric appointments, although it was pretty clear that if Elizabeth and Ray had anything to say about it, that might not happen. And second, she really hoped she and Lainie would be friends—close friends. Whatever her early circumstances had been, Lainie was funny, confident, and easy in her skin. Jess liked that.

Elizabeth sat down and picked up her spoon. Everyone else at the table followed suit, and not for the first time that evening, Jess found herself eating until her spoon scraped the bottom of the bowl.

"Elizabeth, I honestly can't remember having a meal I enjoyed more." Jess finally put her spoon down and leaned against the back of her chair. "I thank whatever gods there be that you were outside this morning when Andy and I came by. I wouldn't have missed this meal for anything."

This time there was no mistaking it. Andy, Ray, and Lainie did exchange glances, but Elizabeth didn't bat an eye. "Well, I'm thankful too." Her blue eyes crinkled in a smile. "I hope this is just the first of many meals you take at this table. Now, why don't you all go on into the living room, and I'll get things put up in the kitchen."

"Nope." Lainie got to her feet and put her hands on Elizabeth's shoulders to direct her toward the living room. "It's your turn at the recliner. I'll get these dishes done in no time."

"Nope." Ray stacked all five empty peach cobbler bowls into one tower, causing his grandmother to gasp a little. "You go sit down too. Put your feet up on the coffee table if Gran will let you get away with it. And take Jess with you. I'll do the dishes and Andy'll help. Right, Andy?"

"You bet. It'll be just like old times." Andy scooped up a handful of silverware and winked at Jess over his shoulder as he headed for the kitchen. "Miss Elizabeth treated everyone like her own. If you were here at mealtime, there was a chair at the table for you. If you were here at bedtime, she found a place for you to sleep. And if chores needed to be done, you did those too."

"I remember those old times." Elizabeth shook her head. "It didn't always work out well for the kitchen."

"Give us some credit, Gran. We might have grown up a little in the last, oh, fifteen years or so." Ray tried to balance an iced tea glass on his forefinger and caught it as it fell.

"Ray! For pity's sake, be careful!" Elizabeth marched across the room to snatch the glass from his hand, but Ray held it out of her reach.

"Just teasing you, Gran. We'll be careful." He grinned and put the glass on the counter just inside the kitchen door. "Go on in and sit down. We'll join you in a little bit."

Even after Elizabeth was settled in her recliner with her feet up and her crocheting on her lap, she seemed to keep an ear directed toward the kitchen, flinching whenever a dish clanked too loudly against another.

Lainie laughed. "Seriously, Gran. Ray does know what he's doing. He's no stranger to the kitchen, I promise you—no matter what he's tried to make you believe since we came back."

"I know. I'm just not used to having men in my kitchen unless they're eating, that's all." Elizabeth rearranged the afghan she was crocheting and wrapped the yarn around her fingers again. "Take that sofa cushion, honey, and put it under your feet. You'll be more comfortable."

Lainie did as she was told and turned to Jess. "How about you? Want to put your feet up too?"

"No, I'm good." Jess smiled at the laughter coming from the kitchen. "Sounds like they're having a good time in there."

"Those two would." Elizabeth shook her head. "They were as different as they could be when they were boys, what with Andy playing every kind of sport you could think of and Ray wanting to draw or paint all the time, but they became best friends as soon as they met in grade school and stayed friends until they both went off to college. Andy was over here so much I came to think of him as one of my own."

"Ray's told me about Andy practically living here." Lainie adjusted the sofa cushion under her ankles and leaned back against the sofa. "He never said much about going to Andy's house, though."

Elizabeth's face took on an expression that was hard to read, and she turned her attention to her crocheting. "No, they didn't spend much time over there. And that was fine with me. I always loved having my boys right where I could see them. But tell us about you, Jess. What was your family like?"

Jess had the feeling that the subject had been deftly and firmly changed, but she complied and told Elizabeth about growing up in Mill Valley.

"My sister's three years older than I am, and she's a research cardiologist in San Francisco. She's the smart one in the family and I'm really proud of her."

"It sounds like you've got a whole family of smart people." Elizabeth raised her eyebrows. "I don't see how you can all be doctors and say one of you is the smart one."

"You don't know Catherine. There's smart and then there's scary smart. She got her MD and PhD at the same time and is doing some pretty impressive work at UCSF."

"I hope I do get to meet her someday. I'd like to meet all your family." Elizabeth looked up as Andy and Ray came in. "All finished in there already?"

"Yep." Ray turned the piano bench and straddled it as Andy took the remaining empty chair. "Didn't break more than two plates and a bowl. Oh, and that little blue bird that's always been on the shelf over the sink? It's sort of toast too. Hope you don't mind."

Elizabeth just looked at him over the top of her glasses, and Ray laughed.

Jess glanced at her watch. It wasn't really all that late, but she had had a long day, and from the looks of it, so had the others. Lainie actually appeared to be dozing on the couch, and the lively conversation had slowed to an occasional comment. She smiled over at Elizabeth. "I think I should be going, but I want to say again how much I loved that dinner. Thank you so much for asking me over. I'm really starting to feel at home here in Last Chance."

"Oh, you're not going already." Elizabeth began to struggle out of her recliner. "It's early yet."

"Don't get up." Jess crossed the room and took Elizabeth's warm hand. "I hope I'll see you again soon."

"I hope so too, honey." Elizabeth patted Jess's hand with her own free hand. "You know where I live now, and I'm almost always at home these days. Don't hesitate to drop in. I love company."

"I'll do that."

"I should be going too, I guess." Andy went to drop a kiss on Elizabeth's cheek before following Jess to the door. "It's been like old times."

"You know, it has been." Elizabeth smiled up at him. "With Ray back home, and now you. I'm counting on seeing a lot of you."

"Don't worry about that. You'll probably get sick of me."

Ray got up and followed them to the front door. "Jess, it was good to get to know you a little better. Glad you came." He turned to Andy and offered a handshake with one hand and a half-hug with the other. "I'm really glad that you're back in town. I thought we might not see you again, except on *Monday Night Football*."

"Good to be back. And I mean that." Andy slapped Ray on the shoulder and followed Jess down the steps. Ray waited on the porch till they reached their cars and then, with a final wave, disappeared back inside.

"That was fun." Jess dug around in her purse for her keys. "I'm glad I got to meet your friends. I really like them."

"They really like you too. I can tell."

"One thing you've got to explain, though." Jess paused with her hand on the door handle. "There was a moment when I caught you and Ray and Lainie looking at each other like I had said something wrong. What was that all about?"

Andy's brow puckered as he considered. "Oh, yeah. I think I know what you're talking about. Didn't know you caught that." His grin was a little sheepish.

"Well, I did, so what was going on?"

"I think it was when you were thanking whatever powers or gods that be, or something like that."

"So?"

"Well, I'm sure you just meant it as a saying, but Elizabeth gets real literal when you talk about God. She'd have been real happy, if the conversation had taken that turn, to tell you that you didn't have to be unsure about what gods there were. She'd have told you that there's just one and then probably joined you in thanking him that she was in the yard too. That's just how Elizabeth is."

"Really? I guess it shouldn't surprise me, considering her age and background, but I have to confess it does, a little. She seems so sharp and aware."

Andy's whoop of laughter caused Jess to raise both hands in an effort to quiet him. "Shhh! They'll hear you through the screen door. What's so funny, anyway?"

"First of all, you're right. Elizabeth is sharp and very aware. And well educated too, for that matter. But as to the rest of what you said—well, as I said earlier, never make the mistake of underestimating Elizabeth Cooley."

"I wasn't aware I had been." Jess felt a little out of sorts. What was wrong with admitting that a country woman of Elizabeth's generation might be a little less forward-thinking than, say, a younger person from the city? It wasn't an insult, after all. Taking a deep breath and reminding herself that she was the fish out of water here and should concentrate on thinking before she spoke, she opened her door and slid behind the wheel. "Well, good night. The run this morning was great. We'll have to do it again sometime."

"What about tomorrow?" Andy leaned down to peer in her open window. "I run every morning, and we might as well run together, unless you really prefer to run alone."

Jess hesitated. Truth be told, she really did prefer a running buddy, someone to keep pace with, and her run with Andy this morning had been great, but it was pretty clear that everyone in town considered Andy Ryan the catch of a lifetime. That wasn't why she had come to Last Chance, and she didn't want anyone, least of all Andy, to get the wrong idea. Then again, he was the one who knew all the trails. Maybe when her schedule really kicked in in a couple weeks, she'd know some too.

"Sure, why not? About 6:00?" Right now she felt as if she could sleep for about a year, but experience told her that like it or not, by the time the sun came up, she'd be up too.

"I'll be waiting outside. See you then." He slapped the roof of her car lightly with the flat of his hand and ambled off to his truck.

Everything looked different in Last Chance at night. There were so few streetlights and it was so dark, but she could see the headlights of Andy's pickup in her rearview mirror, and when she finally did pull to a stop in her driveway, he gave two friendly beeps before he drove by.

# 5

Late summer in Last Chance meant the chile harvest. It meant finding yourself behind slow-moving trucks piled high with deep green pods heading for the processing plant. It meant roadside stands popping up along the Last Chance Highway where you could stop and buy a bushel or two and have them dumped into a roaster and slowly turned over a gas flame while you waited. Everywhere you went, the warm, spicy fragrance of chile, roasting and fresh, permeated the air, and you found yourself thinking about heading over to the Dip 'n' Dine to see what Carlos's special might be. From the time he was a kid, though, for Andy, the beginning of the chile harvest had meant one thing only: football practice.

*Whole different set of butterflies this year.* He shut his big three-ring notebook and leaned back in his chair. There were no windows in his office, but from the clock up on his wall, he guessed it was about sunup. In less than an hour, the summer silence of the building would be broken as football hopefuls began to arrive, and a new season of Last Chance football would begin.

From down the hall, Andy heard the front door open and the soft thud of athletic shoes on linoleum as footsteps approached.

"Hey, Coach." Kev Gallegos, his only assistant, came in and dropped his own notebook on a smaller desk across the room. "Been here long? I didn't think I was late."

"Nah. I got here a while ago. Might as well not sleep here as not sleep at home."

Kev grinned. "I know what you mean. I was up at 3:00 watching those videos from last season again, and I've got to tell you, I'm pretty excited about our prospects this year. There's a lot of potential there. They just need someone to bring it out."

"Yeah, well, that's what we're here for." Andy willed his voice steady and low. Nerves were for other people. The head coach needed to be a rock. "Want to make sure the locker room is ready? The guys'll be here soon."

"Yeah, sure." Kev headed for the hall but stopped in the doorway. "I don't want to get all mushy here, but I got to tell you how honored I am to be working with you. You're the reason I wanted to play football in the first place. I was in sixth grade when you played your last game here, and you made Last Chance seem unbeatable. I couldn't wait to get to high school and be part of that. 'Course, by then you were at U of A, and the streak was broken, and it wasn't the same team. But you know? I keep thinking that maybe I'll get to be part of a different set of Glory Days now. Funny how things turn out, huh?"

"Different team, different time, Kev. This is the season we need to be worrying about, but thanks."

"Well, I just wanted you to know, that's all." He hesitated as if waiting for Andy to say something else, and then, shutting the door behind him, disappeared into the hall.

Andy puffed his cheeks and blew out a gust when he heard the door to the locker room close. This was going to be an uphill battle.

He went back to his notebook and was still at work when his assistant opened the door again some time later.

"They're all here, Coach. We're ready when you are."

"Be right there." He took another deep breath. *Well, here we go.*

The low buzz Andy could hear as he crossed the hall fell into silence when he opened the door, and something over sixty faces turned to greet him. He knew them all, even if he couldn't put one name to a face.

The returning starters were easy to spot; they straddled benches or leaned against the lockers with an easy, territorial confidence. The others, from last year's benchwarmers to the sophomores looking forward to suiting up on varsity for the first time, regarded him with expressions ranging from grim determination to wide-eyed, stomach-churning fear. He stepped to the front of the room.

"Good morning, men. Thanks for turning out." He looked out over the group assembled in front of him. He had the riveted attention of most, but one of the older students against the lockers leaned over and muttered something to the guy next to him and both snickered. That was fine. Guys like that were in every locker room. And they didn't worry Andy at all. "You have the toughest couple weeks of your life ahead of you, and I've got to be honest, not every one of you is going to make it. All you have to do is look around the room and see that we have about twice as many men in here as we can keep, but I promise you that if you give me everything you've got, you'll get a fair shot. If you don't, if you think we just can't do without you, you have a rude awakening coming, because I'll cut you no matter who you are." He made eye contact with the two against the lockers. "Are we clear on that?"

There was an insolent challenge in the look they returned, and Andy glanced back at the clipboard he held. "Okay, the first practice of the day begins at 7:00 a.m. sharp. Get here by 6:45 and start taking laps. At 7:00, Coach Gallegos will blow his whistle and you join us on the field. If you're not on the track, don't bother. You've just missed practice. Three missed practices and you're out. First practice of the day lasts till 10:00. The second goes from 4:30 to

7:00. Same drill; be on the track at 4:15. Weight room is open from 1:00 to 4:00."

He paused and looked out over the boys in front of him, letting his gaze fall on one earnest expression after another. Even the boys leaning against the lockers stood with arms folded over their chests, waiting for what he had to say next.

"I've already told you you're in for the roughest couple of weeks of your life, and you are. You'll be leaving blood, sweat, and more'n likely your breakfast out there on that field every day, sometimes twice a day. But it's worth it. Why else would a sane man put himself through all that? When you put on that uniform and take the field under those lights on the first Friday of September, you'll know what I'm talking about. Now hit the track."

With a low rumble, everyone shuffled to their feet and moved toward the door to the field. Andy stopped them.

"One more thing. There's been a lot of talk in town, and I'm sure you've heard it, about teams gone by and what they did. But that's old news, ancient history, and it doesn't have anything to do with us today. This is *your* time and *your* season. Now make something of it." No one moved and Andy waved his clipboard at the door. "Go!"

In a few seconds, the door swung shut again, leaving the locker room in silence, and Andy checked his roster, still trying to figure out who the two returning players against the lockers were.

"Coach?"

Andy looked up. He hadn't noticed this kid, but he wasn't one who would stand out. Not tall, not big, quiet voice.

"You are?" He looked down at his clipboard.

"Gabe Quintana. Could I talk to you just a minute?"

"Sure, Quintana. What's up?"

"Coach, I really want to play. And I promise to give you everything I've got, but I might have a hard time getting here by 6:45. My mom works the night shift at the hospital in San Ramon, and I can't leave the other kids until she gets home."

"What time does she get home?"

"About 6:30 most days, but some days she can't leave right on time and doesn't get home till nearly 7:00. I'll get here just as fast as I can, and I'll work my tail off when I'm here, but I might be about five minutes late some days."

"What about your dad?"

Gabe's open expression hardened in a second, and he gave a quick shake of his head without elaborating.

"Coach, I really want to play." His words were almost like a mantra. "I've been working the chile harvest for Mr. Sheppard, and he's letting me work from 11:00 to 4:00 and on weekends so I can make practice, but I just don't know if I can make it at 6:45 every day, that's all."

*Oh, man. What do you say to a kid that wants it this bad?* Andy took a deep breath before answering. "Well, Quintana, we have something of a problem then. You know I can't start out making exceptions. It's not fair to the others. I guess my advice would be to talk to your mom and tell her how important it is that you're here on time. It's only about three weeks, and you do get two free passes. Maybe you won't need more."

"Yeah, I understand." Gabe straightened his shoulders, and the grin he gave Andy looked a little forced. "Well, just thought I'd ask. Thanks, Coach."

He turned to leave, and before the door swung shut again, Andy saw him break into a run as he headed for the track. He really did hope Quintana and his mom could work something out. The kid seemed to be carrying way too much weight for someone so young.

He slipped his aviator sunglasses on and walked out onto the field, signaling his assistant to summon the boys from the track. Already the bleachers were dotted with men in jeans or work pants and light denim jackets, hats pulled low to shade their eyes from the sun's rays slanting across the field from the mountains to the east. As he watched, another man emerged from the parking lot behind the field and climbed to a row about midway up. Finding his buddy, he sat down and handed him one of the two steaming Styrofoam cups he carried. Another football season at Last Chance High had begun.

Jess saw them all on the football field when she ran by. Andy had warned her that once football season started, his runs were likely to be predawn and on the track. He'd invited her to join him if she wanted, but truthfully? That really sounded hideous, especially since, thanks to him, she knew some beautiful trails to run now—after the sun was up.

Her first week at the San Ramon Medical Center had been pretty uneventful. She had taken a few back-to-school examinations and diagnosed an ear infection, but nothing major. Next week she was taking the practice of another doctor who was going on vacation, and she was actually looking forward to that. And in another couple weeks, her Last Chance office would be open.

She turned down Elizabeth Cooley's street and slowed to a walk to begin her cooldown. Elizabeth's yard up ahead was empty, and Jess felt a little twinge of disappointment. Elizabeth wasn't outside every day, but when she was, Jess enjoyed the brief conversations they had, though so far she'd always declined Elizabeth's invitations to come in for coffee.

"Well, good morning." Elizabeth opened her screen door and stepped out onto the porch as Sam, her cat, trotted past her and down the steps, tail held high. "It looks like it's going to be a beautiful day, doesn't it?"

"It'll be warm, that's for sure." Jess slowed to a stop at the gate. "How are you this morning?"

"Oh, I'm doing well. I'm always a little stiff first thing in the morning, but once I get myself up and moving, it won't be so bad. Can you stop for a cup of coffee, or do you need to get up to the hospital? I've been hearing some good things about you."

"Really?" Jess had to wonder whom she had heard good things from, since you could count every patient she had seen using both hands and one foot, and none had been from Last Chance. On impulse, she smiled. "You know what? If you take a walk with me first, I'd love to stop in afterward and have a cup of coffee with you."

"Oh, honey, I'm not even dressed." Elizabeth looked down at her robe and slippers. "Just come on in, and I'll walk with you some other day."

"I can wait while you put something on. Don't feel like you have to dress up. You're not supposed to be glamorous when you exercise." She brushed her hair from her eyes with the back of her wrist. "Look at me."

Elizabeth's mouth pinched up, and it looked like she was going to find another reason to refuse the walk, but she huffed a sigh instead. "Oh, all right. Give me about five minutes, but we'd better not see anyone I know."

While she waited, Jess stretched out, using Elizabeth's gate for support. When she heard the screen door open again, she looked up to see Elizabeth in a lavender warm-up suit making her way across the porch.

"Don't forget to use the ramp."

Elizabeth veered slightly and headed for the ramp without answering.

"Is that cane going to be enough support, or do you think you need to take your walker?"

This time Elizabeth did look up, and there was no question that she had been bossed just about as much as she was going to take.

"I can manage just fine the way I am, thank you." She made her careful way down the ramp and gave Jess a tight little smile when she joined her at the gate. "Are you ready to go?"

They had walked for a minute or two with Elizabeth navigating the sidewalk and Jess walking beside her in the street before Jess broke the silence.

"I think you're annoyed with me, Elizabeth."

Elizabeth took a few more careful steps before she heaved a sigh. "No, I'm not annoyed with you, sweet girl. You're just getting the brunt of it, I'm afraid."

"The brunt of what?" Jess kept her voice gentle.

"This." Elizabeth lifted her cane and shook it. "This whole mess. I was doing just fine taking care of myself and my house, driving myself where I needed to go, and then with one little stumble on my porch steps, everything changed. Now I can't take a blessed breath without someone there to make sure I'm doing it right. My sweet daughter-in-law calls me two or three times a day. Ray and Lainie, as much as I love having them with me, moved here from Santa Fe just to look after me. And have you met Sarah, my granddaughter who lives just two doors down? Well, she comes by every day after she gets home from school. She says she wants a cup of tea, but I know she's just checking to see if I'm still upright and breathing. The only reason in the world that they don't hire a babysitter for me now that Lainie's working at the diner is because they make me wear this little help button all the time. Even then they don't want me to leave the house unless one of them is with me, for all the world like I was about two years old. Well, I'm here to tell you that the only thing that has changed is that I'm a little stiffer than I was. Maybe I don't move quite as fast as I used to, but my mind is just fine, thank you very much. And I can still take care of myself."

Jess just raised her eyebrows and nodded without speaking. She had seen Elizabeth fuss gently at her cat, or at Lainie for not resting enough, or even at Andy for not wiping his boots on the welcome mat before coming into her living room, but this was more than that. Elizabeth was frustrated and angry on a level Jess had not seen.

Elizabeth stopped and looked up at Jess. Her cheeks were pink from the exertion of her walk, but her smile was more relaxed, if a little rueful. "My goodness, listen to me talk. I should be ashamed. I've got more family caring about me than you can shake a stick at, and all I can do is complain about it. I need to be counting my blessings, that's what I need to be doing."

She set off again with a determined gait, and Jess fell in alongside her. Truthfully, she understood Elizabeth's exasperation perfectly. It was natural, and Jess didn't think Elizabeth had anything to apologize for, but somehow she felt that the last thing Elizabeth wanted right now was to be set straight—again.

They reached Elizabeth's gate, and Jess held it open for her. If the walk to the end of the block had tired Elizabeth, her slight puffing and her rosy cheeks were the only indication. Her steps were firm and quick until she reached the ramp, and then she stopped, took a deep breath, and grasping the rail with her free hand, more or less pulled herself up the ramp to the porch. Jess followed close behind, and if Elizabeth noticed her hovering, she chose not to say anything.

"Come in the kitchen and I'll get us a cup of coffee." Elizabeth led the way through her little house. "I don't have any coffee cake this morning, but these cookies have oatmeal and raisins, so we'll just call them breakfast."

Jess sat at the table where Elizabeth directed and watched as her hostess moved around the kitchen, filling cups and taking cookies from the jar and putting them on a plate. She still seemed a little breathless.

"There now." Elizabeth finally sat down and smiled across the table at Jess. "This was all I wanted in the first place, just a little coffee and company. Have a cookie. My little friend Olivia and I made them yesterday, so they're nice and fresh."

"I think I met Olivia the first night I was here." Jess took a sip of her coffee. "Didn't someone tell me she was part of your family somehow?"

Elizabeth laughed. "Technically, she's my granddaughter Sarah's niece by marriage, but we got close long before that happened. She comes over after school every day to keep me company."

Elizabeth must have anticipated a lecture because she raised both eyebrows and a forefinger. "Now don't you go telling me that having Olivia every afternoon is too much for me. I get enough of that from everyone else. Olivia is the sweetest little thing you'll ever meet and the highlight of my day."

"I'll bet she is." Actually, Jess had no intention of discouraging Elizabeth from having Olivia over. She had noticed the television was still on and Elizabeth's crocheting piled in the recliner when she came in, just as she had noticed Elizabeth's desire to fuss over and care for anyone who entered her front door. If anyone could keep Elizabeth from sitting all day, Jess had a feeling it was Olivia.

"Elizabeth, I have an idea." Jess leaned both elbows on the table. "I come by here every morning after my run. Why don't you plan on walking with me? We'll take it slow at first and build up your strength. When your family sees you moving around more like your old self, I'll bet they'll ease up a little. And frankly, I'd love the company."

"I thought you and Andy always ran together."

Jess wrinkled her nose. "Not anymore. Football practice started today."

"Ah, well, I should have known. Once football season starts, everything else around town pretty much takes a backseat." Elizabeth took a nibble from the cookie she had just dipped into her coffee.

"So? What do you say? Will you be my walking buddy?"

Elizabeth sighed. "What time would you be by?"

"About this time every morning."

"Every morning?"

"It works best that way."

Elizabeth didn't say anything. She took another sip of her coffee, gazing at Jess over the rim with a slightly furrowed brow and the bluest eyes Jess had ever seen.

Jess picked up her own cup and waited. She was neither Elizabeth's family nor her physician, and she wasn't about to badger her into doing something she didn't want to do. Even if it was for her own good.

"Oh, all right. We'll give it a try." Elizabeth set her cup down with a little clank. "But I'd like to be back home and settled by 9:00 every morning. That's when they run *Rockford Files*, and I like to crochet a few rows while I watch it."

"That won't be a problem at all." Jess held her cup up in salute. "I'm looking forward to this. It's going to be fun."

Elizabeth clinked her own cup gently against Jess's. "Well, we'll see about that."

# 6

"You know, I have this funny pain in my knee sometimes. Not really a pain, more of a twinge, I guess." Juanita set Jess's salad on the table in front of her and bent to rub the offending joint. "It just comes and goes for no apparent reason. There's no bruise or anything. Do you have any idea what it might be?"

"Is it swollen?" Jess knew better than to engage in casual encounter diagnoses, but the question just seemed to pose itself.

"No. There's nothing you can see that might be causing it. It just up and hurts awhile and then it quits." Juanita's forehead furrowed. "What do you think?"

Jess looked at Juanita's knee, covered as it was with thick support hose. "I really can't tell anything without examining it. Why don't you call the office and make an appointment? We shouldn't have much trouble fitting you in."

"Oh, don't worry about it." Juanita's expression relaxed and she flapped a dismissive hand. "I have an appointment with my regular doctor in a couple weeks. If it's still bothering me, I'll get him to check it for me. I just thought since you were here and all that you might be able to tell me something."

She moved off, without a trace of a limp, to ask the next table if they needed any more iced tea, and Jess picked up her fork. *And there you have the second most effective way of dealing with tableside medical consultations—the first being to ask the patient to disrobe.*

Jess looked around the room as she ate her lunch. Every time she came into the Dip 'n' Dine, she felt a little less like a stranger, and that felt good. In the excitement of her plans, she had dismissed her mother's concern that she was moving somewhere where she wouldn't know a soul. She liked people and never had trouble making friends. But she had never encountered a place like Last Chance, where everybody seemed to have known everybody else all their lives. They were friendly and even welcoming, but she still had that feeling that she was company and they were family.

Across the room Lainie Braden, still slim in her uniform, took an order from two men perched side by side on counter stools. Lainie had been new once, but now she was as much a part of the town as the craggy eastern mountains or the faded asphalt highway that called itself Main Street as it ran through town.

Jess munched thoughtfully on a bite of lettuce. *I wonder if I would sound pathetic if I asked her what her secret is. Probably. I'll just give it a little more time.*

As if she could sense Jess's gaze, Lainie looked up and met her eyes with a wide smile. She murmured something to the men at the counter before making her way across the room to where Jess sat by the window.

"Hey there. How are you doing?" She really did seem glad to see her, and Jess felt her loneliness shift a little to make room for the warmth of Lainie's smile.

"I'm fine, but how are *you* doing? Still feeling good?"

Lainie laughed. "I'm feeling great. And if you could turn that into a medical diagnosis and tell my husband and his grandmother, I'd really appreciate it."

"Glad to hear it." Jess let the comment about the diagnosis pass.

"Of course, you probably need to wait till after my appointment, but I'm counting on you."

"Appointment?" Jess hadn't heard about that.

"I know, it's not for another three weeks, but I went ahead and scheduled one. I didn't want to wait to the last minute and then find out you were all booked up and couldn't take any more patients."

"Yeah, that's a real possibility." Jess laughed. "But I couldn't be more tickled. And once we've had that first appointment, you can count on me being in your corner all the way. If at all feasible, Mom calls the shots, I say."

"I knew I liked you." Lainie grinned. "Mom. Wow. I have to get used to that."

"How's that salad? Need some more iced tea?" Juanita appeared at the table and stood just close enough to Lainie that she had to step back a little.

Lainie took the hint and gave Jess a wink as she moved away. "I'll talk to you later."

Juanita watched her go and turned back to Jess with a shake of her head. "That girl is just the sweetest thing ever, and I've loved her since the day she landed in Last Chance, but she does like to visit with the customers. Now, how about a little more tea."

"Thanks." Jess nudged her glass a little closer.

"I just have to ask." Juanita poured the tea and stood back regarding Jess's plate. "Why do you get that salad every time you come in here? I mean, it's good and all, but it's probably the most boring thing on the whole menu. Are you on some kind of weird diet or something?"

"No. I just like salad." With Juanita looming over her, Jess felt a little protective of her plate of greens.

"Well, you must, that's all I can say. Have you even tried anything else on the menu?"

"Um, no. Not for lunch, anyway." Jess looked around the room. All the other diners were eating as if Juanita calling someone on the carpet was nothing new, and Lainie was nowhere in sight. If Jess were anywhere else, she'd ask for the check and flee, never to return, but something told her that she didn't want to burn that bridge. She smiled up at Juanita, trying to keep her voice light. "But you never know. I might surprise you someday."

"Shock me someday is more like it." Juanita gave Jess's plate one last contemptuous glance and sighed. "Well, if that day ever comes, let me know and I'll recommend something. Carlos is the best cook in this part of the state, and it's not his salads that he's known for."

Juanita took her iced tea pitcher and moved off to tend some other table, looking for all the world as if she hadn't just raked a customer over the coals for her menu choice, and Jess watched her go. Some people leaned back in their booth and propped their elbows on the table for a chat; others barely glanced up and went back to their meals. Juanita seemed equally at ease with either reaction. Maybe that was the key. Let Juanita be Juanita; just don't let her under your skin.

Down the road at the high school just past the edge of town, Andy shoved the last of his peanut butter and jelly sandwich in his mouth and brushed the crumbs off his desk. Peanut butter and jelly had pretty much become his diet since football practice started. It was easy to slap on some bread in the predawn darkness before he headed to school in the morning, and it didn't take more strength than he had left when he dragged himself home in the evening. Good thing he liked peanut butter. Or he had before football practice started.

"How'd it go?" Kev came in looking happy and well fed. But then, he went home for lunch.

Andy shrugged. "About like you'd expect, I guess. No one likes getting cut, especially when we're this far into preseason practice. I expect I'll be getting a few calls tonight from dads demanding an explanation."

"Glad it'll be you and not me." Kev leaned over the desk and turned the roster so he could see it. "I guess this is when it gets hard. These last few might play if they were at a larger school."

"Well, it's never easy to let someone go when they really want it." Andy leaned back and clasped his hands behind his head.

"Like this one. Man, he's a fighter. Too bad he's got so many strikes against him." Kev tapped the sheet with a pencil.

Andy leaned to look. "Who, Quintana? Yeah, you're right on both counts. He's got a rough row to hoe, all right. And he is a fighter. That's why I'm not quite ready to let him go yet."

"Really? I had him pegged for next. I feel for the guy, but he has a hard time even making it to practice. And when it comes to raw talent, he just doesn't have what some of these other guys have—guys you'd have to cut to keep him."

Andy didn't say anything. His assistant was right. Gabe was the next logical cut. He was smaller than most of the other players and had already missed two early morning practices. And more than once, Andy had held off summoning the team from the track for a few minutes because he saw Gabe's battered pickup speeding down the highway and throwing up a cloud of dust as it careened into the parking lot. But man, he could scrap. Whether it was drills or a scrimmage, Gabe Quintana went after it like it was the championship game and it all depended on him.

"Well, you're the coach. I'm the first to admit that you know a whole lot more about this process than I do." Kev broke the silence and headed back to his desk. "Say, if you could monitor the weight room this afternoon, I'd sure like an hour or two to go work on my classroom. I'll need to be switching hats back and forth here pretty soon."

"Sure. No problem. I guess I got so wrapped up in what we're doing here that I'd forgotten you have classes to teach."

"Yep. Two American history, one world history, and a government class. Coaches teach around here, unless you're a football hero or something." Kev grinned and raised both hands when Andy glanced up at him. "Sorry, man, I didn't mean that the way it sounded. It's just that we haven't had a full-time athletic director since the Glory Days. I guess the school board's counting on you having your hands full getting another streak like that one started."

Andy shook his head. "Nope, I read the contract carefully. It said coach the football team and coordinate the rest of the athletic program. Not a word about a winning streak."

"Yeah, right. Check again and this time read between the lines; you'll find it, trust me." Kev reached for his hat. "Listen, if I go now, I'll be back in plenty of time to make sure we're ready for late practice. Okay with you?"

"Sure." Andy waved him away and went back to the papers piled all over his desk. He didn't need to go back over his contract to read between the lines. With every interview he'd had before being hired, with every conversation since then that had turned to the Glory Days, with every discussion with Russ Sheppard and the Boosters, over and over he had said the same thing: this is a different time, these are different boys, you can't saddle them with the past. And everyone had nodded solemnly and agreed. And every single one of them, Andy knew, cherished in his heart the belief that the mighty Pumas of tiny Last Chance were poised again to be the talk of the state, maybe even the whole country. He found himself longing for one, even one, conversation that didn't devolve to the Glory Days. And even though he knew exactly the one person he'd like to have that conversation with, he didn't see how he could squeeze it in until after football season.

Jess slowed her car and rolled down the window as she passed the Welcome to Last Chance sign and drove into town. The warm, dry air, golden with sunset and still spicy with roasting chile, slid across her shoulders and ruffled her hair, chasing the chill she still felt after her day in the air-conditioned offices of the San Ramon Medical Center. Her first full day of taking Dr. Benavides's patients while he was on vacation had been long and exhausting but so rewarding. She hadn't put in a day like that since her residency. This, *this* was what she was created to do.

As she pulled up to the town's one blinking stoplight, she saw Andy Ryan's pickup approach the intersection from across the street. She returned his wave and made her turn. If he were on his way home, he ought to be right behind her. A quick glance in her rearview mirror confirmed that, and she smiled. She was even more pleased when she pulled into her driveway and he stopped at the curb.

"Hi there. It's been awhile. How are you?" Jess got out of her car and walked to the truck where Andy leaned across the seat to smile at her through the passenger window.

"Doing great. Busy." He had the nicest smile. "How about you? Still getting those runs in?"

"Oh, yes. Every morning. Then I walk awhile with Elizabeth Cooley. She's amazing."

"Oh, everybody knows that Elizabeth's amazing. She gives Last Chance bragging rights. Right up there with the chile and the Dip 'n' Dine."

"And, of course, the football team." Jess had meant to sound supportive, but she noticed Andy's smile dimmed just a little as he nodded.

"Yep. There's the football team."

"Why don't you come in? We'll dig around and find something to eat." Jess had no idea what was in her kitchen. Certainly whatever they found would bear no resemblance to the feast they had shared at Elizabeth's, but she was pretty sure she could scare something up.

"Nah, I should get on home." Andy leaned back behind the wheel. "Looks like you've had a long day. You probably want to just kick off your shoes and relax."

"That's exactly what I'm going to do. But I don't see any reason why that means you can't come in. I'm not planning on cooking a big meal, if that's what you're worried about, but we should be able to find something to eat while we talk."

"Peanut butter?"

"Ew. No. Sorry, not peanut butter."

Andy opened his door. "Then I'm your man."

Jess cocked an eyebrow as Andy joined her on the sidewalk. "That's your criterion? No peanut butter? Are you allergic?"

"Getting that way." Andy followed her down the walk and into the house. He shoved both hands in his pockets and looked around. "Wow. It's been over ten years since I've been here. Brings back a lot of memories."

Jess had already kicked off her shoes at the door and was heading for the kitchen. She stuck her head back around the corner. "When were you here?"

"Back when I was growing up, Rita and her family were still living here and I knew both her sons. I played football with them, as a matter of fact." Andy followed her to the kitchen and leaned against the doorjamb as Jess rummaged around in the refrigerator. "As you can imagine, Rita was involved in every aspect of the boys' lives. Den mother when we were little, Booster president when we started playing sports. And every Tuesday night, all through junior high and high school, she had the whole youth group from church over for supper and Bible study. I'll bet she made enough spaghetti sauce over the years to float a battleship."

"Sounds like Rita." Jess put some eggs and cheese on the counter and went back to the refrigerator. "I knew the house was hers, of course. I'm renting from her. But I guess I just assumed she'd always been mayor and ran the motel."

"No, she didn't run for mayor until the kids left home." Andy shifted positions and folded his arms over his chest. "And then when her husband Mike died, she bought the motel. I guess it just got too quiet for her here."

"I can understand that. I feel more alive when I'm around people too. I couldn't stand it if all of a sudden I had nothing to do." Setting a tomato and a few mushrooms on the counter next to the eggs and cheese, Jess let the refrigerator door swing shut. "Omelets okay?"

"Omelets sound great." Andy pushed away from the doorjamb and joined Jess at the counter. "What can I do?"

"Here. You can grate some cheese." She reached into a drawer and pulled out the grater. "I'll make some decaf coffee."

As he went to work on the chunk of cheese, Jess glanced up at him. How had she not noticed how tall he was? And how had she not noticed how broad his shoulders were and that his hands were so big that the block of cheese he held all but disappeared? Yep, he was a specimen, all right.

He glanced over and caught her looking. "What?"

Jess laughed. "You. Remember the morning I first met you at the

Dip 'n' Dine? Before Rita even brought me over to introduce me to you, she told me what a football hero you were. And of course, that's pretty much all I've heard about you ever since, but this is the first time I've noticed how well you fit the image. I'll bet if I look in the dictionary under 'jock,' I'll find your picture. Do you have to carry a club to keep the girls at bay?"

"Nope. I just stiff-arm them. Football training can come in handy." Andy went back to his cheese grater, but his smile had disappeared.

"Okay, what'd I say wrong?" Jess folded her arms and leaned against the counter. "Girls don't come after you in droves? What?"

Andy finished his task and dropped the grater in the sink. "I guess I've just never liked the term 'jock.' It's a label—like all labels, I guess—that dismisses anything else I am. Plus, it trivializes the work and drive and even pain that go into playing the best game I can play." His half smile was a little rueful. "Sorry. I guess I'm more tired than I realized. Didn't mean to get all bristly."

Jess was silent a minute. "You know, I get it, and I'm sorry. It's the same with 'geek.' Growing up, I certainly had all the qualifications, and it was never meant as an insult, at least not by anyone whose opinion I cared anything about, but it does trivialize your accomplishments, doesn't it? I mean, *of course* I took all that math and science; that's what geeks take. *Of course* I had a 4.4 GPA; geeks are smart. Well, let me tell you that none of that was handed to me on a platter. I had to work and work hard for it."

Andy just looked at her. "You had a 4.4? Wow, you *are* a geek. I didn't even know GPAs went that high."

Grabbing an oven mitt from the counter, Jess took a swipe at him. "Just go sit down and let me make these omelets."

Andy swung a chair around and straddled it while Jess cracked eggs into a bowl and whipped them with a fork. He didn't say anything, but she felt his gaze. When she slid the last omelet onto a plate and turned around, he was resting his chin on hands he had folded on the back of the chair.

She smiled as she set the plates on the table and went for the coffeepot. "Tired, or just lost in thought?"

"Both, I guess." He got up and pulled Jess's chair out before turning his own around to face the table. "Mostly just thinking."

No one but headwaiters had ever pulled out her chair, and if her earlier attempts at teasing him hadn't fallen flat, she might have told him so. Instead, she just smiled her thanks and sat down.

"Care to share any of those deep thoughts?" She filled their cups and picked up her fork.

Andy appeared to be waiting for something, but after a second or two, he picked up his own fork. "Nothing deep. Just being here in the Sandovals' house got me thinking about all those kids I grew up with. We'd sit around here on Tuesday nights and talk about what we were going to do with our lives. It just never occurred to any of us that we might fail."

"Fail?"

"Well, maybe not fail, but hardly any of us are living the lives we thought we would."

"What did you think you would do?"

His grin looked a little sheepish. "Well, I wanted to play football, of course—college, even the NFL, and then coach."

"And isn't that exactly what you did? I mean, to the letter?"

"Yeah, I guess, but with a couple exceptions. I didn't think I'd be coaching high school football, and I got here about ten years ahead of schedule."

"Why's that?" Jess regretted the question as soon as it left her lips, but she could never seem to learn to be anything but direct.

Andy held her gaze a long moment before looking down and

pushing a bite of omelet around his plate with his fork. When he looked up, all traces of a smile had left his face.

"I wasn't good enough."

"Now, I may not know anything about football, but I know that's not true." Jess was back on solid ground. Helping folks stay positive was part of her training, as well as who she was. "It may have felt that way, but Rita showed me that scrapbook she kept. I just saw the headlines, of course, but it was pretty clear that you were good."

"Ah, Rita." Andy's grin was back, even if it was a little lopsided. "She's a one-woman cheer squad."

"Maybe so, but she didn't write those articles; she just clipped them. So what happened? What brought you back to Last Chance? Unless it's something you don't want to talk about."

"No, it's pretty much common knowledge. I was backup quarterback for the Broncos for about five seasons. Seemed like a lot of that time was spent recovering from injuries that I got when I did get some playing time. Then, when it looked like I was going to get my shot at quarterback, they brought in someone else. And behind me was another hotshot quarterback they had just drafted. I saw the writing on the wall. It wasn't going to happen for me, and since I didn't want to spend the next who-knows-how-many seasons freezing on the bench watching other men play, I retired. If you can call it retiring."

Silence fell in the little kitchen as Andy turned his attention to his omelet. After a few seconds, Jess reached across the table and put her hand on his arm.

"I'm sorry it didn't turn out like you wanted it to. That had to have been rough. But don't forget, the people around here know football, and they watched everything you described unfold. If all I had to listen to was you, I'd think yours was a sad and sorry tale, but everybody in town can relate every detail of your career, and you're still the biggest hero in town."

"Well, their outlook may be just a little limited, not to mention biased." Andy's grin was back.

"I think you're underestimating both the town and yourself." Jess threw her napkin next to her plate and pushed her chair back. "Now, I think I still have some cherry vanilla ice cream in the freezer. Want some?"

# 7

Hi, I'll bet you're Emma." Jess smiled at the little girl sitting on the examination table before turning to extend a hand to the woman sitting on a chair next to her. "Good morning. I'm Dr. MacLeod. And why are we seeing Emma this morning?"

"Where's Dr. Benavides?" The handshake Mrs. Anderson offered was listless and brief, and she didn't return Jess's smile.

"He's on vacation and I'm seeing his patients while he's gone." Jess glanced down at Emma's file. "But if it's important that you see him, I imagine you can reschedule your appointment. He'll be back next week."

Mrs. Anderson huffed a little and resettled her purse on her lap. "No. We're already here, and I had to rearrange my schedule and drive in from Last Chance. But I wish they had told me Dr. Benavides wasn't going to be here when I made the appointment. It was only for her checkup. I could easily have waited."

"You live in Last Chance?" Jess held her stethoscope between her hands to warm it. "I just moved there myself. In fact, I'll be keeping office hours there a few days a week."

"Oh, I know who you are." Mrs. Anderson had a smile of sorts pasted on her face, but she still did not sound very happy. "I'm sure some people will really appreciate the convenience, but when it comes to Emma's health, convenience is the last thing I worry about. I'm sure you understand."

"Okay, let's see how far you can stick out your tongue." Jess decided to let Mrs. Anderson's comments pass and concentrate on her patient. "Come on. Pretend I'm that rotten boy who sits behind you in school."

Emma actually smiled for the first time since Jess had walked in the room, but when her mother cleared her throat, the smile faded and her tongue retreated.

"Oh, my goodness." Mrs. Anderson's laugh was light and brittle. "You don't need to pretend that to stick out your tongue, Emma. Just say 'ahh' for Dr. MacLeod, like you do for Dr. Benavides."

"Ahh." Emma promptly obeyed.

A vague uneasiness came over Jess as she completed her examination, and she found herself checking for telltale marks or bumps. Emma had yet to say one word, despite the questions and comments Jess directed to her personally. Mrs. Anderson, however, did not stop talking.

"You know, I'm afraid I might have given you the wrong impression earlier. It's not that I think Dr. Benavides is more competent than you are. That's not why I'm willing to drive to San Ramon when you'll be right there in town. That's not it at all. It's just that Dr. Benavides has been our family doctor for years. He's looked after Emma since she was a baby." She laughed lightly. "I hope you understand it's nothing personal."

*Right*. Jess continued her examination without answering. *Nothing personal*.

"Well, Emma, how much time do you spend outside?" Jess stood back and smiled at the little girl huddled on the examination table. Emma didn't even open her mouth.

"Oh, if only she had that kind of time." There was that laugh again. "With her piano practice, and her schoolwork, and her chores, there just aren't enough daylight hours."

"Do you like recess?" Jess was determined to get Emma to say something.

Emma shrugged, and her mother answered the question. "They have to force her outside. She'd like nothing more than to be left alone indoors with a book."

"What about friends, Emma? Do you like to play with your friends?"

This time there was no laughter from the chair behind Jess. "My goodness. I thought we were just coming in for a simple checkup. Dr. Benavides never asks these kinds of questions. Is there some reason why you are concerned, Dr. MacLeod? Or are we finished here?"

With a final wink at Emma, Jess turned back to her mother. "We're done. Except that the flu vaccination came in this week. We could give Emma her flu shot now, or you could wait till Dr. Benavides gets back, if you'd rather."

Mrs. Anderson hesitated a long moment before she sighed. "Oh well, we're already here. We might as well get it taken care of now."

Jess had been watching Emma. She had yet to meet an eight-year-old who didn't need at least a little calming at the mention of a shot, but except for a slight flicker of her eyes, Emma was as unmoved as if she had not even heard. There had been no marks or any sign whatsoever of physical abuse on Emma's body, but something was not right, and when Dr. Benavides got back, Jess intended to see if he had any idea what that might be.

"Are you going to the game Friday?"

"Hmm?" Jess looked up from the mug of thick, overbrewed

coffee she was staring into. The morning had been packed, but she still couldn't get Emma Anderson off her mind. "What game?"

"The season opener between Last Chance and San Ramon. What else?" The young nurse shut the door of the cabinet she had been restocking and cocked her head as she turned to stare at Jess. "It's only the biggest rivalry in this part of the state. It was San Ramon that broke Last Chance's big winning streak, you know."

From Theresa's satisfied smile, Jess had little doubt on which side of the rivalry Theresa stood. She shook her head. "No, I don't think so. Friday night I'm going to be home in my sweats with my book and a big mug of herbal tea. It's been a long week, and I'm looking forward to it."

"Seriously? You'd miss the game?"

"Seriously. I am going to miss the game. But you go on and cheer for the both of us." Jess took a sip of her coffee and shuddered as she dumped it in the sink. "Who makes this stuff, and does anyone actually drink it?"

Theresa seemed to be too stunned by Jess's complete disregard of Friday's game to even register the coffee comment.

"But you know that Andy Ryan has come back to coach Last Chance, right?"

"So I've heard." Jess opened the cupboard over the sink and poked through the contents. "Isn't there anything but coffee here? No tea?"

"And you live in Last Chance and everything?"

"Yep." Jess pulled out a box of instant cocoa packets, made a face, and put it back.

Theresa shrugged. "Well, I guess that's your choice, but you'll be the only one in town who won't be at the game. Have fun with your book."

The smile she tossed Jess's way as she left the room was one

Jess knew well. It was the easy, breezy, not-quite-dismissive smile the cheerleader tossed the book-laden geek as they passed in the hall. It had never bothered her in high school. She had a wide circle of friends and a ton of activities of her own, and frankly, she had never felt the slightest desire to be a cheerleader. But she was pretty much on her own here.

Maybe she *should* reconsider. After all, what would it take? Just two or three hours of her life, that's all. Two or three hours sitting on a cold bleacher among a lot of people she didn't know who were screaming about something she didn't understand while watching a bunch of bulked-up boys knock each other down.

*Nope, not happening*. She rinsed out her mug and set it on the drain board. Never in her life had the need for peer acceptance driven her to conform, and she couldn't muster up even a twinge now. Friday night with her book was looking better and better.

By Friday, not only Theresa but nearly everyone Jess came in contact with was talking about the game. As she left San Ramon and headed down the Last Chance Highway toward home, the pickups with "Skin the Pumas" daubed on the back window with white shoe polish gave way to those adorned with "Beat San Ramon" signs. Even the front window of the Dip 'n' Dine had a snarling puma and the words "Go Last Chance High" stenciled across the glass just under the glowing neon Open sign.

"Glad I made it." Jess thought she caught a slight frown on Juanita's face when she opened the door. "I was afraid you might be closing early."

"Well, we were hoping we might, but come on in." No doubt about it, Juanita was perturbed, even though the diner wasn't scheduled to close for nearly an hour. "I suppose you want that salad?"

"I think I'll try something different today." Jess reached for the menu Juanita wasn't quite holding out to her. Being an outsider had its limits. "What's the special?"

"Right there as you came in." Juanita tilted her head toward the whiteboard mounted by the door. "Friday is cheese enchiladas."

"Okay. I'll give those a try. I guess there's no point in asking you if they're good." If Jess thought smiling and trying to engage Juanita in conversation was going to lighten things up, she thought wrong. For once, Juanita was in no mood to chat.

"Red or green?"

"Red or green what?" Jess glanced at her menu again, looking for a clue.

Juanita shifted her weight to her other foot and may have rolled her eyes. "Chile. You want red or green chile on your enchiladas?"

"Oh, that's right. Um, I don't know. Is there any difference, other than the color, of course?"

This time there was no mistaking Juanita's eye-roll, and Jess remembered just a beat too late that Juanita and her husband had a huge chile farm just outside of town.

"Our red can be hotter. But the green's pretty hot too. It's up to you." She tapped her pad with her pencil.

"Green, I guess."

"I'll get this right in." Juanita took the menu and ripped the top sheet off her order pad. "Oh, you want an egg on it?"

"An egg?"

Juanita's voice had the studied patience of a preschool teacher. "Yes, an egg. Some people like an egg on their enchiladas. In fact, I'd recommend it for you. It kind of soothes the bite a little. So, an egg over easy?"

"You know what? Just bring me the salad." Suddenly, Jess was done talking about the special of the day. Truth be told, she was pretty done with talking to Juanita at all. In fact, she had no idea how the Dip 'n' Dine managed to stay open with a waitress who went around picking fights with the customers over their orders.

Juanita didn't say anything. She just heaved a sigh, wadded up the order she had torn off her pad, and wrote another.

"Juanita, I'll take this table." Jess hadn't seen Lainie when she came in, but there she was, smiling and touching Juanita's shoulder. "There probably won't be anyone else coming in. Why don't you go on home? I'm sure Russ wants to get to the game early."

Jess could have hugged her.

"Well, you need to get out of here as much as I do." Juanita still sounded miffed, but Jess noticed that she did hand off the menu. "You don't want to miss the Parade of Pumas."

"I won't miss anything. Ray's coming by for me in an hour. We'll have plenty of time to get there."

"Okay, if you're sure. I'll drop this order off on my way to get my stuff." Juanita's mood had turned on a dime, and she smiled cheerfully at Jess. "You really ought to try those enchiladas sometime. And don't forget the egg. The egg just makes it."

Jess watched her stop by the window to the kitchen before disappearing in the back. "What was that all about?" She kept her voice to a bewildered whisper. "Is it really poor form to want dinner on the night there's a game?"

Lainie laughed. "No, not at all. The season opener is a pretty big deal, which is why Juanita was in such a big hurry. Her husband is president of the Boosters, and they all sit in a special section on the fifty-yard line, and of course, he's in the Parade of Pumas as well. But most Fridays are pretty sane, especially when the team is away. Except for homecoming—then it's *really* crazy."

"Bye now." Juanita came back with her sweater on and her

purse slung over her shoulder. She waved as she headed out the door. "Now don't get so busy talking that you get behind. Ray has to make that parade, and you need to cheer him on."

"We'll be there." Lainie looked toward the kitchen as the ding of a bell signaled Jess's salad was ready. "Be right back."

When she returned, she set the salad in front of Jess along with a small bowl of some kind of stew and a thick white tortilla wrapped in a napkin.

"What's this?"

"This is from Carlos. Juanita's voice has a way of carrying, and he heard your conversation earlier. He said to tell you he'd be happy to make you a salad every time you come in here, but he wants you to just try his green chile stew. It's famous."

Picking up her spoon, Jess regarded the stew with a little frown. "Is it hot?"

"You mean chile hot? Yeah, it's got a little heat to it. That's what the tortilla's for. Spread butter on it, and then if your stew is hot, take a bite of tortilla. It's a perfect combination."

Jess did as she was told, and her eyes closed as the bite of tender pork and green chile warmed her mouth. "Oh, my. I may never order salad again. That is amazing."

"It's a favorite around here. Enjoy." Lainie smiled. "Now, is there anything else I can do for you?"

"Just one thing. What is a Parade of Pumas? It sounds like something the animal rights people would be all over."

Lainie laughed. "No, it's nothing quite so dramatic. It's just a Last Chance tradition that right before the team takes the field at the season opener, every former football player who can still fit in his letterman's jacket—and a good many who shouldn't even try—takes a walk around the track. Everybody cheers and they all wave and feel like heroes again. They go in order of the year they played, with the old guys out in front and last year's graduates bringing up the rear. It's sort of a rite of passage for them."

"Ray takes part too? It just doesn't sound like him."

"Oh, yeah. Once a Puma, always a Puma. In fact, a bunch of guys he played with are coming back especially for this game, since they were all on Andy's team."

"Wow." Jess pushed her salad aside so she could better concentrate on her green chile stew. "And I thought they were serious about football at Cal."

Lainie threw up a hand. "Sister, you have no idea. Now, unless I can get you anything else, I'd probably better get to work. Ray will be here before I know it."

"Go." Jess waved her away. "I'd hate to have you late to the game on my account."

As Lainie grabbed a tray and went from table to table picking up salt and pepper shakers, Jess turned her attention back to her meal. She had come to the Dip 'n' Dine nearly every day since arriving in Last Chance, and the spicy aroma of green chile stew had greeted her every time she opened the door. What in the world had she been thinking to simply order salad without ever investigating that tantalizing fragrance? She tore off a piece of thick, warm, buttered tortilla and used it to wipe the last drops from her empty bowl. Next time, it would be the enchiladas—with an egg.

Ray was just getting out of his truck when Jess pushed through the door and out into the parking lot. His black letterman's jacket with the gold leather sleeves still fit him well.

"Look at you!" Jess raised her eyebrows in appreciation. "That parade must be something to see. I'm beginning to be sorry I'm not going tonight."

"There's still plenty of time. You can change your mind, you know." Ray grinned as he headed for the front door.

"I'm not that sorry." With a wave, Jess slid behind the wheel of her car. "Have fun tonight."

A long line of pickups and a few cars, all decorated in the green and white of San Ramon High and loudly blaring their horns, entered Last Chance from the north and began their noisy procession down Main Street to the high school just south of town. Jess waited until the last car was a block or two down the road before pulling out onto the road behind them. So far, Last Chance had considered her merely uninformed and maybe a little eccentric to willfully miss the season opener, but if she were seen joining the opposition, who knows what damage that might do?

The streets were empty and, except for the sound of honking growing fainter in the distance, silent. To the west, the vivid crimson, coral, and gold of a desert sunset reached high in the darkening turquoise of the sky. Jess sighed and let her head drop against the headrest. Filling in for Dr. Benavides had been exhilarating, and she had loved every moment, but the week had been exhausting. Through it all, the peaceful quiet of a Friday night at home had hung before her like a carrot on a stick, but now that it actually lay before her, Jess felt a little out of sorts. Even in medical school, when her colleagues took advantage of the rare free moment to catch up on their sleep, Jess had wanted company. She missed her friends. People energized her, and an evening sitting cross-legged on the sagging sofa of a student apartment sharing everything from cat videos to solutions to the world's problems to the deepest secrets of the heart was her idea of perfection. Loneliness, always hovering on the edges of her consciousness, moved in and threatened to crush her.

*Enough of that*. Jess rolled down her window and let the warm wind that always picked up at sundown fill her car with the fragrance of sun-warmed mesquite. *You knew it was going to take a while to find your niche when you decided to move to a small town, so just get over it and quit feeling sorry for yourself. Call Mom if you have to talk to someone tonight.*

Jess squared her shoulders as she turned off Main Street and headed for home. Giving herself stern lectures was something she did well, and furthermore, she usually listened. Becoming a part of Last Chance might not be easy, but she would do everything it took.

Just south of town, Jess could see the towering banks of lights illuminating the darkening sky. *Well, almost everything.*

"Mom?" Jess's book kept her attention for almost an hour before the silence grew so heavy she could feel it pressing around her and she reached for her phone.

"Jess! How are you, honey? Everything okay?"

"Oh, I'm fine." At the sound of her mother's voice, Jess realized she didn't feel fine at all. Tears stung her eyes. "I just miss you. That's all."

"We miss you too, but you've wanted a small town practice since you were a little girl, so we can't feel too bad. You're doing what you've always wanted to do."

Jess drew a shaky breath. "Am I?"

"Oh, honey, you sound so sad. What's wrong?"

"I don't know. It's just not what I thought it would be. There's this waitress at the diner who yells at me every time I go in there, and everyone I meet tells me they already have a doctor before I even say anything, and they all think I'm strange because I don't like football."

"My goodness, that is rough." Her mom's voice comforted Jess like a warm hug, but even so, she could hear the laughter just below the surface. "I don't believe I'd go back to a restaurant where the waitress yelled at me every time. Maybe you should find another restaurant and look for some friends who have interests other than football."

"Mom, there aren't any!" Jess knew she sounded like a fourteen-year-old, but sometimes, especially when you were talking to your mom, you just needed to be able to sound like a fourteen-year-old. "Seriously. There is one diner in the whole town, and the waitress yells. And everyone, and I mean *everyone*, is crazy about high school football. They think I'm the weird one."

"I am sorry you're having a hard time of it, honey, but give it time. It always takes a while to adjust to a new place."

"This is all your fault, you know." Jess wasn't ready to listen to common sense. Not yet.

"My fault? How?"

"It's all those stories you told me about your grandpa being the only doctor in that little town. About how everyone in town knew him and called him Doc. About how you'd go with him and wait in the car when he made house calls after dinner, and how you'd stop and get ice cream on the way home."

"My goodness, honey, that was a long, long time ago. Things have changed. Surely you noticed that's not the way your dad and I manage our practices."

"Well, we lived in the city. That's why I wanted to live in a small town."

Jess could hear her mother's sigh come over the phone.

"Well, darling, I'm sorry things aren't like you thought they would be, but as I see it, you have a couple choices. You can admit you made a mistake and cut your losses before you waste any more time. I ran into Moira Conner at the hospital the other day, and she was asking about you. If you want to come home, she'd be the one to talk to."

"But I don't want to come home."

"Well then, it seems like the other thing you can do is decide you're going to succeed in Last Chance. If that means making friends with the waitress, do it. And if you need to go to football games to fit in, do that too. Buy a book and read up if you need to."

Jess didn't say anything. She wanted Poor Baby Mom, not Get a Grip Mom.

"Oh, Jessica." Her mother's voice softened again. "I have so much faith in you. You are an amazing woman and an amazing doctor. You can do anything you want, anywhere you want. That's just who you are. But you are the one who has to decide to do it. I can't do it for you. No one can. Okay?"

"Okay." Jess didn't feel great, but she did feel better.

"Listen, honey, I'm going to have to run. We have tickets for the symphony tonight and your dad's standing at the front door looking at me."

"Oh, sorry to keep you, Mom. Give Dad my love."

"I will. And all our love to you too, sweetie."

Jess punched End on her phone and leaned back against the sofa. Talking to her mom made her realize that she really did want to make a go of it here in Last Chance, and if that meant making friends with Juanita, she'd just have to figure out how. But reading up on football and all that rah-rah stuff? That just might be more than she could bring herself to do.

# 8

The banks of lights had faded to darkness and the parking lot had emptied before Andy finally got in his truck to head home. He had experienced losses on the field before, both at the University of Arizona and when he played for Denver, but never here before tonight. Not once. Funny. You'd think with all the talk of the Glory Days since he'd been back, he would have at least considered that at the end of every one of those eighty-four games, some team had straggled off the field in exhausted silence while the fans and players of the mighty Pumas of Last Chance celebrated their invincibility. Well, tonight it was San Ramon who celebrated.

Main Street was silent and empty when he drove back through town. It usually was this time of night, but back in the day, when win piled upon win, no one wanted to go home, and pickups piled with his friends slowly drove Main Street from one end to the other before turning and driving back the other way or heading up to San Ramon to find someplace to eat that actually stayed open past sundown. Man, that seemed like a long time ago, and when did he start feeling so old?

The phone in his pocket vibrated, but Andy ignored it. In the first place, his pickup hadn't been equipped to handle hands-free calling, and he'd never bothered to have it installed, but more than that, he could not think of one person he wanted to talk to right now. As he passed by Jess's house, with its still lit windows, he glanced over out of recently acquired habit and shook his head. *Nope, not even her.*

By the time he turned off onto the dirt road that led to his house and his headlights picked up the long, low adobe sitting under an ancient cottonwood tree, his phone had signaled several more calls.

*Too bad. They're just going to have to wait till morning.*

When he turned off his ignition and the house sank back in darkness, he sat in the cab a moment listening to the night wind toss the branches of the old tree before opening the door and heading for the front door.

*Okay, shake it off. You've got a team meeting tomorrow at 10:00 and another game to get ready for next Friday. You need to let this one go.*

He fixed himself a couple peanut butter sandwiches and poured a large glass of milk before he settled on the sofa, and by the time he'd finished one and downed the glass of milk, he was actually starting to feel a little better. Digging into his pocket, he pulled out his phone. It was too late to call anyone back even if he wanted to, which he didn't, but it wouldn't hurt to see who called. One message from Russ Sheppard, two from his mom, and three from people he didn't know. If he were anywhere else, he might have wondered how the strangers got his number so fast, but this was Last Chance. If anyone had his private number, everyone had his private number. He sighed as he hit Russ's message. Might as well get this over with and see what the mood was.

"Andy, this is Russ Sheppard. I imagine you and the boys are feeling kind of low right now, but I want you to know we're real proud of the effort you made tonight. San Ramon has always been a tough competitor, and this was just one game. We're still looking for big things from you all, so put this one behind you and move on to the next. We're with you all the way. If you need anything at all, just let us know. That's what we're here for. Get some rest now, and we'll talk to you soon."

*Could be worse.* Andy took a deep breath and blew it out. *Now Mom.* If he knew for sure she just wanted to ask about the game, he'd let it wait, but there was always the possibility that something was wrong. He played the first message.

"Hi, honey, it's Mom. This is the big night, and Aunt Barb and I couldn't be more excited. We'll be praying for you all evening, so give us a call the minute the game is over, okay? Hang on a second . . . Aunt Barb says, 'Go Pumas!' Love you!"

Andy leaned back against the sofa. He'd call in the morning. It was an hour later in Oklahoma, anyway. From the time stamp on Mom's second call, he guessed it was probably one of those that came in while he was on his way home from the game. Again the desire to put the game behind him, at least till morning, fought with the worry that somewhere between the first and second message, some disaster had befallen. And again, that responsibility he felt for his mom won. He hit Play Message.

"Hi, hon, it's me again. I'm thinking the game must be over now, and I'll bet you're worried about it being too late to call. Well, don't worry about that. Aunt Barb just made us a big bowl of popcorn and *The King and I* is fixing to come on TV. We're going to be up for a long time yet, so you call us, you hear? We won't be able to sleep a wink till we hear from you. Love you! Hang on . . . Aunt Barb sends her love too."

Andy felt a flash of annoyance. He could picture his mother and his aunt sitting in their robes and slippers eating popcorn and watching the old musical with the phone in easy reach. And he had not the slightest doubt that they would wait up until he called. Mom always waited up. He hit Call Back and dropped his head against the back of the sofa.

"There you are! We were starting to get worried."

Andy hadn't been able to get his mom to use the mobile phone he bought her, but he had been able to get caller ID on her landline.

"Hi Mom."

"Ooh. I don't like that tone. I guess things didn't go like you hoped?"

"Nope." How did she get so much from two words?

"Oh, I'm sorry. What was the score?"

"Six to 31."

"Oh, dear. Well, you'll do better next time. Was it a good game? Everyone played well and no one was hurt?"

"I don't know that I could call a 6 to 31 loss a good game, but no, no one was hurt." Andy was more than ready to let his mom get back to her popcorn and movie, but she seemed to be settling in for a good chat.

"Well, that's good. We've been praying for safety for everyone. We even asked for prayer at church Wednesday night. We'll call in our praise report first thing tomorrow."

"Praise report. Okay then. I guess you didn't think to pray for a win."

There was a long pause on the line, and Andy could almost hear his mother carefully choosing her words.

"Well, honey, that just doesn't seem right. I know those other boys wanted a win just as much as you did. But we did pray that it would be a good game where everybody did their best and no one got hurt and that the Lord would rest his favor according to his will."

"Apparently that was on San Ramon." Andy really wanted to get this phone call over with before he said something he'd wind up having to apologize for.

"Andy, you just don't know how the Lord is going to use this game. Don't let this get out, or I may find myself banned from at least four states I can think of, but I really don't think the Lord puts much store in who wins or loses football games. I think he cares a lot more about how the game affects people's character and what they need to grow closer to him. That's why I always feel such peace putting it all in his hands." She gave him a moment or two to respond if he felt like it, which he didn't, and when she spoke again her voice was warm. "Darlin', I know you're disappointed. Believe it or not, I'm disappointed too. I'm so disappointed I could cry. But I do believe the Lord had his hand on this game, however it ended. And we can have faith that good is going to come from it."

A wave of tenderness swept away the irritation that had been chewing at him since he first realized he was going to have to call his mom, and he felt the tension slide from his shoulders. Personally, he didn't see the harm in praying for a win, especially if his mom did the praying. Her conversations with God were as easy and natural as his were with Kev, and he was pretty sure that all she'd have to do was ask. And he was just as sure that she wasn't going to do that. Mom was always going to be Mom.

"Okay, I'm going to let you get back to your movie now. I'm ready to call it a night, even if you two party animals are still going strong." He smiled into the phone. "When are you going to come see me? I'm getting the old place all fixed up. I'd like for you to see what I've done."

Silence grew, and in the background Andy could hear someone singing.

"I just don't know about that, honey." When she did speak, her voice was carefully measured. "But we'd love it if you were to come see us. When can you come? Thanksgiving?"

"I can't promise Thanksgiving. We might still be in the playoffs, not that tonight is any indication of that." Andy recognized a subject being changed when he heard it. "But what about Christmas? I can spend about a week at Christmas. How would that be?"

"Christmas? You mean that? Hang on." Andy waited while she imparted the news to Aunt Barb. In a minute she was back. "We are just beside ourselves, but can't you stay longer than a week? We just never get to see you."

"We'll see." Actually, Andy had planned on getting some serious work done on the house during Christmas break, but going into that now with his mom might mean another forty-five minutes on the phone. "Right now, though, I've got to get to bed. Love you, and give Aunt Barb a hug for me."

"I love you too, honey. Christmas! I just can't wait. I think we'll have to get ourselves a real tree this year."

After he hung up the phone, Andy leaned back against the sofa and looked around. There had not been a lot of money to keep the place in good repair when he was growing up, and after he left, it really started to fall apart. The various renters and caretakers he had found over the years only slowed the process, but now, as he found the rare block of time to work on it, it was slowly becoming the home he intended to live in for the rest of his life. And when it was beautiful again—when not even the most careful observer could find where a fist-sized hole in the wall had been patched or a door had been kicked in—maybe he and his mom could both finally forget.

"Things always look better when the sun comes up." How many times had he heard his mom say that? Well, it wasn't the only thing she was usually right about. Andy finished his stretches and headed down the dirt road at an easy run. The sun had yet to crest the mountains and a light wind still held the cool of an early autumn dawn, but as the landscape lightened, so did his outlook. In a few hours, when he met with his team, they could talk about last night's game with an optimistic look to the future.

He hadn't been running long when he spotted another runner ahead on the trail that skirted town, and even if, as far as he knew, Jess wasn't the only other adult in Last Chance who ran every morning, the sheen of copper in her hair would have given her away. He quickened his pace until he pulled alongside her.

"Mornin'."

Jess's cheeks were red and damp curls framed her face, but she smiled a greeting through even puffs of breath.

"You got a head start on me, I see. Mind if I join you?"

Still no words, but she smiled again as she shook her head, and he shortened his stride a little to match hers.

The dawn wind died as the sun finally found its way over the top of the San Ramon range and flooded the valley around Last Chance with light. Except for the occasional flutelike song of a meadowlark or the melancholy call of a mourning dove, the only sound was the soft and rhythmic thud of their feet on the dirt path, and though at that moment Andy felt as if he could run forever, it wasn't long before he felt the sweat trickle down his back and his own breaths were deep and measured.

Andy could probably have run another mile or so by the time they reached the vacant lot in the cul-de-sac and walked through to Elizabeth's street, but Jess was clearly ready to call it a morning, and Andy decided he'd rather cool down with Jess than take off and leave her behind.

"Whoo, that was good." Jess stretched her hands over her head and laced her fingers before dropping them again and rolling her shoulders. "Sometimes I have to just about kick myself out the door in the mornings, but I'm always glad I do."

"Still go every morning?" Andy inhaled deeply to regulate his breathing.

"Just about. Elizabeth and I keep each other honest."

"Elizabeth Cooley?" Andy laughed. "She's the only Elizabeth I know."

"And she's the one I'm talking about, smarty. We walk for a while after my run. I'll be stopping off at her house when we get there. Want to come with us?"

"Wish I could, but I've got a team meeting at 10:00. We need to look at video and talk about last night's game."

"Oh, yeah, the game. How'd it go?" Jess pushed her fists into the small of her back and arched.

"Not so good, thanks for asking. We took a loss."

"Bummer." Jess swung her arms in big circles. "Well, here's Elizabeth's house. Thanks for the run. Maybe we can do it again sometime."

"Yeah, sure." *Bummer? Yeah, I guess you could call losing the opening game of the season to San Ramon a bummer.*

"Okay then." Jess started up Elizabeth's walk. "See you."

"Wait." Andy wasn't quite ready to see her disappear in the house. "What are you doing later?"

Jess shrugged. "Laundry, grocery shop, the usual."

"Have lunch with me. My meeting won't last much past noon. Meet me at the Dip 'n' Dine at about 1:00?"

"The Dip 'n' Dine?" Jess seemed hesitant. "I don't know. I think I got on the wrong side of the waitress when I was in there last night. In fact, that seems to happen a lot. I don't think she likes me."

"Juanita? I'm sure she likes you." Andy grinned. "If she didn't, you wouldn't be wondering about it. Believe me, you'd know. She takes great pride in being known for speaking her mind."

"I had noticed she didn't seem to hold much back. It seems like that would drive away customers. How does she get away with it? I mean, isn't the owner even a little concerned about it?"

"He tries to keep her reined in, from what I hear, but Juanita is just Juanita. He pretty much has to take her as she is or let her go."

"And? It seems like a pretty obvious choice to me."

"You mean he should fire her? Believe it or not, that would be the worst thing he could do. Juanita may get under everyone's skin, but she's one of ours. And even though she can be a pain, and everyone loves Chris, the town would line up behind Juanita in a heartbeat. Chris has only been here a couple years, and Juanita was born here."

"Wow. Makes me wonder what I've got myself into." Jess was starting to look worried, and Andy wanted to erase those little frown lines that had appeared between her brows.

"You picked a good place full of good people; I can promise you that. And there are worse traits than loyalty. Just give them a little while to get to know you."

"And don't do anything that would make them choose sides." Jess didn't look all that reassured.

"I can't see that happening." Andy glanced at his watch. "I've got to get going. Lunch at 1:00?"

"Okay." Jess's smile finally broke through, and it made Andy want to smile too. "As long as you sit between me and Juanita. She still scares me."

"Are you kidding? You're going to have to protect me. She'll have plenty to say about last night's game. And it won't be 'Bummer.' See you later."

As Andy started back the way they had come, the front door opened and Elizabeth came out onto the porch. He called "Good morning" and picked up his pace. If he allowed himself to be drawn into conversation with Elizabeth, he'd be late for his meeting for sure.

Les Watson's pickup passed him before he got to the end of the street, and Les slowed down to lean out the window.

"Better step on it, son. They're gaining on you."

Andy grinned and raised a hand in greeting as he ran past the slow-moving pickup. *Nope. It never gets old.*

"I'm so sorry I missed Andy." Elizabeth made her careful way down the ramp from her porch to the front walk. "It's been a while since I've seen him. I guess he's been busy, what with football practice and school starting and all. I just wish I could have given him a hug and told him there's a lot more football to play yet."

Jess raised an eyebrow as she held the gate open for Elizabeth. "Don't tell me you were at the game too."

"Oh, no, honey. I haven't been able to manage those bleachers in years. But I heard all about the game when Ray and Lainie got home last night. I don't mean to be telling Andy his business, but it sounds like his defense could use a lot of work. And with two missed field goals, he may need to rethink his kicker too."

"Really." Jess was staring, but Elizabeth was too busy navigating the sidewalk to notice. "I had no idea you were so knowledgeable. How do you know so much about football?"

"Oh, I must have seen a hundred games right here in Last Chance, and then we took in all the road games when the boys played. And of course, between dinner table conversations and having the boys and their friends talking about it all the time, it was hard not to pick it up."

"The boys? That would be Ray and who else?" Jess took Elizabeth's elbow to steady her when she faltered a bit.

"Well, both my boys played—that would be Joe Jr. and Jerry—and all my grandsons. And of course boys I knew from church, and sons and grandsons of my friends. There was always someone I knew to cheer for."

"Were they all there at that Parade of Pumas last night?" Jess hid her smile. This was a side of Elizabeth she had never seen.

"Most of them. Joe Jr. was there, and his boy Justin, and of course Ray. Steven's still at the academy, or he would have been there too."

"What about Jerry? Does he not live around here?"

Elizabeth's eyes grew misty and her smile a little sad. "Jerry never was in the parade. He enlisted in the Marines the day after he graduated from high school, and, well, he was killed on patrol in Vietnam. It was June 17, 1973."

"Oh, Elizabeth, I'm so sorry." Jess slid an arm around Elizabeth's shoulder and squeezed. "I didn't know."

"Of course you didn't know, dear. Why should you?" Elizabeth patted the hand that still held her shoulder. "He's always in my thoughts, of course, but especially at this time of year. He did love his football, and he was good too. Maybe not quite as good as Andy, but still better than anyone else our family has produced. Don't tell anyone I said that, though."

"I wouldn't dream of it." Jess gave Elizabeth's shoulder a final squeeze and dropped her hand. "But listen, anytime you feel like talking about Jerry, I'd be happy to hear some stories. He sounds pretty amazing."

"I might take you up on that sometime." Elizabeth smiled up at Jess, and her eyes were still misty. "I just hate acting like Jerry never existed, and it only upsets my family when I try to talk about him. Joe Jr. won't even stay in the room, and most of the others never even knew him."

Her steps grew slower, and she seemed lost in her thoughts. Finally, she squared her shoulders, lifted her chin, and blew out a deep breath. "Well, enough of that. Please excuse an old lady for getting all caught up in the past. Sometimes it seems like a hundred years since Jerry left, and at the same time I almost expect he'll be coming in looking for something to eat, all of eight years old."

"There's nothing to excuse, believe me." Jess wondered at the tears stinging her own eyes. "I was serious. I'm not going to push it, but I really would like to hear about Jerry anytime, and I mean that."

"All right. I'll keep that in mind." Elizabeth took a few more firm steps before she stopped and her shoulders drooped again, ever so slightly. "But I'm finding myself a little tired this morning. Would you mind if we cut our walk short today? I could fix you a cup of coffee."

"Of course we can call it a day, although I'll have to pass on the coffee. I've got a lot to get done today, and I guess I'm meeting Andy at the Dip 'n' Dine for lunch."

"Oh, really?" Elizabeth smiled. "Well, I'm sure he can use the support. Give him my love."

"I'll do that."

They reached Elizabeth's gate, and she stopped with her hand on the gate's latch. "Thank you for the walk, dear. I've so enjoyed our times together and I hope you'll still come see me, but I'm afraid it's going to be getting too dark and cold here pretty soon for me to take my walks in the morning. My little friend Olivia and I will just have to do that after school."

"That sounds like a good decision. I'm not sure yet what I'm going to do when the days get real short, anyway." Jess tried to hold the gate for Elizabeth, but she was waved away. "If there's anything at all I can do for you, just let me know. Promise?"

"I will do that." Elizabeth had already started up the walk but stopped and turned to look at Jess. "You know, if you mean that, there is something you can do."

"Of course I mean it. What do you need?"

"Well, I could use a ride to church tomorrow. Ray and Lainie left for Santa Fe before dawn this morning because he's part of a show that's opening in a gallery up there, and Sarah and Chris had made plans for a quick getaway themselves after the Dip 'n' Dine closes this afternoon. Of course, when they realized they were both going to be away this weekend, they tried to change their plans, but I wouldn't hear of it. I had about made up my mind I was going to stay home tomorrow, but if you really don't mind . . ." Her voice trailed away.

"Of course I don't mind. I'd be happy to take you to church. What time shall I come by?" It had been years since Jess had been to church on a Sunday morning, but going tomorrow with Elizabeth just seemed right somehow.

"Ten-thirty should give us plenty of time. And I do thank you." Elizabeth's smile was warm. "I do hate missing church, and the worst thing about getting old is having to depend on others to get me there."

Jess stood on the sidewalk watching Elizabeth carefully making her way up the walk. She knew better than to try to help. That issue had been settled quite firmly on the first day she and Elizabeth walked together.

When Elizabeth finally reached her front door, preceded by Sam the cat, who seemingly appeared from nowhere, she turned and waved before going inside. Jess returned the wave and after a second headed back home at an easy pace. It was beyond her how someone so frail could exude so much strength.

# 9

"Well, my goodness, do you cook at all?" Juanita met Jess at the door of the Dip 'n' Dine and showed her to a booth by the window. "Not that we don't love having you come in, of course. But eating out every day of the week is bound to get expensive, even if you are a doctor."

"I don't eat out every day of the week. I think this is only the fourth or fifth time I've been in this week." How did Juanita always manage to put her on the defensive, and why did she feel compelled to explain, anyway?

"Five times in one week might not seem like much to you, but nobody I know eats out that much, unless they have something to celebrate." Juanita handed her a menu. "Here you go. Do you want to look at this, or should I just bring you a salad?"

Jess took the menu. "Actually, I'll wait a bit to order. I'm meeting someone."

"Oh?" Juanita perked up. "Anyone I know?"

"Naturally." Jess smiled up at her but offered no other information, and after Juanita waited a moment or two, her mouth got a little pinched and she turned away.

"I'll go get you some water. Just let me know when your friend shows up."

Jess watched her go. On her way to get the water, Juanita stopped at a table or two, and from what Jess could discern, she was just as brusque and plainspoken there as she was when she spoke to Jess. The difference was that the diners at those tables looked up and smiled and, after exchanging a few words with her, went back to their meals and conversations as if Juanita's attitude was just part of the Dip 'n' Dine ambience. And who knows? Maybe it was.

"Think you'll be ordering soon?" Juanita was back with the water. Her mouth was still pinched and she did not meet Jess's eye as she put the glass on the table. "Things can get kind of backed up on Saturday afternoons."

Jess took a closer look at Juanita's face. Had she actually hurt Juanita's feelings? She'd have sworn Juanita didn't even have any feelings. Feeling a little guilty, she tendered a peace offering. "I sure hope so. Andy said he'd meet me here right after his team meeting, and he didn't think it would go much past noon. But if you need the table, I'd be happy to wait for the next one."

"No, of course not." With Jess's conciliatory tone and her curiosity assuaged, Juanita seemed ready to let bygones be bygones. "I'm sure he'll be along soon. I'm not a bit surprised he's taking more time than he expected to with those boys, though. Last night was not pretty."

"So I heard." Jess pulled her glass of water closer. "I know Andy was feeling pretty low when I saw him earlier this morning."

"Well, he shouldn't." Juanita's brook-no-nonsense tone was back. "And I'll be the one to tell him so when he gets here. There are plenty of other games to win this season; this was just the first one. Of course, it was the one and only game we'll play this year with San Ramon, our archenemy, so it does mean they have bragging rights all year long, and let me tell you, when it comes to bragging, no one can do it better than San Ramon. But let us just win the rest of our games, and they'll get real quiet real quick. You wait and see." She gave the table a sharp rap with her knuckles for emphasis.

"All right, then." *No pressure. Just have a near perfect season and all is forgiven.* "It looks like they've got their work cut out for them."

"If anybody but Andy was head coach, I might be a little worried, but I just have a feeling that once they get their feet under them, there will be no stopping that team." She glanced past Jess into the parking lot just as the ding of a bell signaled an order ready to serve. "Here's our boy now. You tell him what I said, and I'll be back to take your orders in a minute. Although with you ordering those salads every time you come in here and Andy always getting a bowl of green chile stew, I could just as easily save myself a trip and go ahead and put your orders in now."

She headed off toward the kitchen as the door opened and Andy came in. Before he had taken three steps, someone had grabbed his attention and his hand, and he stopped for a minute to talk. His eyes lit up and his smile widened as he spotted Jess, but again someone reached for his arm as he passed, and again he stopped. By the time he reached their booth and slid in across from her, his smile looked a little wooden.

"Whew. I've had backfields that were easier to get through than that was."

"I'm glad you made it." Jess grinned and pushed the menu across the table to him. "At least everyone was friendly. I didn't see any torches or pitchforks."

"Not this time. They all told me not to worry about it, that there were still plenty of other games to win this season."

"Juanita made almost the same comment. Sounded kind of ominous when she said it."

"It sounds ominous when everyone says it, although I'm sure

they think they're being encouraging. But you know what? I came back to Last Chance to coach the football team, not to worry about what the town thinks. Russ can do that. He's the Booster president."

"Russ can do what since he's the Booster president?" Whether Juanita was on her way to their table to take their order or whether she just heard Russ's name mentioned and came over, Juanita clearly believed that any conversation that involved her husband involved her as well.

"Hi, Juanita." Andy flipped his menu open and just as quickly flipped it shut. "I was just saying that I was going to let Russ and the Boosters run interference with the town for us, so we can just concentrate on the season. You know how things can get."

"You don't have to say another word." Juanita flapped a hand at him. "Forget Monday morning quarterbacks. They're just amateurs compared to our Saturday morning, biscuits and gravy quarterbacks. You would not believe the things I've heard in here this morning. They talked like the one and only thing that causes a team to win or lose is the coaching. But I just told them, 'Give the boy some time. He just got here. We'll get our team back, you just wait and see.'"

"Well, I appreciate it. Glad you've got my back." Andy's smile looked forced as he handed the menu to Juanita, not that she noticed. "I'll have the green chile stew and maybe some extra tortillas, if you please."

"Absolutely." Juanita tucked the menu under her arm and pulled out her pad. "And a salad for the doctor, right?"

"You know, I think I'll try those chicken enchiladas we talked about last night. With green chile." Jess tried to look nonchalant, as if she were an old hand with chile of all sorts, but Juanita's double take and raised eyebrows as she turned to go secretly delighted her. "Oh, and please put that egg on it."

Jess didn't know what she was expecting when she turned back to

Andy after placing her order—maybe a "wow" or an "atta girl"—but he was just gazing out the window at an eighteen-wheeler that was rumbling its way through town. Feeling a little silly that she had expected some kind of a reaction from him just because she ordered enchiladas, Jess waited until Andy looked back at her.

She smiled. "Still here. Where are you?"

He shook his head as if to clear it. "Right here. Game's over. I'm not going to think about football again until Monday morning." He blew out a huge gust of air. "So what are you doing with the rest of the day?"

"Like I said, just the laundry, cleaning, grocery shopping."

"On a beautiful day like this one? You've got to be kidding. Come on, we can do better than that. The laundry and cleaning aren't going anywhere."

"Yep, you've got that right. They're just sitting there waiting for me."

Andy acted as if he didn't hear her. He leaned forward on his elbows, and for the moment, Jess could believe he actually had put last night's game behind him. "Have you seen the Gila Cliff Dwellings yet?"

"No. What are the Gila Cliff Dwellings?" Despite her chore list, Jess found herself drawn to his enthusiasm.

"It's an ancient village built into some caves in the side of a cliff. It's small, not like Bandelier up north of Santa Fe or Mesa Verde in Colorado. They think maybe a dozen or so families lived there back in the thirteenth century, but it's really something to see. Let me show you around this afternoon; it would only take about an hour and a half to get there, and the drive is beautiful."

"The drive to where is beautiful?" Juanita appeared at their table with a tray of food. "Here you go. Green chile stew and green chile enchiladas. Careful, that plate's hot."

She looked from Jess to Andy and waited. Obviously, her question had not been rhetorical.

"I'm trying to talk Jess into going up to the Gila Cliff Dwellings with me this afternoon. She's never been." Andy unwrapped a thick tortilla and spread butter on it.

"Oh, then you've got to go. There's no question. And Andy's right. It's a real pretty drive. It's a little early to see much color, but there might be some." She turned to Andy. "And it wouldn't hurt you to get out of town for a while, either. Kind of let things settle down a little bit."

*Settle down? Maybe there are torches and pitchforks out there after all.*

Jess took a tentative poke at her enchilada with her fork. It looked so *big*. And it still bubbled around the edges. This would take some figuring out. She looked up when the silence told her that some kind of response was expected.

"Sounds great. Let's get out of town for the afternoon. We'll just let Monday take care of Monday's problems."

"All right, then." Juanita seemed pleased that thanks to her, yet another problem had been tidily taken care of. "You two go off and have a good time. And you just tell me if you don't think that enchilada doesn't put your plate of rabbit food to shame."

After giving the table one last satisfied look and asking them if they were sure they didn't need anything else, Juanita left them to their lunch. Jess poked her enchilada again. It didn't look like any enchilada she had ever seen. It was flat, for one thing, spilling chunks of chicken and fragrant green chile sauce from between stacked corn tortillas, and there was that fried egg sitting on top. She took a tiny taste. The flavor of the green chile was rich, earthy—and hot! She tried to look casual as she reached for her glass of water.

"No, wait." Andy put his hand on her arm to stop her. "That'll just make it worse. Here, take this buttered tortilla. This is what you need."

She stuffed a bite of the warm bread in her mouth, and it did help. Andy smiled in sympathy.

"You don't like hot food? I should have warned you."

"I love hot food!" Jess ate another bite of tortilla. "Indian food and Thai are two of my favorites, but most Mexican food I've eaten has been pretty mild. I sure wasn't expecting this."

Andy laughed. "I know what you mean. It's not the same elsewhere, is it? The thing you need to keep in mind is that this food didn't come north through Mexico to get here. Spaniards settled here around five hundred years ago, and using the things they could get to grow here in this high and rocky place, and learning a lot from the Pueblo Indians, they came up with this. It's probably more accurately called New Mexican than Mexican. Personally, and without a shred of prejudice, I think it's the best food in the world. I'd be happy to eat it for breakfast, lunch, and dinner."

"You wouldn't have much of a stomach lining left." Jess took another bite, followed by another quick bite of tortilla. "But I have to say the flavor is amazing, almost worth the pain."

"Ah, first you get used to it, then you crave it. Wait and see." Andy spooned in a large bite of green chile stew. "Besides, it doesn't do a thing to your stomach lining. In fact, New Mexicans have the lowest per capita incidence of stomach problems in the entire country."

Jess just looked at him. "You made that up."

Andy shrugged. "Maybe. But so what? Some of the most interesting facts I know are completely made up."

"Promise me you'll never go into science."

"No worries. At least not the kind of science you're talking about. I'm back where I want to be, doing what I want to do—

coaching football, making stuff up, and eating as much of Carlos's cooking as I can get."

Andy's mood really did seem to lift the more they talked, and Jess found herself laughing at a silly streak he had never shown before. But when she saw a middle-aged man in boots with his belly hanging over his wide leather belt begin to make his way toward their table, she had a feeling all that was about to change. And she was right.

"Andy? Sorry to interrupt your lunch, but I hadn't had a chance to welcome you back yet."

Andy's face split in a grin, and he stood up and grabbed the man in a half hug, half handshake. "Rob! Good to see you, man. Saw you sporting that letterman's jacket last night. Still looking good."

"Well, it's getting a little tight, that's for sure. I'd hate to have to snap the thing up."

Andy laughed and turned to Jess. "This is Rob Ellis. Rob was my hero growing up. He made moves on the field you'd swear couldn't happen. He was just the best there was."

"A lot of good that did me." There was a note of bitterness in Rob's voice that belied his smile. "But I've got a lot of hopes pinned on my boy. You think he's got a chance to go the distance?"

"Your boy?" Andy's confused frown dissolved into a delighted grin. "Ellis! Of course! I don't know why I didn't make the connection. Man, you've got a kid in high school? I can't believe it."

"Yeah, sometimes I wonder where the time went myself." He hitched his jeans. "But here's the thing. I really want Zach to have the chance I never had. By the time you were playing, we were right smack in the middle of the Glory Days and all over the news. Scouts actually came to watch you play. But when I played, we were just another fly-speck high school in the middle of nowhere playing other fly-speck schools just like it, and nobody gave a darn."

"I wouldn't say that, Rob. You were Last Chance's golden boy. I think if we'd have had a town square, they would have erected a statue of you right in the middle."

"Yeah, well, Last Chance doesn't offer full ride scholarships to Pac-12 schools, now does it?"

There was no mistaking the bitterness in Rob's voice now, and Andy's smile faded. "Yeah, I caught some breaks, all right. I'm the first to admit it."

"Hey, I didn't mean to get all gloomy on you." Rob's smile was back, even if it didn't quite reach his eyes. He slapped Andy on the shoulder. "You deserved everything you got and then some. But I'm thinking that just with you being here, the team's going to get some attention, and then if they start winning, why, the scouts'll be swarming. My boy'll get his shot, like I never did."

"You never know, Rob. I wish I could look into the future for you, but I can't." The pleasure that had spread over Andy's face at seeing an old friend had faded, and he just looked tired.

"Well, keep an eye on him. He's got all the raw talent he needs; he just needs some development. The coach we had last year was worse than useless."

"That's what I'm here for." Andy extended his hand. "Rob, I can't tell you how good it is to see you again. I know I don't need to ask if I'll see you at the games."

"Oh, I'll be there. I bring my own video camera to film the games so Zach and I can go over them together." He clapped his hand into Andy's. "It's been a real pleasure. I'm looking to see some great things from the team from here on out."

With one last slap on the shoulder, Rob turned to go, but before Andy could sit down, he turned back.

"One more thing. I just can't help thinking that if you'd played Zach a little more last night, the score might have been less lopsided.

I've seen him play a lot more than you have, and I know what he can do. I can guarantee you that three of those turnovers would not have happened if he had been on the field." He raised his hand in a salute. "Well, that's it. Good seeing you, Andy. Ma'am, a pleasure."

Andy slid back into the booth, and Jess watched Rob make his way back through the diner to the door. When she looked back at Andy, he was staring out the window again, watching Rob Ellis climb into his truck.

"Is he one of the Saturday morning biscuits and gravy quarterbacks Juanita was talking about?" Jess smiled when Andy turned to look at her.

"Rob? Maybe. I guess. But you know? Everything he said was true. He was good, more than good. He just played in the wrong place at the wrong time."

"Is his son as good as he thinks he is?"

"Yeah, Zach's good. I don't know if he wants it as bad as his dad does, though."

"Did your dad turn up at the games with a video camera too? And bug the coaches for you?" Jess grinned.

"Nope, Dad didn't make it to a lot of my games." Andy just glanced down at his watch and signaled Juanita for the check. "We need to get going if we want to see those cliff dwellings. They're in a canyon, and you lose the light early."

# 10

Andy had second thoughts about taking Jess to the Gila Cliff Dwellings almost as soon as they got in his truck and headed out. After all, if some of the other prehistoric sites had been described as cities carved from stone, Gila could barely be considered a village. It was sort of the Last Chance of cliff dwellings, but maybe that was what made the place so special to him.

"I hope I haven't oversold the place." Andy glanced over at Jess. She looked good sitting on the other side of his truck, like she belonged there. "Don't be expecting the Seven Wonders of the World. It's pretty small."

"What? No pyramids? You might as well turn around and take me home." When Jess turned to smile at him, he noticed how the sun shining through her reddish-gold hair made it seem to glow. "Actually, just getting out of town is a treat. I haven't had time to do much exploring. I had no idea there were so many mountains here. I guess I pretty much thought it was all desert."

"Seriously?" Andy kept his eyes on the road. It was too easy to get distracted if he looked over at her. "How much time had you spent here before you moved?"

"Not that much, I guess. I came out to talk to Dr. Benavides, of course, and to meet the other doctors in the practice. I didn't have time to do a lot of sightseeing then, though. It was sort of a quick visit."

"How did you wind up here, anyway? I guess I just assumed that you wanted to live in New Mexico, but it doesn't sound like you'd even been here before."

"You don't have to know every inch of a place to think about living there." Jess was beginning to sound a bit defensive. "And for your information, I have been to New Mexico before, just not this part."

"Oh, where have you been?" Andy had a feeling it was time to let the subject drop, but he really was curious.

"Well, we drove through the southern part when I was in middle school, and I've also been to Santa Fe."

*Santa Fe. And she didn't see the mountains.* Andy opened his mouth to say something and closed it again. It definitely was time to let the subject drop.

"Of course, I was only about five at the time, and the only thing I can remember is Native Americans selling jewelry from blankets on the sidewalk," Jess went on. "But I did not move to a state I had never even visited. So there."

"Okay, then." Andy didn't even try to hide his grin. "You're practically a native. Well, it's a great big state and I'd love to show it to you. Maybe after football season is over, we can do some exploring."

"I'd like that, although finding time when we're both free might be a little tricky. Dr. Benavides is trying to ease into retirement, so I'm taking more of his patients, when they let me, and my branch office in Last Chance opens this next week. So even though deep in my heart I'm thinking I'll probably have more time than I know what to do with, I'm really hoping that will change soon."

"Hey, congratulations." Andy glanced over at her again. "So

Last Chance is finally getting its own doctor. Good for us. Shall we hope for an outbreak of plague? That ought to get things going."

"Right. That's exactly what we should hope for." Jess shot him a look. "No, I'm not looking for an epidemic. Just wishing a few more local folk would be as pleased in practice as they are in theory."

"You just need to give it a little time, that's all. They'll come around. If you've got Dr. B. on your side and he's trying to retire, that's all you need. You'll be busy."

Jess made a little sound in her throat and reached for the volume knob on the radio.

Taking the cue, Andy stopped trying to be helpful. But he couldn't help it. He had this pep talk reflex that triggered every time he sensed discouragement. It was useful in the locker room, and face it, if he hadn't been able to talk himself through some mighty tough times when he was a kid, who knows where he'd be now? But clearly Jess had heard all she wanted to hear.

He let the sounds of his classic country station fill the cab of his truck, and as they drove, any tension there had been between them dissipated into the warm, early autumn afternoon. He even found himself singing along with an old Kenny Rogers tune, and when he caught Jess smiling at him, he cranked up his volume and beat the time on the steering wheel to see if he could make her laugh outright. She did.

The parking lot was empty when Andy pulled in, and the only sound he heard when he got out of his truck was the rustle of a soft wind through the cottonwoods and pines.

"It's so quiet. Are you sure it's open?" Jess got out of the truck and stood by the door.

"It's open. There's a pay station at the trailhead." Andy joined her and took her hand. "We just lucked out. No one's here but us. Come on, but don't look until I tell you to."

"All right. Just don't let me walk into anything." She kept her eyes on the ground in front of her as Andy led her along the asphalt path.

"Here." Placing his hands on her shoulders, Andy turned her to face the looming cliff in front of them. "Look up."

Jess slowly raised her head. "Oh my." The words came in a whisper.

High above them, carved by the winds of millennia, caves peered out across the valley like hooded eyes. Even from where they stood below, crumbling stone walls were visible in the shadowy interiors. Andy let silence reclaim the moment before he spoke again.

"Come on, let's go up and look." He led the way up the winding path until they reached the first of the caves. It ran deep into the mountain, with low stone walls still marking off the rooms.

"Who lived here?" Her voice was hushed and reverent.

"An ancient people. They were long gone before the Mescalero and the Navajo ever came to this area."

"Why did they leave?"

"No one knows. Maybe there was a drought and the creek down there dried up; maybe they were forced out by invaders. As you can see, there are only a few dwellings, so the population couldn't have been that big. The first Europeans to explore the ruins found tools here, and corn in the storage bins. It was as if the residents all walked off one day and never came back."

Jess found an outcropping of rock near the edge of the cave and sat on it, wrapping her arms around her knees and hugging them close. Andy joined her. The narrow valley below them was already caught in shadow, although the sun still painted the tops of the cottonwoods yellow-green and warmed the face of the pockmarked cliff where they sat.

Jess lifted her face to its rays and closed her eyes. "That sun feels good, and I'll bet the people who lived here liked it too." She opened her eyes and looked at Andy. "Do you think that's why they chose these caves to build their homes?"

"Probably didn't hurt." All Andy's trepidation at bringing her here had fled. She seemed to see here what he did. "Plus there was the water and the ready-made shelter."

"I still wonder what made them leave." She closed her eyes again. "Listen. The wind in the trees almost sounds like they might be coming back."

"Well, if they are, they'll be taking off again. Here come the invaders."

Below them, in the parking lot, two passenger vans came to a stop and about a dozen boys poured out, joined by a few adults. As the adults tried to gather the boys and give instructions, and as the boys yelled over each other and scattered, Andy reached for Jess's hand and pulled her to her feet.

"It's going to get real busy here in a minute. Let's try to get a head start. There are a few more dwellings I want to show you."

Andy led as they made their way across the cliff face single file, stopping in each cavern for a few minutes, but the spell had been broken. The tumult behind grew closer until the first boys caught up with them in the last cave.

"Okay, can we go now?" The tall, skinny blond kid who got there first called back to the nearest leader. "Boooring."

"Really? You think this is boring? Did you even look at it?" Jess smiled at the boy and her tone was teasing, but he just glanced at her and headed back the way he came.

"Charming child." Jess raised an eyebrow as she turned back to Andy.

He shrugged. "He's what? About thirteen? Comes with the territory. At least he's been here, and maybe someday when he doesn't have to be so cool, he'll remember and come back."

"I'll bet you never found this place boring, not even when you were thirteen."

"I had a different kind of life than these guys." Andy reached for her hand as they headed back down the path to the parking lot. "My guess is that this is a scout troop working on some merit badge or other. I never had much time for things like scouts."

Andy realized as he spoke that he had left himself open for the next question—*What kind of life did you have?*—but Jess never asked it. She just stopped, looked back up at the ancient ruins, and sighed.

"This was amazing, Andy. Thank you so much for sharing this place with me." She looked at him with a pensive expression he couldn't quite read. "I'm so glad we had it all to ourselves for a while. It was like going seven hundred years back in time."

"All part of the service." Andy opened her door and walked around the truck and climbed in the driver's side. Being with Jess was easy and made him feel good. He never worried that she was more interested in the football player than in the man. She had made it abundantly clear that the football player didn't impress her in the slightest. There was something freeing in that, and he realized he wasn't ready to let the day go. Not yet. "Since you're not sure when we can do this again, why don't we take the scenic route home so I can show you a little more of the country?"

He saw her glance at her watch and frown.

"Hey, if you've got to get back, I understand." He pulled out onto the highway. "It was just a thought." *Take it easy, Ryan. Don't push it.*

"Oh, why not?" Jess grinned at him as she relaxed against the seat. "The day's pretty much gone anyway, and besides, I'm curious about what you call scenic if this isn't it."

The western sky had gone through crimson and coral and was already shading to deep purple by the time Andy drove his pickup back into Last Chance. He had been right. As hard as it had been to imagine, the narrow road that wound through the mountains on their way home could indeed be called the scenic route. The afternoon had been just what she didn't know she needed, and Jess felt as relaxed and peaceful as she had in a long time.

"Hungry?" Andy slowed as they approached the Dip 'n' Dine. "Want to get something to eat before we call it a day?"

"I don't know." Jess looked out the window at the couple heading for the last car in the parking lot. "It looks like they're trying to close. I went in at closing time last night. It's not a mistake I want to make twice."

"Seriously? That doesn't sound like Chris."

"Oh, I never saw Chris. I'm not sure he was even there. It was Juanita who made me aware of the protocol."

"Ah, that explains a lot. Okay, no Dip 'n' Dine." He picked up speed again. "So, how about my place? I've got a couple steaks I can grill."

Jess hesitated. There was nothing left of the sunset but a deep red glow on the horizon, and the stars were coming out. It had been a lovely day, but it was over.

"It's just that I feel responsible." Andy looked so serious when he glanced over at her. "If it weren't for me dragging you off, you'd have a houseful of groceries by now and probably be insisting that I have dinner with you. Fixing you a steak is the least I can do."

Jess laughed. Maybe the day didn't have to be over just yet. And truthfully, she was curious. The paved street that ran past the house she rented from Rita turned into a dirt road at the end of the block, and she had wondered where Andy wound up when he drove past. "Okay, since you put it that way. I guess it is your fault that I'd be eating my last yogurt for dinner if I went home."

Jess felt the slight jolt as Andy's truck left the pavement behind and headed down the dirt road to stop in front of a long, low house with a deep front porch running the length of it. For a moment before she reached for the door handle, Jess just sat and looked at it. She wasn't quite sure what she had expected—maybe a rustic bachelor cabin or something—but it certainly wasn't this. For one thing, it was by far the biggest house she had yet seen in Last Chance, and despite the building materials scattered around and a few raw boards nailed to the steps and front porch, it could have been abandoned. She got out of the truck and stood by the door.

"Come on in." Andy came around and took her arm. "But be careful. There's lots to trip over, and it's nearly dark."

He guided her up the steps and led the way inside. Jess stood and looked around while Andy switched on some lights. The room was huge, though nearly empty of furniture, and carved beams traversed the high ceiling.

"I'll get us warmed up here in just a minute." Andy knelt in front of the kiva fireplace dominating one corner and lit the kindling nestled under the teepee of logs leaning against its back wall. He got up, dusting his hands. "There, that ought to do it. Come on in the kitchen, and I'll get those steaks going."

Jess followed him and again stopped at the door. She didn't know what she had expected the kitchen to look like, but it certainly wasn't golden oak cabinets, almond-colored appliances, and wallpaper with little chickens on it. Andy moved about the kitchen, pulling steaks from the fridge and potatoes from the pantry, but eventually he must have noticed her silence because he stopped and looked at her.

"What?"

"Um, nothing. What can I do to help?"

"Not a thing. Just pull up that stool at the breakfast bar and keep me company."

She did as she was told, propping her elbows on the creamy Formica counter, and watched him work for a while. Finally, she had to say something.

"So, how long have you lived here?" It didn't begin to touch on all the things she was curious about, but it was a start.

Andy looked up. "This time? About two or three months, I guess."

"This time?"

"Yeah, I grew up in this house, but before last summer, I hadn't been back since I graduated from high school."

"You grew up here?" Jess looked around. Clearly, the house was built to be a showplace, but its rundown condition was due to more than neglect. She could see where holes in the walls had been patched, and there was a long scorch mark next to the window as if curtains had once caught fire. "And you haven't been back, even to visit?"

"No point." Andy went back to peeling potatoes. "No one I know was here. Mom had her stuff packed, and I drove her to her sister's in Oklahoma the day after I graduated."

"And your dad?" Jess knew she was likely treading where she shouldn't, but she couldn't help herself.

"Dad had moved on a couple years earlier. Do me a favor and get the iron skillet out of that cupboard over there, would you?" Andy didn't look at her and was starting to look a little grim around the mouth.

"Sure thing." Jess hopped off her stool and went to look for the skillet. She could have kicked herself. She *always* had to ask the next question. It was a good trait for a doctor but not so good when getting to know someone. They sometimes felt a little invaded.

Gradually, as Andy finished preparing their steaks and fried potatoes and they took their plates to the living room to eat in front of the fire, the easy, peaceful air Jess had so enjoyed all day returned. The conversation was relaxed and comfortable, centering on trivial things like the events of the day and people they both knew. Only two subjects were never touched—the history of the strange old house, and last night's football game.

Andy and his house were still on Jess's mind the next morning. Clearly, the house had seen violence, but that could have happened after Andy and his family had moved away. Tenants? Squatters? Briefly, she considered asking Elizabeth what she knew, and just as quickly, she dismissed that idea. In all her conversations with her, Elizabeth had never once approached anything that could be construed as gossip, and Jess was pretty sure that was exactly how Elizabeth would categorize such a question. Jess smiled to herself. She had never given other people's opinion of her much thought before, but Elizabeth's high regard? That was something worth hanging on to.

She could see Elizabeth standing at the window when she drove up, and by the time she got out of her car and headed up the walk, Elizabeth had appeared on the front porch.

"You are so sweet to pick me up like this." Elizabeth handed her Bible to Jess and reached for the railing of the ramp leading from the porch to the sidewalk. "I suppose it wouldn't have hurt me to stay home one Sunday, but I do hate to miss."

"No problem at all. I'm glad to do it." Jess smiled and followed slightly behind as Elizabeth made her way to the car waiting at the curb. She knew better than to offer any assistance. She had quickly learned that if Elizabeth needed help, she would ask for it.

"You know, of course, that I had an ulterior motive in asking you to take me to church this morning." Elizabeth sounded pretty pleased with herself.

"Oh?" Jess waited until Elizabeth had settled into the front seat before handing back her Bible.

"Yes. You've been saying every week that you were going to try to get to church on Sunday, and something's always come up. So I just thought I'd give you a little help."

Jess shut the passenger door and went around to slide in behind the wheel. She smiled over at Elizabeth as she started the engine. "So Lainie and Ray are home lurking behind the curtains?"

"No, they're in Santa Fe." Elizabeth laughed. "You know I'd never fib to you. But it did occur to me that this might be just the chance you were looking for to get there."

Jess fell silent as she drove the few short blocks to church. What was there to say to that?

"And here we are." Jess turned into the church parking lot and came to a stop under one of the two elm trees that shaded the little lawn in front of the church. She turned to smile at her passenger. "Tell me, do you always get your way?"

"Not always." Elizabeth unfastened her seat belt. "But most always."

Jess was not exactly a stranger to church. She and her family were members of a church back in Mill Valley, and they went fairly regularly when Jess and her sister were little. But as the years went by, they went less and less, until by the time the girls headed off to college, it was pretty much a Christmas and Easter thing. And since then, truth be told, Jess had gone hardly at all. Even so, nothing about her previous experience at church had prepared her for the Church of Last Chance.

Small and plain, the church could hold possibly one hundred fifty people, if they squeezed together on the pocked and polished wooden pews. It had a platform with a pulpit and a choir loft at the front, a piano on one side, and an organ on the other. And that was all.

People didn't slip into their pews and silently read their bulletins until the service started; they stopped in the aisle to greet a new arrival, they leaned over the back of their pews and waved to get the attention of someone sitting a few rows behind them, they even got up and crossed the room to speak to someone on the other side. Jess was a little nervous following Elizabeth down the aisle. She was accustomed to footsteps silenced by thick carpet, light filtering through richly colored stained glass windows, the pipes of the organ rising majestically against the wall. You know, church. What had she allowed herself to be drawn into?

Elizabeth stopped at the third pew on the left and stepped back. Jess slipped in and sat down next to Andy before she knew he was there.

"Morning." Andy seemed mighty pleased with himself at her surprise. "Fancy seeing you here."

"Good morning." Jess must have looked as puzzled as she felt, because Andy's grin widened. "Did I tell you I was bringing Elizabeth to church this morning?"

"Is that why you think I come to church? I'm here every Sunday."

His tone was teasing, but Jess was embarrassed. She had sounded a little presumptuous, and she knew it. She felt her cheeks warm as she looked away.

"Hey." Andy bumped her shoulder with his own. "I was just joking with you. Ray called and asked me to take Elizabeth to church for him, then he called back and said you were going to. So yes, I knew you would be here, and I knew where you'd be sitting too. So go ahead and feel stalked. You're entitled."

Jess started to reply when she felt a slight nudge from Elizabeth's elbow. Sometime in the last few minutes, everything had changed. The room was silent except for the softly playing piano, and everyone had taken their seats. An atmosphere of anticipation filled the room as the organ joined the piano. The music swelled as a door to the choir loft opened and the choir filed in. Juanita was up there, and her husband, Russ. Jess wasn't sure why that surprised her, but it did. Before she could give it much thought, though, the choir director faced the choir, raised both hands, and nodded to the pianist, and they began to sing.

Jess was astonished at how good they were. Not that they could be taken for a professionally trained chorale, but their song was so authentic, so heartfelt, that Jess felt tears sting her eyes. She even found herself seeing Juanita in a different light, and that probably was the thing that surprised her most. Maybe there was more to Juanita than she knew.

The rest of the service was as pleasing as the music. The minister, who Elizabeth introduced as Brother Parker after the service, was warm, easy to understand, and to the point, even if she'd never have been able to keep up with his Scripture references if it weren't for Andy's help. There was no yelling, no pulpit pounding, no flinging of guilt, and no snake handling. Truthfully, she wasn't really expecting snake handling, but you hear things.

"So, what do you think of our little church?" Andy eased out into the crowded aisle with her after the benediction had been pronounced.

"I like it." Jess was a little surprised to hear herself say it. "It's not at all what I was expecting, but I really liked it."

"What were you expecting?" Andy raised an eyebrow.

"Jess, honey, come here." Elizabeth reached for her. "There are some people I'd like you to meet."

Gratefully, Jess turned away. She really did not want to tell Andy what she had been afraid of. In fact, now that she thought about it, she felt kind of silly.

# 11

How was your vacation?" Jess sat down in the chair across from Dr. Benavides, cradling a cup of coffee.

"I felt pretty good till I got here this morning." He looked up from the file open in front of him and gestured at the stack waiting for his attention. "Did you see anyone while I was gone?"

"I saw as many as would let me." Jess shifted in her seat. "A few who had appointments, especially those who didn't need urgent care, said they'd reschedule and come back when you were here."

"Well, they rescheduled." He sighed and went back to his file. "Is that fresh coffee?"

"I'm sorry?" The question seemed to come from nowhere.

"Is that coffee fresh? It can taste like mud." Dr. Benavides glanced up.

"Um, yes. It just finished brewing." Jess hesitated a second while the silence grew. "Would you like me to get you a cup?"

"Please. With some nonfat milk and one and a half sweeteners." His attention had already returned to his files.

Jess got up and went to the break room. Getting Dr. Benavides his coffee wasn't the problem; in fact, maybe she should have offered when she came in and sat down. But his peremptory attitude rankled a bit. She was a colleague, after all.

He didn't acknowledge her, or the mug of coffee she placed on his desk, and after a second or two, she moved toward the door. He stopped her by slapping his file closed and leaning back in his chair.

"We've got to figure something out. I want to retire someday, sooner rather than later, and at this rate it's not going to happen. Besides, it's a big waste of resources having you just hanging around making coffee while I work myself to death."

Jess slipped back into the chair in front of his desk, feeling a little as if she had been called into the principal's office. Surely he didn't think this was her idea.

"So this is what we're going to do." He glared over the top of his glasses. "I want you to make rounds with me at the hospital, get to know people so they'll feel a little more comfortable with you."

Jess nodded. She wasn't sure how that would work on the days she would be in Last Chance, but now didn't seem like the best time to bring that up.

"I'm going to be cutting my office hours back, and there'll be no more of this." He slapped the files of the patients who had rescheduled while he was gone. "I don't know what the desk was thinking letting people reschedule their appointments for when I got back. What'd they think I was taking a vacation for, anyway?"

Jess cleared her throat. "That might be my fault. They were so upset when you weren't here that I told them they could reschedule if they weren't comfortable seeing me."

Dr. Benavides just looked at her a moment. "Oh, you did, did you? Well, let me tell you right now that if you start out mollycoddling your patients like that, setting aside valuable time for them and then letting them waltz out of here for no good reason without using it, you'll wind up good and sorry in a hurry, and either working twice as hard as you should be here, or sitting in an empty office over there in Last Chance wondering where your patients are."

"Well, I am sorry. I just didn't want you coming back to a bunch of angry patients."

"They can get mad on their own time, not mine." He took a sip of his coffee, scowled at it, shot Jess a look over the top of his glasses, and set it back on his desk before going back to his work.

"All right. Message received. It won't happen again." Jess was aware of the stereotypical image of the old irascible family doctor barking orders at everyone like a drill sergeant. She had always thought it a television cliché or something from the distant past. Apparently, Dr. Benavides hadn't received that memo, or had wadded it up and tossed it if he had. She was betting on the latter.

"There is one more thing, if you have a minute."

Dr. Benavides seemed a little startled when he looked up and found her still sitting in front of his desk. "Shoot."

"Sue Anderson brought Emma in for a checkup while you were gone."

"Everything all right?"

"Oh, there's nothing wrong with her health."

He smiled. "They're a great little family, aren't they? I've taken care of all three of them since they were born."

Deciding that she'd better tread lightly, Jess chose her words carefully. "Emma is an exceptionally well-behaved child, don't you think?"

"I wish all my patients were like Emma, and that includes a good portion of the adults as well. Why? Was there a problem?"

"No, not at all. Well, Mrs. Anderson was a little upset to find me here instead of you, but the examination was fine. It's just that . . ." Jess took a deep breath to give herself time to marshal her thoughts. "It's just that Emma sat up there on the examination table and didn't say a word. Mrs. Anderson answered every question I directed to Emma. And when I suggested it was time for a flu shot, Emma never even blinked. I've never seen that in a child before. It's just not natural behavior for a child of Emma's age."

"You don't think so?" Dr. Benavides was starting to sound impatient. "Well, for the first twenty-five years or so I was in practice, that's exactly how children behaved. It was what was expected of them. It's only been in the last fifteen or twenty years that there's been all this negotiating with kids in the doctor's office, promising them this or that if they'll just stop screaming and let the doctor examine them. I'll tell you what, if more parents were like Sue Anderson, the world would be in a lot better shape than it is. I know my job would be a lot easier, that's for sure."

Jess suspected that Dr. Benavides's memories of the past were a little rosier than reality would decree, and that his take on the present was a little harsher, but she also knew it was time to let the subject drop. She got to her feet.

"Well, thank you for your time. And again, I'm sorry I allowed things to stack up for you."

He nodded distractedly and opened another file. "Tell Theresa to make another pot of coffee, would you? And have her bring me a cup; she knows how I like it. Oh, and don't get too involved in anything. We're leaving for rounds at the hospital in about twenty minutes."

By the time Thursday rolled around, Jess was more than ready for her first day in her Last Chance office. It had taken all her resolve to drive right past earlier in the day when she headed for San Ramon and her obligatory rounds with Dr. Benavides, especially as her assistant Eva's car was already in the parking lot and the lights were on inside. But now, as she was on her way back to Last Chance, she could feel apprehension begin to do battle with her excitement. What if this was a colossal mistake and she wound up having to close down the office and return full time to Dr. Benavides's office? Frankly, she wasn't sure she could do that.

He had been a bit blunt when they first started talking about Jess's working with him and very clear about what he expected, but Jess liked that. She appreciated clarity and assumed he would warm up when they got to know each other better. Wrong. In fact, if anything, he had grown even more brusque and imperious. She knew his first name was Alonso, but she had never heard anyone use it. Certainly she had never been invited to call him anything but Dr. Benavides. He didn't call her anything, although she had heard him refer to her as Dr. MacLeod when he spoke of her to others.

Jess knew she had a few appointments that afternoon, mostly due to Rita's relentless promotion of what she called Jess's grand opening, but the white van in the parking lot surprised her. As far as she knew, her first appointment wasn't until this afternoon, 1:00, to be precise. Could someone have called Eva that morning for an appointment—all on their own?

Excitement pushed apprehension aside as she drove around to the back where the door to her office was located. She tried to muster a manner of cool professionalism. She was, after all, only doing what she had spent years preparing for, what she had in fact already been doing at the family practice in San Ramon, and what she planned to do every day until she was at least as old as Dr. Benavides. But in her heart of hearts, she really expected trumpets to blow and confetti to fall when she fitted her key in the door and let herself into her office. She was home.

Slipping into her crisp white lab coat, Jess went to find out who the van belonged to. She found him kneeling behind the desk in the waiting room checking the telephone's connection to the wall.

Eva leaned on the desk, chatting and giggling. She looked up when Jess walked in.

"The phone wasn't working right, so I called and Chad came right over."

"Yep, almost got you up and running." Chad didn't look up.

"What's the problem?" Jess peered over his shoulder as if that would tell her something.

"Nothing much. Just a little hitch in the system. Be done in a sec."

"I see." Jess did not, but Chad didn't seem inclined to explain further. "Eva, could I see you a minute?"

"Sure." The smile on Eva's face faded to guardedness as Jess turned to lead the way back to her office.

Jess closed the office door behind them and folded her arms. "Okay, what's going on?"

"Going on? Nothing." Eva's eyes were wide with innocence. "The phones wouldn't work, and I just called Chad to come fix them. He's almost done."

"Why didn't you call me first? If there's a problem, I need to know about it."

"The phones were out, remember?" Eva grinned. "That's why I called Chad in the first place."

"And you called Chad how? On your cell phone?"

Eva didn't answer, but her pout said a lot.

"Look, Eva, don't get me wrong." Jess took a deep breath and smiled. The last thing she needed was to alienate her office assistant, even if she was on loan from Dr. Benavides's office. If Eva walked, she'd have to close up again until she found a replacement. "I appreciate your taking the initiative to get a major problem solved. We can't operate without phones; I know that. But I do need a heads-up before we obligate ourselves for unexpected expenditures, okay?"

"Well, you don't need to worry about that." Eva seemed only slightly mollified. "Chad's doing this as a favor. There's no charge."

"The phone company does favors?" Jess did not like the sound of this.

"Well, he's not actually on the clock. His shift doesn't start until later, but when I called, he just came on over."

"I see." Things actually were becoming clearer, and Jess found herself wondering if there ever had been anything wrong with the phones. That may have been just a convenient story concocted when they saw her drive in.

"All done here." The voice from the waiting room was muffled by the closed door.

"Okay, go take care of that for us, would you? Thank him for me, but remember, we need to do everything on the up-and-up here. That means service calls made during business hours and invoices recorded and paid. Are we good with that?"

Eva may have rolled her eyes as she left, but Jess let it go. For the time being, at least, it was just going to be the two of them here at the Last Chance office, and Jess wanted a team, not the reverential hierarchy Dr. Benavides presided over.

"Good morning. Is the doctor in?" Rita's voice, unmistakable in its brisk enthusiasm, floated down the short hall from the waiting room. "I don't want to bother her if she's busy, but if she's got a minute. . . ."

"I'm absolutely free at the moment, Rita." Even if Jess had determined to appear cool and professional, the delight in Rita's smile was contagious, and Jess found herself returning it as she walked in. "What can I do for you?"

"Look at you!" Rita beamed. "You're a doctor!"

Jess held out her arms and twirled once. "So it would appear. I have the outfit, the office, everything but the patients."

"They'll come. Don't you worry about that." Rita set a big, fluffy fern in a pink foil–covered pot on Eva's desk. "Here. I brought you a little something to celebrate your grand opening. I just wish we could have done more."

"The plant's perfect, Rita. Thank you." Jess smiled. "And thanks for understanding about the grand opening."

"You know I wasn't talking about a bouncy house and hot dogs in the parking lot, right? Or a free blood-pressure clinic. Although now that I think about it, that might not have been a bad idea. But I wish you would have let us do something to let folks know you're here."

"But you have." Jess was developing a real fondness for the dynamo who was her landlord and first friend in Last Chance. "I think you've introduced me to every single person in town—twice!—and told them they need to come here instead of going clear up to San Ramon. If I didn't know better, I'd swear they were jumping into doorways or heading off the other way when they see us coming."

"Honey, if I let a little thing like that stop me, this town would have gone to pot years ago." Rita adjusted her glasses and peered at Jess over the rim. "You've got to have a tough hide if you want to get things done in a place like Last Chance. Besides, I've learned the art of turning up before they see me coming."

Jess grinned. "I had no idea. I thought those were all chance encounters."

"And that's my plan." Rita adjusted her purse on her arm and headed for the door. "Oh, there is one thing. Every quarter we have a little reception at the town council meeting called 'Meet the Council.' Folks come to find out what's going on and to express their concerns, if they have any. They're all welcome at every meeting, of course, but if you give one a special name and serve cake and coffee, they're more likely to come. Anyway, the next one is three weeks from Monday, and I think it would be a real good idea if you came and told us a little about yourself. You know, where you came from, what your family's like, why you chose Last Chance to settle in."

"Oh, I don't know, Rita. I think they all know me by now, don't they?" Jess had no idea how many people came to these Meet the Council nights, but she was pretty sure she had to have met all of them. Rita was nothing if not thorough.

"I think you should come. You'd be surprised how people loosen up when they have a plate of chocolate cake in their hands. And there should be a pretty good crowd this time. Andy Ryan has already said he'd come, and I know folks are going to want to come see him."

Frankly, Jess wasn't all that heartened at the thought of having a captive audience thanks to the popularity of the new football coach. Rita must have read her thoughts in her expression, because she flapped a dismissive hand.

"Oh, don't worry about the crowd coming to see Andy. He's a hometown boy, and this town's crazy about football anyway. Just take your blessings where you find them and make the most of it. You don't have to say one thing about your new office if you don't want to. Just tell us about yourself. Folks around here like to know their neighbors."

Jess sighed and shook her head. As much as she liked Rita, she was beginning to understand why people ducked into doorways when they saw her coming. The woman did not know the meaning of the word *no*.

"Perfect!" She did, however, recognize surrender. "You won't be sorry. I know it made a world of difference for Chris Reed. He was the first new business owner in Last Chance for probably twenty years, and you'd have thought he'd come to steal the silver, the way folks treated him. But all they needed was to get to know him to realize what a sweetheart he was. It will be the same with you."

"People think I've come to steal the silver?"

"No, of course not, but some folks still need a little time to get used to newcomers." Rita glanced at the clock on the wall behind the desk and grabbed at the doorknob. "Good night, look at the time. I meant to just pop in and drop off the plant, and here I've been talking your ear off like neither one of us has anything to do. Don't forget—7:00 p.m., three weeks from Monday night at the community center. It will be fun, especially if the team has a few wins by then to crow over."

She breezed out, leaving the waiting room feeling even emptier than it had. Jess took a deep breath and slowly let it go.

"Well, it looks like I'm going to Meet the Council three weeks from Monday."

"Yep." Eva was doing something to her phone and didn't look up.

"Do you think the team will have a few wins to crow over by then?"

"Don't know. Maybe. But since I'm from San Ramon, the only Last Chance game I care about is the one they played last week." She looked up from her phone with a triumphant little smirk. "And they got pounded."

"Let's call it a day." Andy walked up to his assistant coach. "It's starting to get dark."

Kev nodded and blew his whistle, waving his arm in a circle around his head before pointing to the sports complex. Straggling in groups of two or three, the players pulled off their helmets and headed for the locker room. Kev and Andy fell in behind.

"So, what do you think, Coach? Are you liking what you see?" Kev untied his sweatshirt from around his neck and pulled it over his head.

Andy nodded. "Yeah, I think so. Most of these guys really want to play ball. What they might lack in innate talent, they make up for in drive. Unfortunately, there are a couple who have what it takes but want to skate by. I'll take drive over so-called talent any day, so I think we have what it takes to win some games."

"Win *some* games? I think folks are counting on a lot more than some, Coach. Doesn't sound like you've got a lot of confidence in the team."

"The season's young yet. We've got a lot of games to go." Andy grinned and slapped Kev on the shoulder as they entered the building. "Tell Zach Ellis I want to see him in my office before he goes, would you?"

Andy was sitting at his desk about fifteen minutes later going over his notes when he heard a tap on his door and looked up to see Zach Ellis standing in the doorway.

"You wanted to see me, Coach?"

"Yeah, come on in." He gestured with his chin toward a chair on the other side of his desk. "Have a seat."

Zach dropped into the chair and slouched against one arm. He gazed at Andy without saying anything, as if waiting for his coach to explain the summons.

Andy ignored the little flare of annoyance he felt. Zach's attitude was bordering on insolent, but Andy hadn't called him into the office to chew him out. He decided to let it go. This time.

"I saw your dad last weekend. Did he mention it?" Andy leaned back in his own chair and smiled.

"Yeah. He said."

"I never connected you with him. I don't know why. I guess I just never thought of him as being old enough to have a kid in high school."

"Mmm." Zach lifted his chin in recognition that Andy had spoken.

"I guess every kid who wants to play football has a hero. Your dad was mine. Every time he played, I'd get as close to the field as they let me and memorize every move he made. I just wanted to *be* Rob Ellis."

"Lucky you." Zach smirked. "You turned out to be Andy Ryan instead."

Andy stopped smiling and folded his forearms on the desk. So much for pleasantries.

"Your dad, whose opinion I respect, by the way, thinks you have what it takes to make a football player. Do you?"

Zach shrugged. "You're the coach."

Andy took a moment before answering. It couldn't be clearer that Zach was doing everything he could to get some kind of a rise out of him, and he was just as determined not to take the bait. There might be occasions when he jumped all over Zach. That was just part of the job. But Andy would be the one who decided when and why that would be, not Zach.

"You're right. I am the coach. And with all respect to your dad, if all I had to go on was what I've seen so far, I'd say he was dead wrong."

Zach shifted slightly in his chair, and the smirk left his face.

"Look, Zach, what's going on? Your dad's obviously seen something. Why haven't I seen it?"

The silence in the office grew while Andy waited for an answer. Finally Zach shrugged and looked away. "What's the point?"

"What do you mean?"

"I mean, what's the point?" Zach's voice rose. "I mean, look at my dad. I've heard people who've watched him play say he was even better than you were."

"He probably was."

"But because he played in this little Podunk town, no one ever knew that. There was no scholarship for him; there wasn't even any college for him. He's been working as a county lineman since he graduated from high school." Zach's voice shook. "Every year, he puts on an old letterman's jacket that he can't even snap up anymore for the Parade of Pumas. And everyone says, 'Ooooh, there's Rob Ellis. He was so good in his day,' and he feels like a big shot one more time. I'm never going to let that be me."

Andy leaned back in his chair. Whatever he had expected, it was not this. "Does your dad know how you feel?"

Zach shook his head. After a moment he swallowed and cleared his throat. "No. He was my hero too, you know. It was a big deal being Rob Ellis's kid. I just don't want to wind up having lived my best days before I turn eighteen."

"So what do you want, Zach? Is there something you'd rather be doing?"

He sighed. "No. That's the thing. I gotta say I love the game. In fact, when I found out you were coming, I thought I might get a chance to do something after all. But shoot, we were pathetic last Friday, and if you want to know the truth, I don't think we have much of a chance this week either."

"You may be right. In fact, if everyone put forth the effort at practice you did this week, I'd say we're almost guaranteed a loss." He paused and held Zach's gaze a long moment. "But I'll make a deal with you. If you give me all you've got from this minute on, and I mean a hundred and ten percent, and if you're as good as your dad thinks you are, I'll help you get your shot. But I've sure got to see a whole lot more than I've seen so far." Zach started nodding and Andy waved him toward the door. "You better get on home. It's getting late. Your folks will wonder where you are."

After Zach left, Andy leaned back in his chair and folded his arms across the top of his head. Rob was biased, of course, as every father was, but Andy had noticed an easy grace in Zach when he was on the field, so maybe there was something there. He had no idea if Zach could get a scholarship at a top school, but he could probably get one somewhere, and all a kid really needed was a chance.

# 12

The roar of Puma pride that had permeated every corner of the town when Jess arrived in Last Chance had quieted to a low grumble by the night of the town council meeting. Last Chance High's record stood at 1–3, and even their single win gave more cause for complaint than for triumph.

"You are a brave woman." Andy slid behind the wheel of his truck after closing Jess's door and started the engine. "If you had suddenly decided you needed to go to this thing on your own, I sure would have understood. I hope you brought your doctor stuff, because there will be blood."

"I may have a Band-Aid or two in my purse. If there's not too much blood, that ought to work." Jess turned to smile at Andy, but he looked pretty grim for someone who had just made a joke. She leaned back against the door so she could see him better. "Are you serious? Rita said this was just a friendly get-together."

"Nah. I'm just kidding." Andy threw her a quick grin. "Folks take their football pretty seriously, but other than the occasional parking lot fistfight, they don't get violent."

"Fistfight?" Suddenly the very benign, warm and friendly event Rita had promised was appearing to Jess in a whole new light. She didn't have much to say for the rest of the short drive.

Andy pulled into a parking space at the community center and shut off the ignition.

"Look." He reached across the seat and enveloped Jess's hand in his own, giving it a little shake. "Everything is going to be fine, okay? There will not be blood; there will be no fights. First of all, Rita would never allow the chief ingredient of a parking lot fistfight to cross the threshold of a town council meeting. She serves coffee only. And second, these are good folks. I've known them all my life. Sure, they'll have some tough questions, but I'm okay with that. It's just part of my job."

When Jess got out of the pickup, she was beginning to feel a little better, and when Andy joined her and gave her a wink and a smile, she almost relaxed. But when he pushed the door open for her and she walked past him into the hall, he leaned down to whisper, "But keep the Band-Aids handy just in case."

Rita spotted them the minute they came in, waving and tucking her clipboard under her arm as she bustled across the room to greet them.

"There you are! I was beginning to think you weren't going to come."

Jess glanced at her watch. It was ten minutes to 7:00 and the room held maybe twenty people, including the half dozen or so seated at a long folding table at the front of the room. She exchanged a glance with Andy.

Rita appeared to be too busy with her clipboard to notice. "So, here's the schedule."

She ran through the night's agenda without looking up from her clipboard or even taking a breath, and when she finally looked up with a smile and said, "Any questions?" Jess found she had none. In fact, she would have been hard pressed to repeat almost anything Rita had just told her. Only one thing registered with her. She would be introduced and speak before Andy.

Rita gave them about two seconds to respond before continuing. "All righty then. We'll be starting here in seven minutes, so go on and mingle."

She gave Jess's arm a little pat, but her gaze had already landed on a new arrival she clearly needed to talk to before the meeting began, and waving her arm to flag him down, she took off again.

Jess turned to Andy, but before she could say anything, a man in well-worn jeans and a blue plaid shirt approached them and nodded. "Evening. Nice to see you, ma'am. So how are we looking for Friday, Coach?"

As two or three more men ambled over to join a conversation that obviously didn't include her, Jess looked around the room. A few more people had arrived, bringing the total to around thirty. Most stood chatting in groups of three or four, and a few were drawing coffee from a large urn into Styrofoam cups. Jess took a deep breath. *Time to mingle.*

When Rita called the meeting to order a few minutes later, Jess was laughing with two older women and the recently married daughter of one of them. As much as she appreciated that Rita had taken her under her wing and introduced her to everyone she could think of, Jess couldn't help noticing that when she was on her own, people didn't seem to have that deer-in-the-headlights expression they assumed when Rita loomed up before them. In fact, everyone was downright friendly and welcoming, and for the first time since she arrived in Last Chance, Jess began to truly feel she might belong here one day.

Finally, after the Pledge of Allegiance, the opening prayer, and Rita's extravagant introduction, Jess found herself standing before the small crowd. She recognized Russ Sheppard sitting at the council table, and Juanita was there in the second row. A few of the others also looked a little familiar, but the only smile came from the young newlywed she'd spoken with before the meeting.

She smiled back and looked out over the small assembly as she took a deep breath. "Hi, I'm Jess MacLeod. Rita asked me to tell you all a little about myself, but my goodness, anything I could say after that introduction would only take the gloss off. I'm tempted to stop right here."

There were a few chuckles and some more smiles, and Jess relaxed. The twenty minutes Rita had allotted her went by much faster than she imagined they would, and before she knew it, she was asking for questions.

The faces were friendly enough, but there were no questions, and after a moment she smiled and said, "Well, thank you for listening. I loved getting to know some of you tonight, and I intend to get to know all of you better. I think one of the best decisions I ever made was coming to Last Chance, and I hope to be here a long, long time. Rita told me that this was just supposed to be a friendly get-together, but you know that I can't sit down without giving at least one bit of medical advice: flu season's on its way, so don't forget to get your shot."

The crowd chuckled and applauded as Jess joined Andy on the first row. She leaned over to whisper, "Piece of cake. A lot of worry for nothing."

"For you, maybe." Andy crossed his arms and leaned back in his chair.

"And now, I'm pleased to introduce someone who needs no introduction." Rita stood at her chair behind the long folding table and beamed, first at Andy and then at the room.

For someone claiming Andy needed no introduction, Rita certainly had a lot to say about him, his years growing up in Last Chance, and his football career after he left. She finished up by saying, "Let's welcome Last Chance's own hometown hero, the boy who made us proud—Coach Andy Ryan."

The applause that greeted Andy as he stepped to the front was less than tepid, even for a small crowd, and Jess, remembering how much that single smile had meant when she was up there, gave him one of her own.

"Well, I'm guessing that you didn't come out tonight to hear about me." He leaned his weight on one foot and shoved his hand in his jeans pocket. "I'm thinking you came to talk football."

"You got that right." The muttered comment came from somewhere in the middle of the room.

"Then let's talk football." Andy shifted his weight and gave a half grin. "I don't need to tell you that we've had a rough start to the season. Shoot, you were there. You saw it. But as you know, with nearly half the team last year graduating, we've got a young team. There's a lot of potential there, though, and I think you're going to see some good football before the season's out."

In an easy, relaxed manner, Andy went on to talk about the team, its weaknesses and strengths, his confidence in them, and his belief that despite the year's disappointing beginning, a winning season was still within their grasp.

"So keep coming out to support your team." He was beginning to wrap things up, and Jess became aware of movement and a slight restlessness behind her. "If you're a parent, keep it upbeat. Believe me, between me and Kev Gallegos, they get all the coaching they need, and then some. Just keep that Puma pride up; we'll do the rest. Now, I'll bet we have some questions."

Almost before he finished speaking, Jess heard the scraping of chairs against the linoleum floor. Andy pointed over her head to someone behind her. "Yeah. Les." Jess looked over her shoulder to see a wiry older man with a salt and pepper mustache and denim jacket get to his feet.

"I get what you're saying, Andy. The boys, most of 'em anyway, do lack experience, and like you say, your toughest teams were stacked there at the beginning of the season." He paused a beat or two. "But what in Sam Hill happened with Otero Valley? I don't think Otero Valley's won a dozen games in the last ten years, and we beat 'em by one lousy point. One! And if they'd 'a made that field goal in the last thirty seconds, they'd 'a beat us too." He stared at Andy as if he couldn't believe he even had to ask the question, threw up his hands in a gesture of hopelessness, and sat down, still shaking his head.

"What can I tell you, Les? Other than to say that upsets sometimes come out of nowhere. That's why they call them upsets. Otero fields an experienced team this year, and we've got young players at nearly all positions. But don't forget, whether you win by forty points or by one, they still put that *W* in your column. Your team won that one. Be proud of 'em."

Almost before Andy finished speaking, someone else got to his feet, and frustration that had been building since Last Chance lost its second game began to spill all over the community center hall. Jess knew of the Glory Days, Last Chance High's eighty-four-game win streak, of course. It was Last Chance lore. But if she thought it was an impressive, once-in-a-lifetime occurrence, clearly the people in this room did not. As far as they were concerned, by returning to Last Chance, Andy Ryan had implicitly promised the return of the Glory Days as well. And the disappointment that it wasn't going to begin this year, with this team, was almost palpable.

Andy, though, kept his cool. When he spoke in specifics about the technicalities of the game, it mostly floated over Jess's head, but his theme never changed: these were good, if inexperienced, kids. They were working hard and they were getting better with every game. Last Chance had a lot to be proud of.

Gradually, Jess felt the tension in the room ease. People seemed to relax in their chairs. At least, Jess didn't hear near the shifting and shuffling she had heard earlier, and the questions seemed more about gaining information than making accusations.

Finally, Rita rose to her feet. "I think we have time for about one more question. We do have a little business to take care of tonight, and the sooner we get it taken care of, the sooner we can cut that cake in the back."

"I have a question, Andy." The voice behind Jess was slow and calm, but there was no mistaking its grim edge. Jess turned around to see Rob Ellis standing in the back, his hands shoved deep in his pockets.

"Hey, Rob. I didn't see you come in." Andy grinned. "Shoot."

"It's just this." He folded his arms across his broad chest. "My boy, Zach, is a senior, which means unless he gets a scholarship somewhere, he's got exactly seven games left and he's done playing football for good. I've watched him and worked with him since he was big enough to hold a football, and he's good. Anyone who's ever seen him play can tell you that." A murmur of assent rippled over the crowd. "So what I want to know is, is he gonna get his shot? You don't play him enough. You've lost three out of four games, and you still don't play him enough. He's your best player. It doesn't take a rocket scientist to see that, just a good coach. I get that you've got next year's team to develop, but what about this year? What about *my* boy?"

The room fell completely silent, and the easy smile Andy had worn since he stepped to the front of the room faded. From her vantage point in the front row, Jess could see a muscle along his jaw clench. Before he could say anything, Rita spoke up again.

"I think that's a question that's better dealt with in your office, Andy, if you don't mind. We really do need to get the business meeting started. But we do want to thank you, Coach Ryan, and you too, Dr. MacLeod, for coming out to talk to us tonight." She beamed and brought her hands together in loud applause. As the rest of the room joined in and Rob banged out the back door, Andy took his place beside Jess in the front row.

He didn't say anything or even look at her, but that muscle in his jaw still clenched, and she could hear his quick and angry breath gradually slow to normal as Rita brought the meeting to order. True to her promise, all the business was quickly dispatched, and in moments the meeting had been adjourned.

"You okay?" Jess leaned over to whisper as the crowd behind them shuffled to its feet and a buzz of conversation filled the room.

"I'm fine." He stood up and took a deep breath as he held out a hand to pull her to her feet. "As I said, it's just part of the job."

"Andy?" Les came up and offered his hand. "I need to tell you how sorry I am that I flew off the handle like that. I had no cause to do that, and I feel real bad about it. You're right. A win's a win, and I'm proud of those boys for pullin' it off."

Andy took the calloused old hand and shook it. "I'm proud of them too, Les. Thanks for coming to tell me, but it's all right. Don't give it another thought."

"But I do. I feel like I set the tone for the whole evening by jumping down your throat right off the bat. And it got ugly there at the end. I'm just sorry about that."

"Les, that was not your fault." Andy clapped him on the shoulder. "To tell the truth, it went a lot better than I thought it might. I was expecting maybe tar and feathers."

"Tar and feathers, my foot. You ought to know by now that we never get the tar and feathers out till the end of the season." He shook Andy's hand again and nodded toward Jess. "Ma'am."

As Les headed off toward the table where Rita was handing out squares of chocolate cake, Jess cocked her head as she watched him go. "Isn't he the guy who keeps telling you to run faster or they're going to catch you when you're out running?"

"Yeah, that's Les, all right." Andy smiled and shook his head. "He's battled some demons in his day, but let me tell you, you're not going to find a more stand-up guy anywhere than Les Watson. If the world were filled with Les Watsons, it would be a better place."

Having seen the spider veins in Les's cheeks, Jess had a pretty good idea what demons he had battled. "He does seem like a nice guy. How's he doing?"

"Les? I guess he's doing great. There was an alcohol-related accident involving some kids a couple years ago that he felt responsible for, even though he wasn't anywhere near it at the time. From what I hear, that was it for him. It's been a struggle, but so far he's come out on top."

"Good. I like him."

"Me too. Now, I figure if we can run the gauntlet to the cake table, and eat some of Rita's cake, we will have done our bit and can leave. What do you think?"

"I think you've got a plan."

A few minutes later, when they did walk out into the cool October evening, Andy reached for her hand. Jess had never been much for hand holding, but Andy seemed to like it, and Jess discovered that when she was with him, she liked it too.

"Well, the official word is that you're going to be a mom, and it will probably happen around March 16." Jess smiled as she pulled off her latex gloves the next afternoon and took a seat on the little stool in her examination room. "How have you been feeling?"

Lainie Braden swung her legs over the side of the examination table and sat up. "I'm feeling great now. I did get tired pretty easily for a while, and there was a time or two when I was afraid I was going to lose my breakfast, but I never did."

"Good for you. Well, you're doing great. You need to keep taking those prenatal vitamins. And you need to have some blood work done and an ultrasound. I'll give you some paperwork to take to the lab at San Ramon General, and I should see you again in about eight weeks. Other than that, just keep doing what you're doing. Do you have any questions?"

Lainie held her hands to her cheeks. "So, I'm really pregnant?"

Jess laughed out loud. "You had doubts?"

"No. No, I knew up here." She tapped her head. "It's just that nothing's happening, except I have to pee all the time."

"Believe me, a lot is happening. You just can't see it yet, but you will." Jess stood up. "Now, I'm going to let you get dressed. If you think of any questions or have any concerns at all, call me. That's what I'm here for."

Lainie, still wearing a spacy grin, nodded.

"I'm serious, Lainie. Call *me*. You're going to get more advice than you know what to do with from everyone you see and hear horror stories that'll make you wonder what you got yourself into. Everyone loves to enlighten a first-time mom. But you don't have to listen."

Lainie nodded again.

"Repeat. 'I don't have to listen.'"

"I don't have to listen."

"There you go, girlfriend, and don't forget it." Jess reached for the door. "I really am so happy for you, and tell Ray congratulations for me, would you?"

She left Lainie, still sitting in her paper robe smiling into the near distance, and went to her office, slipping off her lab coat as she closed the door behind her. Lainie was the last appointment of the day. She hadn't exactly worked herself to death since she opened her office in Last Chance, but there had been at least a few appointments every day. She was especially pleased about Lainie. Besides being one of the first people Jess had met when she got to town, Lainie had become a friend, one of the few she had found time to make. It would be great to see her through her pregnancy and deliver her baby.

The schedule for tomorrow sat on her desk, and Jess was going over it when her cell phone rang and she saw Andy's number displayed.

"Hi." She smiled into the phone.

"I've got an injured player. Can you see him, or should we head on up to the ER in San Ramon?" Andy minced no words.

"What kind of injury? Do you need to call an ambulance?" There was only so much she was equipped to do in her small office.

"No, it's just a cut across his forehead, but I'm pretty sure he'll need stitches. We're already on our way. I just need to know if we can stop at your office or if we should go to San Ramon."

"Bring him over. We'll be able to take you right in."

His voice relaxed a little. "Sorry to call on your personal phone, but that's the only number I have."

"No problem. Listen, I need to go get ready for you. See you in a minute."

Putting her lab coat back on, she went to find Eva, who was sitting at her desk with her jacket on, closing down the computer. She looked up when Jess came in. "Well, I scheduled Lainie Braden's next appointment, so that should be it. Okay if I leave now?"

"I need a suture setup in examination room two. They're bringing someone over from football practice."

The look Eva gave Jess clearly said, "You've got to be kidding," and Jess ignored it. "Hurry, please. They'll be here in just a few minutes. In fact, I think that's them now."

Through the front window, Jess saw Andy pull his truck next to the front door and say something to the person sitting next to him on the front seat. He got out and went around to open the passenger door and help a dark-haired kid wearing a blood-splashed jersey and clutching a roll of gauze to his head make his way to the door. At first glance she could hardly believe he was a football player. Certainly he did not fit any idea of a football player she had ever held. He was about her height, maybe five-foot-six, and weighed perhaps a hundred and forty pounds.

She ran to open the door for them and took his other arm as they came in. As they headed down the hall, Eva passed them on her way out of the examination room. Jess hoped the others didn't catch the disgruntled look Eva shot them as they went by, but a flash of irritation went through her.

"Eva, you can go now. I'll finish up here."

"Really? If you're sure." Her voice was all concern. "I mean, I can stay if you want me to."

"We're good. See you tomorrow."

Jess had neither the time nor the inclination to deal with Eva at the moment. From the moment Dr. Benavides's office manager had asked her to work, at least temporarily, with Jess in Last Chance, Eva had been unhappy. Clearly, she felt as if she had been banished to the boonies and was openly counting the days till she could return to the high echelons of civilization represented by San Ramon. Jess left her standing in the hall.

"Here. Can you get him up on the examination table?" Jess reached for the latex gloves.

"I can get up myself." Still holding the roll of gauze against his forehead, her patient did manage to get up on the table, although he swayed a bit as he sat there.

"Okay, let's see what we've got here." Jess smiled at him as she took the gauze from his hand and examined the cut. At least the bleeding had stopped. "What's your name?"

"Gabe. Gabriel Quintana."

"Well, Gabe, I've got some good news and some bad news for you." She gently cleansed the wound as she talked. "First of all, the cut isn't as bad as all this blood might lead you to believe. The vessels are pretty close to the surface on the head, so cuts tend to bleed a lot. But—and here's the bad news—you are going to need stitches, and that's going to take you out of football for at least a while."

"Man." He glanced over her shoulder at Andy, who was still standing in the doorway. "How long will it keep me out?"

"Depends. If it's just the stitches, maybe a week, ten days. But it's hard to imagine you taking a shot to the head like you must have taken without getting your brain rattled too. If you have a concussion, we'll just have to see."

Jess finished cleaning the long cut and reached for the antiseptic.

Gabe winced as she began applying it. "Is this going to take long?"

"Got an appointment?" Jess went on with her work.

"I gotta get home. The kids go to a neighbor's when my mom leaves for work, but I've gotta go get them and give them their dinner."

"We called your mom, Gabe." Andy spoke up. "She told us to do whatever needed to be done, and she'll get here as soon as she can. She's on her way now. Don't worry about it."

"Man, they hate it when she has to take off. I need to go."

Gabe was getting agitated, and Jess wanted him calm. She glanced over at Andy. "We're about to get started here. Why don't you go out and wait for Gabe's mom in the waiting room? You can tell her what happened when she gets here."

She turned back to Gabe with a warm smile and put her hand on his shoulder. "How're you doing?"

He shrugged.

"I guess that's kind of a silly question, isn't it? Okay, here's what we're going to do. I'm going to inject a little anesthesia into the wound. You won't like it much, but you've probably dealt with a lot worse today, even before you got hurt. Then, after it gets numb, I'll put the sutures in. It won't take long. We might even be done before your mom gets here."

He nodded and closed his eyes while she injected the anesthesia.

"Gabe, open your eyes and look at me." She looked closely into his eyes when he did. "Now, I want you to follow my finger with your eyes without turning your head. Can you do that? Okay, good job."

As she put in the sutures, Jess asked Gabe questions about his injury, about his family, about his plans for the future just to keep him talking, and when she heard his mother come in the front door, she was tying the last knot.

She could hear Andy trying to tell Gabe's mom about the accident, but since his voice was heading their way, Jess had a feeling he was chasing her down the hall to do so. She came through the door and went straight for Gabe, putting both hands on his shoulders and holding him at arm's length for a better look.

"*Mijo*, what happened? Are you all right? There's so much blood." She turned to look at Jess, as if demanding an explanation.

"Hi, Mrs. Quintana. I'm Dr. MacLeod." Jess tried to make her smile reassuring. "Gabe's doing fine. He's got twelve stitches in his forehead, and even though he doesn't show signs of concussion, I'd advise you to take him up to the hospital for testing. You can't be too careful with a head injury."

"Absolutely." Gabe's mom was carefully examining his stitches.

"Can I take him home first to change his shirt and to get my other kids settled, or is it an emergency?"

"More of an urgency than an emergency." Jess smiled. "You need to take him as soon as you can, but it can wait till you get your kids settled, and I'm sure Gabe would like to get out of that shirt. Now, if you let me get that cut bandaged, you can be on your way."

Mrs. Quintana stepped out of the way, and Jess dressed the wound.

"Don't take the bandage off for at least forty-eight hours. Keep a clean bandage on it after that, and be sure to keep it dry. If there's swelling or redness, come right in. Otherwise, I want to see you next Monday after school. And no football until I say so, got it?" She looked first at Gabe, then at Andy. Both nodded. "Okay then. That's it!"

All four walked into the small waiting room, and as they passed the desk, Jess took one of her cards from its rack and wrote on it before handing it to Mrs. Quintana. "Would you call me when you get Gabe home tonight? That's my cell number on the back. I want to hear how he's doing. Don't worry. I'll be up."

Mrs. Quintana looked at the number and nodded. "Sure."

"Thanks." Jess opened the door and locked it behind them. She watched Gabe and his mom get in her car and drive off before turning to Andy. "Would you tell me why someone as small as Gabe is playing football?"

If she thought Andy would offer excuses, she was wrong. "Because he wants to. And because he's good. And because he has more drive and heart than most of the rest of the team put together. I hate it that he got hurt; you have no idea how much I hate it. But that's football, and I'm not going to be the one to tell him he can't play."

Jess was silent a moment. "All right then. I guess that's clear enough."

After a long moment, Andy looked at his watch. "I guess I better get back. Practice is over, but there are some things I need to do."

Jess nodded and unlocked the front door for him. "Okay, well, good night."

"'Night." Andy went out and got in his truck. It had gotten dark since he brought Gabe in, and his headlights flashed across the back of the office as he backed out and drove away.

Jess locked the door behind him. Suddenly her lab coat felt stiff and itchy, and she realized that all she wanted was to go home, take a long bath, and curl up with a book and a cup of tea. She took a deep breath, held it, slowly exhaled, and headed to the back to clean examination room two.

# 13

Jess was right. The bath was exactly what she needed, as were the tea and the book. And when she lit a fire in her fireplace and put on her oldest, softest flannel pjs, the day began to sort itself out. It hadn't really been that bad. In fact, she had looked forward to Lainie's appointment. Things didn't start going downhill until Andy called, and that was only because of the attitudes she had to deal with. She had been annoyed, though not surprised, by Eva's fit of pique that she was asked to stay a few minutes late; she was going to have to talk to Eva about that. But it was Andy's stance when she suggested Gabe might be a little small for football that surprised her. He seemed almost angry, and frankly, Jess just didn't get that.

The phone on her coffee table buzzed, and Jess made a grab for it. Gabe's mom hadn't checked in yet, and she was anxious to hear how he was doing.

"Hi." It was Andy. "Have you heard anything yet?"

"Nope." Jess leaned back against the sofa cushions and tucked her feet up under her. "I was just thinking Gabe's mom should be calling soon."

"Will you call me after you talk to her and let me know how he is?"

"I really can't. There are all kinds of regulations, but I can tell his mom you're concerned and that you've asked that she call you."

"Would you do that? Tell her I won't keep her long, I just want to know he's okay." A short, awkward silence followed, and Jess was about to say good-bye when Andy spoke again. "Listen, I'm sorry I barked at you earlier. You didn't have that coming."

Jess silently agreed. She thought her question had been perfectly reasonable. "So, what was the deal?"

"Just touchy, I guess. It seems every time I talk to anyone these days, the first word out of their mouths is *why*. 'Why did you . . .' 'Why didn't you . . .' 'Why don't you . . .' Anyway, I think I took it out on you, and I'm sorry. I shouldn't let it get to me like that."

"Okay, since we have that settled." Jess chose her words carefully. "Keeping in mind I'm his doctor and not someone who's trying to help you coach the team. Don't you think he's a little small to be playing football?"

There was another long pause before Andy blew out a long sigh. "Don't underestimate Gabe. He's not real big, but he's strong, and he's fast. And he loves the game. He didn't get hurt because of his size. He just cracked helmets with another player. It happens."

Sensing she was stepping out on thin ice, Jess retreated. "Okay, backing off here. I'll just patch 'em up when you send 'em my way."

"You could come to a game, you know." The tension in Andy's voice had eased a little, and Jess could almost hear his attempt at a smile. "See for yourself what the attraction is."

"Maybe I will one of these days." Jess took the olive branch he offered, even if she really could not see herself ever sitting on a cold bleacher watching a bunch of guys run into each other and fall down. "Listen, I really do need to get off the phone, though. I'm waiting for Mrs. Quintana's call."

"Oh, sure. Don't forget to ask her to call me, okay? I'll be up."

Mrs. Quintana called less than ten minutes later, and Jess could tell by her voice that her news was good.

"Sorry I'm calling so late. I needed to make sure the kids were all right first and get Gabe all tucked in. He's going to be okay. He just needs to stay in bed for a couple days. That's all."

"That's terrific news, Mrs. Quintana. I think it would be a good idea to wake him up every three hours through the night, though, just to be on the safe side. He may not like that much, but as you say, he's going to be in bed all day long tomorrow anyway. You're the one who'll be missing sleep."

Gabe's mom chuckled. She had a low and easy laugh. "Please. Call me Marta. When anyone calls me Mrs. Quintana, it usually means one of my kids is in some kind of trouble. And don't worry. If I were still at work, I'd be up all night anyway, so checking on Gabe isn't going to be a problem. Waking people up when they're trying to sleep is what I do best."

Jess smiled. Marta seemed like someone she'd like to get to know. "I noticed you had on scrubs. Do you work at the hospital?"

"Yes, I'm an LPN at San Ramon General. And I've been wanting to tell you how glad I am that you came. It's time Last Chance had its own doctor."

"I appreciate that. I'm glad I came too. Now, I'm going to let you get some rest. You've had quite an evening. I'll call in the morning to see how Gabe did through the night, but it sounds like he's in great hands."

"I think he'll be fine. He complained all the way home about a chemistry test he'll be missing tomorrow and falling behind in calculus, which is Gabe being normal." She laughed. "Good night, Doctor."

"Good night, and it's Jess." She stopped herself just before she hung up. "Oh, Coach Ryan asked that you call him and tell him how Gabe is. He said he'd be up late."

"I'll call him right away. Have you gotten to know him at all? He is such a good man. I've lived in Last Chance all my life. Both my brothers played football, and my cousins, and I don't think there's ever been a coach who cares as much about the boys as Andy does. I know he's worked really hard to help Gabe out." She laughed. "Listen to me. I said good-bye and then started in talking your ear off again. Good night, Doctor. And I mean it this time."

"Good night." Jess ended the call and put her phone back on the table. Maybe Marta was uncomfortable calling her by her first name, or maybe she just hadn't heard Jess's request, but Jess did hope they could be friends.

"How's Quintana?" Kev came into Andy's office after his last class. "Sorry I couldn't wait till you got back. I got everything wrapped up here and Tina was counting on me to get home. She has her bunco game on Tuesday night."

Andy sat back in his chair and rubbed his eyes. "He's going to be okay. He got a few stitches, and they're keeping him home for a day or so because of that rap on the head, but he'll be back."

"But not by Friday?"

"Nope, and probably not by next Friday either. I'm not sure when he'll be ready to play."

"Man, I do not need to hear that." Kev folded his arms and leaned against the doorjamb. "I think we had a real good chance to start turning things around with these next few games, but with Quintana out . . ."

"Yeah, it's a hit, all right." Andy went back to the notebook open in front of him. "But that's part of the game."

"You know, I got to hand it to you, Coach." Kev pushed away from the doorjamb and shoved one hand in his pocket. "I wouldn't have given you two cents for Quintana when he showed up for practice last August. Too small, too scattered, and no experience to speak of. He pretty much spent the season sitting on the bench last year. But you saw something that sure escaped me. I guess that's why they pay you the big bucks, huh?"

Andy looked up from under his brows. "Yeah, right."

Kev laughed as he headed to the locker room. "I'll go make sure things are set up for practice. See you in a few."

Andy could hear the players begin to arrive for practice as he worked, and when a light tap came at his open door, he looked up expecting to find one of them standing there.

"Hi, Andy. Dare I approach the inner sanctum?" A slender woman with blonde hair curling around her shoulders smiled at him from the doorway.

"Heather!" He got up and crossed the room to take both her hands in his. When he bent down to kiss her cheek, he noticed her eyes were still as blue as an early morning sky. "I'd heard you were still in the area. Thought I might run into you sometime. I didn't think it would be here, though."

"Okay, you caught me. I came to find you." She laughed up at him as he led her to a chair in front of his desk. "I forgot that my boys had flag football today after school, so I got here to pick them up way too early. When I realized I had a half hour or so to kill, I took a chance that you might be free and I could say hi."

He sat down behind his desk and leaned on his folded arms. "I can't get over it. You haven't changed a lick in, how long? Nearly ten years?"

"Longer. We didn't see much of you after graduation."

"Wow." Andy felt a twinge of guilt. He had really intended to stay in touch with Heather, and in those early days even dreamed of coming back for her someday. "Has it been that long? Can't be."

"Time does fly when you're having a good time." She tucked a strand of hair behind her ear, just like she used to, and smiled again. "But we can save this for later. I want you to come to dinner. James would love to see you again, and my boys are dying to meet you. Telling them I was homecoming queen in my day got a big yawn from them; telling them you were my escort elevated me to superstar status."

"Sure. I'd like to see James and meet your boys." Andy got to his feet. Silence from the nearby locker room told him that Kev had already taken the team out; he needed to get out there. And Heather needed to go get her sons. "Almost any day but Friday. Just let me know."

"Saturday? About 7:00? James has taken over the family chile farm, so you know where to find us." She gathered her purse and stood up. Andy walked her to the door. "Oh, and feel free to bring someone with you, if you'd like. There's always room for one more."

Andy took a deep breath. Bringing someone might be a good idea. "Yeah, there is someone I could bring with me. Let me talk to her and I'll get back to you."

"Great. Anyone I know?" Heather stopped in the doorway and raised an eyebrow. She was doing that funny little thing with her mouth that she always did when she was about to worm a secret out of him.

"Nope. She's new in town. She's the new doctor, as a matter of fact, so she may be on call or something. I'll call you in the next couple days to tell you if she'll be coming."

Both eyebrows were up now. "The doctor. Wow. You do move fast. Be sure to warn her she's coming to a farmer's house. Nothing fancy."

"She won't be looking for fancy. That's not her style." He gave Heather a quick good-bye hug. "You'll like her."

"If you like her, I'm sure I'll like her too." She put a hand on his shoulder and stood on tiptoes to kiss his cheek. "Now, I've got to run and get my boys. They'll think I forgot them again."

Andy stood in the doorway of his office watching her as she hurried down the hall and out the door. It couldn't have been ten years. She looked just like she did when she was seventeen. Not even the fragrance she wore had changed.

As Jess headed down Last Chance Highway Friday evening, she passed a long line of cars and pickups decorated with black-and-gold streamers and white shoe polish proclaiming Puma pride heading up toward I-10. She waved as she went by and gave a little double tap to her horn in solidarity, and in doing so unleashed a cacophony of whoops and blaring horns that she could still hear in the distance as she drove into Last Chance. Clearly, as the week had gone by and game day approached, the frustration and even anger displayed Monday night at the town council meeting had changed again to hope. And for Andy's sake, how she wanted them to be right.

The lights were still on in the Dip 'n' Dine, and a few cars were still in the parking lot as Jess drove into town. Since the folks going to the game seemed to have already left, she took a chance and pulled in. Lainie had assured her that the Dip 'n' Dine did not close early on game days, no matter what Juanita said, and truthfully, she wanted a little company, even that of strangers. Friday night was for welcoming the weekend and not a night she wanted to go home and eat yogurt.

She pushed the door open with a cautious eye out for Juanita, but it was Lainie who crossed the dining room to greet her.

"Hey, look who's here." Lainie gave her a hug and looked around the room. "Where would you like to sit?"

Jess shrugged and glanced at the row of booths by the window. "Doesn't matter."

"Over here!" A petite woman with dark, curly hair smiled and beckoned.

"Okay with you? Sarah was just telling me she wanted to get to know you." With Jess's nod, Lainie led the way to the table.

"I hope you don't mind." Sarah reached across the table and took Jess's hand as she slid in the booth across from her. "I'm Sarah Reed. That's my husband, Chris, over there. I'm just waiting for him to finish up here and get ready to come home. Say hi, Chris." Chris looked over from the cash register where he was dealing with customers and waved. "Anyway, everyone I know keeps telling me how terrific you are. I don't know how I wound up being the only person in town who hasn't met you yet."

"Different circles, I guess." Jess found Sarah's smile infectious, but then she guessed most people did. "I feel like I know you, though. Elizabeth has shown me your wedding pictures and told me all about you. Second-grade teacher, right?"

"That sounds like Gran. Family is her favorite topic of conversation—well, her second-favorite topic, anyway."

"Oh? What's her first?"

"How much time have you spent with Gran?" Sarah sat back and cocked her head.

"Some. Not as much as I'd like, though. I really like her."

"Everybody loves Gran, and I'll leave it to you to discover her favorite topic of conversation—which you will, believe me."

"Are you all ready to order?" Lainie appeared at their table and Sarah looked up as she handed the menu back.

"I'll have the stuffed sopaipilla, beef, with red chile."

"All right. How about you?" She turned to Jess with a smile. "Have you had time to decide?"

"Um, I don't know." Jess hadn't even looked at her menu. "What Sarah's having, I guess, and some iced tea."

"Good choice." Lainie tore the sheet off. "I'll get this in and bring your tea."

After she left, Jess leaned across the table. "What did I just order?"

Sarah laughed. "You know what sopaipillas are, right?"

"Yeah, you put honey in them."

"Well, in this case you don't. You fill it with a mixture of ground beef and onions and Carlos's secret spices and cover it with red chile sauce, or green, if you like it that way. As my granddad used to say, 'It's so good it ought to be against the law.'"

Lainie came with their iced tea just as the last of the other customers went out into the night, and Sarah scooted over and patted the seat next to her.

"Come sit down for a minute. There's no one in here but us now."

Lainie sighed. "I'm afraid if I sit down, I might not get up."

"All the more reason for her to sit down, right, Jess?" She continued patting the seat until Lainie, with a glance toward Chris, did scoot in next to her.

"You do look tired, Lainie." Jess tore a package of sweetener open and stirred it into her tea. "You don't want to overdo it."

"I'm fine, really." Lainie leaned her head against the back of the booth and closed her eyes for a moment. "We just got slammed earlier with folks trying to eat before they headed out to the game, and Juanita had already talked Chris into letting her go a little early. She and Russ never miss a game if they can help it."

Jess shook her head. "I still can't get used to all this devotion to high school football. Am I really the only person in town who doesn't care?"

Lainie opened one eye and tapped her own chest, indicating

there were at least two, but Sarah clearly could be counted among the faithful.

"I'd be there every week if I could. In fact, before I got married, I never missed a game if I could help it. That's how I knew it was Friday night—frozen pizza, a football game, and a good scary movie. It was the best."

Lainie patted Sarah's hand without opening her eyes. "Poor baby. Sorry you've got it so rough now."

"Well, we're usually there by halftime for home games." Sarah didn't even seem to notice Lainie's sarcasm. "And I still watch my movie when we get home, but the frozen pizza has been banished forever. Chris makes great pizzas from scratch, but it's just not the same, you know? They don't have that unique cardboard flavor."

Jess laughed. How had she missed getting to know Sarah?

"Here you go. Be careful, though. The plates are hot." Chris arrived tableside and set plates brimming with steaming red chile sauce in front of Jess and Sarah.

"Oh, I'm sorry, Chris." Lainie moved to get out of the booth. "I didn't even hear the bell."

"It didn't ring." Chris put a hand on her shoulder. "It's okay. Take it easy. We're done for the day. But if you ladies want dessert, you'd better order now. Carlos is cleaning the kitchen."

"None for me, thanks." Jess looked up from gingerly poking her stuffed sopaipilla with a fork and smiled. "This is going to fill me up. I can tell that right now."

After getting a similar response from Sarah, Chris nodded. "Okay. Enjoy your dinners. And take your time."

As he ambled away to turn off the Open sign and dim the dining room lights, Sarah reached across the table to grab Jess's free hand. "I know! Come over to my house. Chris made a triple chocolate cheesecake last weekend, and there's still some in the freezer. We can eat cheesecake and watch my movie. This one is called"—she paused for effect—"*The House Down the Road 4*. Come on, who can say no to cheesecake and a good horror flick? You come too, Lainie."

"Nope. Goin' home." Lainie had closed her eyes again. "I'm going home, taking my shoes off, putting my feet up, and watching whatever Gran has on TV—*Colombo*, *Hawaii Five-O*, doesn't matter."

"But you'll come, won't you, Jess?" Sarah was clearly in the mood to do a little Friday celebrating herself.

Jess grinned. "Sure. Why not? Does it matter that I haven't seen *The House Down the Road 1*, *2*, and *3*?"

The first thing Jess noticed when she opened Sarah and Chris's front door to go home a few hours later was that the wind had picked up and was howling through the cottonwood tree in the front yard, ripping dying leaves from the branches and pulling them up into the black sky. The second thing she noticed was how dark and empty and full of shadows the quiet street had become. And, of course, the third thing was how very far her car, parked at the curb, seemed to be from the warm light pouring from the front door.

*Would you get a grip? It was just a movie, and you're a scientist. What is your problem?*

"I'm going to stand right here and watch until you get in your car, and I'll leave the porch light on until you're gone." Sarah's voice at her elbow made her jump, and Jess turned to tell her that wouldn't be a bit necessary.

"Thanks, I'd really appreciate that."

*Well, how embarrassing was* that *to have to admit?*

Jess forced herself to walk casually to her car, and when she was safely locked in, had sneaked a quick peek to the backseat, and had started the engine, she waved Sarah back in the house.

As she drove down the street, past Elizabeth's house where a light still shone from behind drawn curtains and Sam sat like a loaf in front of the door, she found herself smiling. Despite spending most of the evening with her face buried in a sofa pillow, she had had a good time, a really good time.

The distant racket Jess had begun to notice as she approached Main Street had grown to almost deafening proportions as she came to a stop at the blinking red light that hung swaying in the wind over the intersection. Two school buses, still adorned with butcher paper banners proclaiming "Pluck the Eagles" and "Here Come the Pumas" passed by, leading a seemingly endless procession of cars and pickups, all with horns blaring and passengers leaning out the windows shouting at the empty street.

If anyone still left in Last Chance had turned in early, Jess had a feeling they were awake now. She also had a feeling that they didn't mind a bit.

# 14

"Here you are! It's been so long, I thought maybe you had forgotten how to get here." The strikingly pretty woman who opened the door reached up to kiss Andy on the cheek before turning to Jess and extending her hand. "And you're Dr. MacLeod. I'm so glad to finally meet you. Come in! Come in! James, they're here."

"Please. Call me Jess." Jess spoke to no one in particular since all attention had returned to Andy.

"Great game last night." The dark-haired man with a goatee, who must have been James, got out of his chair and met Andy in the middle of the room with a half hug and a handshake. "It's been way too long. Good to see you, Andy. Welcome home."

"And these rascals are Ethan and Tyler. They have been out of their minds since I told them you were coming. I hope you don't mind, but I told them you might autograph their footballs." Heather turned to two boys, each clutching a football, huddling together behind their dad. "Oh, for Pete's sake, boys, don't you think we should at least let him get in the door before you bring those things out? Now, why don't you come shake hands and show that you've learned a few manners."

"Hey, guys, how're you doing?" Andy grinned and shook each small hand. "I hear you play a little football yourselves."

"Yeah, flag." Ethan spoke with studied nonchalance. "We don't get to play tackle till middle school."

"That's time enough. You'll still get plenty of football in." He reached out his hand. "What you got there?"

Without a word, Ethan handed over his football, and Andy took it. "Got a felt-tip pen?"

Tyler, who had yet to say anything, produced the pen, and Andy autographed the footballs, one after the other.

Jess, still standing near the door, watched as Heather posed Ethan, Tyler, and Andy for pictures. Not until Andy looked over at Jess with a shrug and a half smile did Heather seem to remember Jess was there.

"Oh, my goodness, I am so sorry. This family just lives and breathes football, and once we get started, there's no stopping us." She gestured toward the sofa. "Come meet the gang while I go get dinner on the table. Andy, you do the honors."

Heather disappeared into the kitchen while Andy introduced Jess to James and the boys. James nodded and said, "Ma'am," the boys didn't say anything, and everybody found places to sit in the small living room.

James shifted in his chair and cleared his throat. "So, how do you like Last Chance so far?"

"The longer I'm here, the more I love it. Are you a native?" Jess's cheek muscles were beginning to hurt from smiling.

"Yup. So are the boys here. Heather too, for that matter. We all are."

"Wow." Jess nodded, still smiling. "You don't see a lot of that where I'm from."

"Z'at right?" Clearly, James was a man of few words.

Jess glanced over at Andy, watching the conversation, if you could call it that, with his ankle resting on his knee and one arm draped across the back of the sofa. *Anytime you want to chime in here, Andy, feel free.*

While Jess cast around trying to think of something else to say, James addressed Andy. "Gotta say, Andy, those boys keep playing like they did last night, and we might just see a winning season yet."

"You were at the game?" Andy deftly caught the ball Tyler threw him and lobbed it back.

"Are you kidding?" Heather stuck her head around the corner from the kitchen. "I'm surprised you couldn't hear us. I was hoarse this morning, I screamed so much. That was the most exciting game I've seen in years. And Tyler, no football in the house."

"Oh, man! When 84 intercepted that pass in the end zone and ran it 104 yards for a touchdown, I just went crazy. I was screaming so loud." Ethan was actually bouncing in his chair with the memory.

Tyler grinned and bounced a little himself but had yet, as far as Jess could tell, to say a word. Clearly a boy who would take after his dad.

"When the lead kept changing hands during the first half, I thought I was going to die." Heather had abandoned the kitchen and perched on the arm of Ethan's chair. "But the second half was all Last Chance."

"45–21." Ethan collapsed against the back of his chair in satisfaction, lightly tossing his autographed football.

"Yup," said James.

"Sounds exciting, all right." Truthfully, Jess had no idea what they were talking about, but there was no question that some remarkable football had been played.

"Weren't you there?" Ethan stopped tossing his football and stared at her.

"Um, no, I didn't go to the game." Jess felt a little warm.

"*Why not?*" Tyler did have a voice after all, and he could sound downright indignant too. Who knew?

"Come on, boys, don't badger Dr. MacLeod." Heather tousled Ethan's hair. "Doctors don't get to do everything they want to, you know. They have to take care of sick people, and people don't always pick a good time to get sick, right, Dr. MacLeod? Were you on call last night?"

"Well, no, I wasn't." Everyone was looking at her. What could she say? That she was watching *The House Down the Road 4* and eating cheesecake?

Finally, Andy came to her rescue, if you could call it that. "Actually, Jess isn't a real big football fan yet, but I think we can change that once we get her to a game, don't you, Tyler? She just doesn't know what she's missing, that's all."

Jess shot a look at Andy. She had hoped he would say that not everyone liked football and that not everybody needed to, but when she looked at the incredulous faces of the boys and the polite but stiff smiles of the parents, she realized he had probably done her a favor. After all, they had just arrived, and it could wind up being a long evening.

"Tell you what." Heather got to her feet and put her hand on Jess's shoulder as she headed back to the kitchen. "You sit with us at the next game, and we'll tell you what's happening on the field. Once you know what's going on, you'll be hooked."

"If I can, sure." Jess took a deep breath. "But as you said, my time's not always my own. I'll have to see how things are next Friday."

"Fair enough. I'll give you a call Friday to see how things are going. Now, guys." She glanced at her watch. "Dinner will be on the table in twenty minutes, so get all this football talk out of your system, because once we sit down, we're going to talk about something Dr. MacLeod might be interested in."

"Oh, no." Jess held up a hand. "Don't stop on my account. Maybe I'll learn something. And *please*, call me Jess."

Heather smiled without promising anything and gave Jess's shoulder a pat. "Why don't you come in the kitchen with me? You can keep me company while I get dinner on the table." She led Jess from the room while calling over her shoulder, "Remember, guys, twenty more minutes and we change the subject, so make it count."

Jess gave up. They could call her what they wanted and talk about whatever they felt like. She'd do her best to keep up, and let it go at that.

"What can I do to help?"

"Not a thing." She pointed at a stool. "Just sit right there and talk to me."

Jess climbed on the designated stool and looked around. "I love all your chiles. Red is such a happy color for a kitchen."

Heather looked up from her stove and shrugged. "It's more my mother-in-law's taste than mine. I don't even know if they sell red chile wallpaper anymore, although I'm sure you can still find all the chile light switch covers and trivets you want at any souvenir shop in the state. A complete kitchen remodel is on our 'someday list,' but every time it gets anywhere near the top, something comes along and bumps it back down." She bent down to pull a pan of corn muffins out of the oven. After setting it on a wrought iron trivet adorned with red and green chiles, she turned around and leaned against the counter, tucking a strand of hair behind her ear. "So, how did you meet Andy? Obviously not at a football game."

"I met him my first day in town, actually. Rita took me to the Dip 'n' Dine to meet people, and he was there having breakfast." Jess tried not to feel as if she were being quizzed. "Then a day or so later, I ran into him while I was out running, and we became running buddies until football practice started."

"Ah, old friends then." Heather's smile was warm and friendly, and Jess wondered at the little wave of uneasiness that rippled through her.

"Not when compared to the history you all have, of course. Andy told me that the three of you go way, way back."

"I guess we do at that, the three of us." Heather made a little face that Jess couldn't read. "What did he tell you about us? I should get a chance to defend myself, don't you think?"

"Nothing that needs defending, I promise." Jess grinned. "Just that you all had met in Sunday school even before you started kindergarten and had been friends all your lives."

"Yes, that's all true."

Andy really had not said much about these old friends he said he wanted her to meet, but clearly Heather was looking for something more, so Jess dug deeper, trying to remember anything else he might have said.

"Oh, he did say that one of the best things about coming home again was the chance to reconnect with old friends."

"There's nothing like reconnecting with old friends, is there? Unless it's making new ones." Heather's shoulders seemed to relax a bit, and the smile she turned on Jess was warm and confident. "Now, if you wouldn't mind helping me get these platters on the table, we can call the guys."

As Heather had decreed, there was no football talk at the table, and at the beginning of the meal, she made every effort to include Jess, but gradually and inevitably, the conversation turned to old times and old friends. Attempts to bring Jess up to speed regarding who and what they were talking about grew cumbersome and finally stopped, though whenever anyone glanced her way to include her, Jess would nod, or smile, or raise her eyebrows to show interest. Truthfully, though, Jess was fine with the arrangement. She was learning more about the people and times of Last Chance during this meal than she had learned in all the weeks she had been in town. And at least they weren't talking about football.

As the evening continued, Jess began to be aware that she was not the only spectator at the table. Ethan and Tyler didn't even feign interest and were excused as soon as they had eaten enough to satisfy their mother, but James didn't seem to have much to say either, and the more Heather turned her attention exclusively to Andy, the quieter her husband became.

"So, James . . ." Jess found the briefest of lulls in the conversation. "What about you? What were you doing when all this was going on? Did you play football too?"

"Oh, sure, some." James looked up from his plate and leaned back in his chair. "Not like ol' Andy here, but I played. Of course, my biggest problem was that football and the chile harvest overlapped until October, and my dad needed me here, so it took some doing."

"The problem was, and still is for that matter, is that this farm is too small to be able to hire out the harvest but too big to do it all by yourself." Heather took control of the conversation again. "So at harvest, it's all hands on deck. We just finished up the harvest last week, and I, for one, am ready to catch my breath."

"Now what happens?" Jess turned back to James. "I've been seeing those chile roasting stands going up all over. Will you open one of those?"

"Naw. We just take 'em over to the cannery."

"Again, it's just a matter of capital." Heather again. "And capital can be hard to come by on a farm this size."

James nodded his assent, and Heather went back to talking about the old days with Andy.

Jess found herself wondering about the two of them. James was nice enough looking, but Heather was stunning, and while James was quiet to the point of silence, Heather's warmth and vivacity would seem to put her in the center of any crowd. They had to have married young, maybe even still in their teens, to have kids as old as Ethan and Tyler. James must have felt her gaze, because he looked up. She smiled and went back to her meal. What a shame that Heather and James's story was not one that was being recounted this evening. Jess would have loved to know what it was.

"Thanks for coming with me tonight." Andy glanced over at Jess as they bumped down the dirt road to the highway that led back to Last Chance. "It couldn't have been much fun, though. All we did was talk about the good old days."

"I'll take the good old days over you-know-what any day." Jess stretched her legs out in front of her. "At least I know what you're talking about, even if I don't know who you're talking about."

Andy laughed. "You know, you surprise me. You seem like such a try-anything-once kind of girl, and yet you've dismissed football without ever seeing a game, not even one."

"I'm not such a try-anything-once girl. I've never bungee-jumped off the Golden Gate Bridge, and I'm fine with that. I've never jumped out of an airplane with a parachute either, but that one might still be on the table. I haven't decided yet."

"Seriously?" Andy stared at her so long that Jess cleared her throat and pointed to the road. "You're comparing jumping off a bridge or out of an airplane with sitting in the stands watching a simple high school football game?"

"Well, I'm just telling you that football's not the only thing I've given thought to and decided not to do, that's all."

"I just want you to watch it, not play it."

Jess sighed. "Why is this such a big deal to you, anyway?"

"A couple reasons, actually. Number one, like it or not, Last Chance is a football town. And even if whether or not you like the game doesn't make much difference where you're from, it makes a huge difference here. I'm not saying that you'll never be accepted here in Last Chance if you hate football, but it will take a lot longer, and that's just a fact."

Jess felt her shoulders tighten. In the first place, she didn't think she needed anyone running interference for her in Last Chance. She was getting along very well, thank you very much. And in the second, what concern of his was it anyway? She pursed her lips and stared out the windshield.

"Do you want to know the other reason?" Andy seemed to have noticed the sudden chill in the cab of his truck.

Jess just looked at him before turning her attention back to the road in front of them.

"Okay, here's the other reason why it is such a big deal."

Did he think she had said she *did* want to hear the other reason?

He took a deep breath. "It's because I'd like to get to know you better, that's all. And I want you to know me. And that means knowing at least a little about football. It's what I've done with my life. I don't know that I could say it's who I am, but it comes as close as anything else."

He pulled up in front of her house and shut off the engine. Jess took off her seat belt and folded her arms as she leaned back against the door.

"So, how many games would I have to go to in order to know you better?"

"Well, that depends on how quick you are. Can you pick things up pretty fast?"

Jess narrowed her eyes. "I'll see your football and raise you neurobiology and organic chemistry."

Andy raised an eyebrow. "All right, then. Sounds like you're pretty confident, so here's a suggestion. Homecoming weekend is in three weeks. Go with me. Everyone in town will be there. There's a big bonfire on Friday night, and the game's Saturday afternoon, and it ends with a dance that night. It'll be fun—and you'll get to see what it's all about."

"Just the game, or everything else?"

"I was thinking everything. The bonfire, the game, the works."

She thought a minute. "And that will fulfill the football requirement?"

"Let's just say it will let you know if you want to know more. That's simple, isn't it?"

Jess finally smiled. "Okay. I have never in my life been to anything remotely involved with homecoming, but this does sound like it could be fun. Especially the bonfire and the dance."

He shook his head. "I don't know. Maybe you are hopeless."

"Well, what am I going to learn just sitting there watching? It's still going to look like a bunch of guys running into each other and falling down. It's not like you're going to be sitting with me and explaining everything, you know."

"You have a point." He drummed his fingers on the steering wheel for a moment. "I've got it. Why don't I pick you up for church tomorrow? After church we can go up to San Ramon and grab a burger and then go back to my house to watch the Cowboys-Eagles game. I can explain what's going on and you can ask any questions you might have. Then at the homecoming game, you can have at least an idea of what's happening."

After a long moment, Jess heaved a sigh. "All right. But just little bites, okay? Don't try to make me an expert with just one game."

"I couldn't even if I wanted to, but I can help you understand that it's more than just a bunch of guys bumping into each other and falling down. And who knows? You may even like it."

"Yeah, right. See you tomorrow." Jess got out of the truck and gave Andy a halfhearted wave before heading up her walk. When she decided to leave San Francisco and make a life in a tiny New Mexico town, she thought she had considered every possible pro and con to make the most rational choice possible. But clearly some had escaped her.

When Andy stopped his truck in front of Jess's house the next morning, he could see her watching for him at the front window, but he got out anyway and met her halfway up her walk.

"Good morning. These are for you." He handed her a sprig covered with diminutive purple blossoms.

"They're so sweet." When Jess held up the spray to get a better look, Andy noticed the roots were still attached. "What are they?"

"I don't know. They were growing in my yard. I thought they were pretty." Andy's mom had been a great gardener and remnants of her garden still appeared every year, but Andy was beginning to suspect this was a weed.

"Do I have time to take it back in and put it in water?"

"Nah. There are plenty more where that came from. You can get a whole batch when you come over this afternoon, if you want 'em."

When Andy opened the door for Jess and she climbed up into his truck, he noticed the care with which she placed the sprig of flowers next to her on the seat. He wished he could get it away from her, if only to take the roots off. He felt like a fourth grader trying to impress his best girl with a dandelion.

Almost as soon as they got to church, Andy was surrounded by people who wanted to go over Friday's game play by play. It was great to see smiling faces for a change, but to tell the truth, for once, he did not really want to stand there and listen to everyone rehash the win. What he wanted to do was find a place and sit next to Jess. But when that began to look like it might be difficult to achieve, she told him not to worry about her, and the next thing he knew, he could see her sitting between Elizabeth and Lainie in the third row on the left. Both women seemed delighted to see her, of course. He'd be delighted too, if he were sitting there with Jess.

Even after the choir started coming in and Lurlene turned around to raise the congregation to their feet for the first hymn, the football cadre that had him surrounded in the back didn't want to give up. By the time Andy finally broke loose, his choices were to clomp down to the front of the church and try to squeeze into an already packed third row, or to find a lonely spot near the back. He chose the back, but he wasn't happy about it.

# 15

Hi, Gabe, how're you feeling?" Jess walked into the examination room and smiled as she looked up from the file folder she was reading.

"Fine, I guess." Gabe sat on the examination table in jeans and a letterman's jacket, his feet dangling off the edge.

"You guess?" She put down the file and scrubbed her hands. "Any problems?"

"Yeah. A few. When can I go back to practice?"

"Well, let's see." Jess carefully removed the immaculate bandage and examined the sutures on his forehead. "These look great. Someone's been taking real good care of this. You?"

"My mom."

"I thought as much. Tell her she did a great job. This wound is as clean as any I've ever seen after a week. I'll take these sutures out now, and if you keep taking good care of it, you should be good as new in a few weeks, except for the dashing scar you'll have."

"So when can I go back to practice?"

"I can't say right now, Gabe. Not tomorrow, that's for sure." She picked up the scissors and snipped the first of the sutures in Gabe's forehead. "Have you had any headaches?"

"Not since the first day."

"Blurred vision?"

"Nope."

"Dizziness?"

"Nope."

"All really good signs." She finished snipping the sutures and began gently pulling them from Gabe's skin. He winced. "But you've got to keep taking good care of this cut on your head. You don't want it to open up again. Then we'd be back to square one."

"*Man*. I gotta get back." He shifted as if he were about to hop down and bolt.

"Gabe, you will. But it's going to take a little time." Jess folded her arms and looked closely at the restless young man on the table in front of her. He seemed to worry way too much for a seventeen-year-old kid. "What's the rush?"

Gabe hesitated and seemed to grow even more anxious as he did. Finally, he looked up at her. "I heard this kid on the team, Zach Ellis, and he said Coach was going to get this scout he knows from the University of Arizona to come look at him. I know he's coming to see Ellis, but maybe he'll like what he sees in me too. I know I could never get the same scholarship Ellis could get, but any little bit would help."

"Well, Coach Ryan told me you were good, and fast, and had a lot of heart, so who knows?" She smiled at him. "When's the scout coming?"

"That's just it. We don't know. So every game I miss is a game where he might have been there. I have to get back now. If I don't get a scholarship, I'm not going to college. It's as simple as that."

"Can your parents help at all?"

Gabe's laugh was bitter, and he looked away. "Are you kidding? It's all my mom can do to keep us all fed. She can't send anyone to college. That's why I need to go, so I can help the kids when it's their turn."

"And your dad?" Jess had to ask.

Gabe met her eyes, and the expression she saw there was far beyond his years. "My dad can't help us."

"Okay. It looks like you're on your own. But you're not the first kid to face that. So, seriously now, how realistic is it that you get a football scholarship to the University of Arizona?"

His head jerked up and Jess held up a hand. "Keep in mind that until yesterday afternoon I didn't know a first down from a referee, and I still don't know much more than that. All I know about your ability is what Coach Ryan told me, and I told you what he said. So, with all that said, how realistic is it?"

He slumped. "Not very, I guess. Pac-12 schools can recruit pretty much anywhere they want."

"There are other types of scholarships, you know. I heard you mention chemistry and calculus the other night. Those aren't easy classes. How're you doing in them?"

"Okay, I guess. B's, sometimes an A-. Not all that great."

"And do you have a job?"

Gabe shrugged. "Just on the weekends. I work for Mr. Sheppard on his farm. I don't get a lot of hours in, but I can at least buy my own clothes and stuff."

"Okay, look." Jess sat on the little stool and ticked off the list on her fingers. "Your mom depends on you to help with the kids, right?"

He nodded.

"And you have a job, and you have football practice as well as games, and you're taking some really tough classes at school."

He nodded again.

"Gabe, something's got to give, and I'm afraid it's going to be you. You've got to make some choices. How's this for a scenario? You choose a state university, and with a combination of scholarships, loans, and part-time jobs, you put yourself through. You won't be the first one to do it, and if anyone has the drive and discipline to pull it off, it's you. You'll need to get those grades up, though. There's nothing at all wrong with a B, but for top scholarships, you'll need top grades. And the more you get in scholarships, the less you'll need in loans." It pleased Jess that Gabe looked interested, even animated as she talked. He needed some dreams that didn't depend on a miraculous football scholarship. "What *do* you want to do when you get out of school?"

"I don't know." He shrugged yet again. "When I was a kid, I always wanted to be a doctor, but that's not going to happen."

"Why not?"

He just looked at her. "I don't know. It's just one of those things kids want to be, like an astronaut. You don't really do those things when you grow up."

"Is that so? I just wish you'd told me that about eight years ago. You could have saved me a lot of really hard work."

Gabe ducked his head and grinned up at her.

"Tell you what." Jess stood up and Gabe hopped down from the examination table. "Let's find a time when we're both free, and I have a feeling that will be harder for you than for me, and let's get together and come up with a plan. There's no reason why you can't be a doctor, or anything else you want to be."

The animated look she had seen in his eyes when she talked about his future began to fade almost as soon as she stopped talking, and he just nodded.

"Gabe, listen to me. I'm serious. You can do this. I know you can. You call me and we'll get started, you hear?"

He started to shake her hand but stuffed his own in his front pocket instead. "Okay. I'll call."

"You do that. Keep taking good care of that forehead, and

remember, no football until I say so." She walked him to the door. "Oh, by the way, Gabe, when's your mother's day off?"

"I don't know. It varies."

"Have her give me a call too, would you? There's something I'd like to talk to her about." She laughed at the worried look he gave her. "No, it's not about you. Not everything's about you, you know."

Jess stood in the window and watched Gabe get in his battered truck and drive off. No wonder Andy wanted to keep him on the team. He did have more heart and determination than any five people Jess could think of, but even that could only stretch so far. She wasn't kidding when she said something had to give. And she could only hope that he followed his head as well as his heart.

"Hey, Coach, you got a minute?"

Andy looked up to see Gabe Quintana standing in the doorway. "Hey, Gabe. Come on in. Shouldn't you be in class?"

Gabe shrugged and edged into the room. "Nah. It's just homeroom. I got a pass."

"So, how're you doing?"

"I'm doing all right, I guess. Stitches are all out, anyway."

"Come here. Let me take a look at that." Andy tipped his head to get a better angle under the overhead light. "Man, that's some angry-looking scar you've got there. It looks like you tangled with a machete."

"It's okay. The doctor says it will fade in time, but I'm always going to have a scar."

Andy grinned. "It'll make you look dangerous."

"That's what she said, only she said dashing."

"Well, if the men find you dangerous and the ladies find you dashing, what more could you ask for? I know you saw the doctor on Monday. Did she say when you could come back?"

"Not for a while yet. Not this week, and maybe not next week either. She's afraid it might open up again."

"Well, she's the doctor. I guess we have to go by what she says. We don't want you coming back before you're ready." Andy started to go back to his work, but Gabe didn't move, except to shift his weight and pick at a fingernail. "What's up, Quintana? Is there something I can help you with?"

"Well, Coach, it's, um . . . I'm thinking of quitting the team."

Andy didn't say anything, but he gestured to the chair in front of his desk, and Gabe sat on the edge. Five minutes ago, if he had been asked who on his team would be most likely to quit before the season was over, Gabe Quintana would have been the last, the very last name he would have come up with. He waited for Gabe to explain himself.

"It's like this, Coach. I love the game, you know I do, and like everybody else in town, I always dreamed of being the next Andy Ryan. But look at me." He spread his hands and looked down. "I'm five seven and weigh 145 sopping wet. I'm not going any further than running back at Last Chance High. I mean, look what happened last Friday. I couldn't even play and you won 45–21. You don't need me."

"So why quit halfway through the season during your senior year? There are a half dozen games left and that's it."

"Yeah, I know, and it's killing me thinking I'm not going to play. But in another seven months or so, I'll graduate, and then what? If I don't get a scholarship of some kind, college is out for me, and I'll get a job at the chile cannery or working for the county. I want more than that."

"I still don't see what quitting football has to do with getting a scholarship. You weren't pinning all your hopes on a full-ride football scholarship, were you?"

Gabe sounded embarrassed when he laughed. "No, not since about tenth grade. I have to admit that I daydreamed about the scout that you're bringing over to watch Ellis seeing me play and being bowled over, but reality set in. We both know that's not going to happen."

Andy sat back in his chair and threw up his hands. "I just don't get what you're talking about, Gabe. Just tell me, and make it as clear as you can."

"Okay, it's like this." Gabe leaned his elbows on his knees and clasped his hands between them. "We both know I'm not going to college on a football scholarship, so my only chance is an academic scholarship. But I need to get my grades up, and the way things are right now, I just don't have the time to do that. Something's got to give, and I guess that something is football. Dr. MacLeod is going to help me in the afternoons when I'd ordinarily be at practice."

"Dr. MacLeod?"

"Yeah, she says I'm taking all the right courses, but I need to try for A's instead of B's. On the days when she's in Last Chance, she's going to let me study in her office and help me out if I need it."

"Does she know that you're quitting football?"

"Oh, yeah. She didn't exactly suggest it, but when I said that's what I was going to do, she sort of nodded like she thought it was a good thing to do."

"Well, Gabe, you know what you need to do. I can't say this makes me happy. Quitting the team midseason is just not something I understand. But here's what I'm going to do. Since your doctor said you might not be back for another couple games, I'm going to leave your name on the roster until then. You can come back anytime during the next two weeks, no questions asked, but after that, well, your resignation is accepted. Fair enough?"

Gabe swallowed hard and nodded.

Andy got to his feet and extended his hand. "All the best to you, Gabe, and I mean that. You're a good man. Wish I had more like you."

Gabe shook his hand, and for a moment, Andy thought he was going to say something, but he just swallowed again and left. Andy heard his boots going down the hall until the sound was replaced by that of the big front door opening and closing.

Dropping back in his chair, Andy leaned back and rubbed his eyes. What did Jess think she was doing? Forget Gabe for the moment, although Andy didn't think for one minute that he wouldn't wind up regretting his decision. When someone just disappeared from the team in the middle of the season because he changed his mind, team morale suffered big-time. Each man had to know he could count on everyone else and that everyone else counted on him. That's what being a team meant. You didn't just quit.

He yanked his desk phone over to him and started jabbing in her number, but before the connection was made, he hung up. If he remembered right, she'd still be making rounds in San Ramon. Besides, he needed to cool off before he said anything. If he talked to her now, he was bound to say something that would probably end all hope for any kind of a relationship, present or future. And even though at the moment, he was so mad he could spit nails, he didn't think he wanted to risk messing things up for good.

Jess smiled in satisfaction when she checked her schedule of appointments when she finally got back to Last Chance after doing rounds at San Ramon General with Dr. Benavides. Whatever his intentions were in making her do rounds with him, patients were not flocking from San Ramon to Last Chance to see her, but people from Last Chance were making appointments, a few more every week. Today an older man she hadn't met yet was coming in with something that sounded very much like gout; Kaitlyn Reed, who owned the salon, was coming in for a checkup; and Sue Anderson, of all people, was coming for a consultation—although she refused to give even a hint as to what she wanted to consult about. Then, after office hours, Marta Quintana was stopping by. Hopefully, the trend would continue, and she'd wind up running from patient to patient like she was beginning to do in San Ramon, but for now this was nice—busy enough, but not so busy that she couldn't spend as much time as she wanted with each patient.

The first patient did, indeed, suffer from gout, and Jess gave him an information sheet about what he should and shouldn't be eating and drinking. He handed it right back to her.

"But this is all the stuff I like to eat. Can't you just give me a pill or something?"

"I'm afraid it doesn't work that way, Mr. Crawford. This is a diet-related condition, and changing your diet is what's going to help." She held out the sheet, and he snatched it out of her hands and glared at it.

"Well, If I'da known this was all you were going to give me, I'da gone up to Dr. Benavides in San Ramon. I thought you were new and modern and would have all kinds of miracle drugs."

"Sorry, and just so you know, Dr. Benavides would have said the same thing I did." Jess smiled at him. "But if you follow those instructions, you ought to be feeling better in a few days, and if you're not, just come on back."

He was still grumbling when Jess left his room and walked across the hall to find Kaitlyn Reed perched on the examination table in a paper gown. She had only been around Kaitlyn a few times but had really liked her. In fact, the more time she spent with that convoluted Cooley clan, headed by the doughty Elizabeth Cooley, the more she liked all of them. Of course, Kaitlyn wasn't a Cooley, but her brother, Chris, was married to a Cooley, and that more or less put her in the family. All quite complicated, unless you were from Last Chance. Then you were born knowing how it all fit together.

"Hi, Kaitlyn." Jess checked the file she had pulled out of the rack on the door. "Just a checkup today?"

"Yes, time for my annual."

"Good for you." Jess checked the form Kaitlyn had filled out in the waiting room. "No problems? No concerns?"

"Well, there is something I need to talk to you about." Kaitlyn, who always possessed a quiet confidence that Jess admired, today seemed almost embarrassed. Jess waited. "Um, from my teens until I came to Last Chance last year, my life, um, the way I lived it, wasn't really anything to be proud of."

She looked at Jess as if she hoped to find understanding there, and Jess nodded to encourage her to continue. She did.

"Well, I'm a new person now, and I'll probably be married within the year to a really wonderful man, and I just want to make sure that everything is the way it should be, you know?"

"I think I do. So in addition to the regular tests, you want a thorough blood work-up?"

"Yeah. I guess that's what I'm asking."

"Sure, I can order that for you, and there are some other tests I can do too. Do you have any symptoms you're worried about?"

"No, nothing at all. But I want to know for sure."

"That's a smart thing to do, Kaitlyn." Jess began her examination. "So, you're getting married? Tell me all about your groom. Is he from Last Chance?"

"Yes, he was born here. His brother is Ray Braden, Lainie's husband, and his cousin is married to my brother."

"Oh my, another Cooley. I was just thinking what a terrific family they are. So when are you getting married?"

"Probably sometime in the spring. He's just finishing at the Law Enforcement Academy and got his first choice of assignments. He'll be a state policeman right here in this part of the state. So we'll wait until he gets all settled in his new job. I don't want a big wedding."

Jess reached for Kaitlyn's hand and helped her sit up. "It seems to me that from what I've seen, even an intimate family wedding is going to be a big wedding. Where do you draw the line?"

"That's my problem. Unless you run off, any wedding around here is a big wedding." Kaitlyn sighed. "But Steven should get back soon, and we can start figuring all this out. It's too hard to do on the phone."

"I can see how it would be." Jess smiled and looked at her notes again. "Well, we won't know for sure until all the tests get back, but everything looks just fine. I'll write out an order for a blood work-up, and you can take it to the lab at San Ramon General. I'll call you either way, just to set your mind at ease."

"Thanks so much, Doctor." Kaitlyn took her hand and kissed her cheek. "I was so worried to have to talk about all this, and you made it so easy. I'm really glad you're going to be my doctor."

"Me too, and please, my friends call me Jess." Jess had never had a patient kiss her in gratitude before, and to tell the truth, it was kind of nice.

"Oh, and one more thing." Kaitlyn stopped Jess as she picked up Kaitlyn's file and headed for the door. "I guess everyone probably assumes Steven and I will be making some kind of announcement, but we haven't yet, so I'd appreciate it if you didn't say anything. Okay?"

"Couldn't if I wanted to." Jess gave her a wink. "It's all confidential in here."

Leaving Kaitlyn to get dressed, Jess went to find the last scheduled patient of the day, Sue Anderson. All Sue would tell Eva when she made the appointment was that she wanted a private consultation with Dr. MacLeod. This, coupled with the fact that both Mrs. Anderson and Dr. Benavides had alluded to a lifelong professional relationship, made Jess more than a little curious.

Sue was fully dressed and waiting in the other examination room when Jess walked in.

"Hello, Mrs. Anderson." Jess sat on the stool as Mrs. Anderson was seated on the only chair in the room. "This is all rather mysterious. How can we help you?"

"I don't mean to be mysterious." Sue Anderson sat with ankles together, clutching her purse on her lap. "But I do need you to assure me that this conversation will be entirely confidential."

"Of course, that goes without saying."

"Even from Dr. Benavides."

"If you wish." Jess made a note. "Now, what's up?"

Mrs. Anderson took a deep breath. "It's Emma. You know what a sweet child she is."

"I have met Emma." Jess smiled.

"And so well behaved. People have remarked on what a good little girl she is since she was two. Since she was *two*! I hear people talk about the terrible twos and I have no idea what they're talking about."

"Yes, she is remarkably well behaved. I noticed that right off when I met her." Jess felt a surprising pang of compassion for Mrs. Anderson. Clinging to the illusion of perfection can be so exhausting. "But I think you're worried about her for some reason. Am I right?"

After a moment, Sue nodded. "Yes. Yes, I am, a little. She doesn't have many friends, for one thing. She is so much more mature than other children her age, and I think they're intimidated by that. Children can be so cruel, and I think it upsets her more than she tells me. She's started pulling at her eyebrows, and it's really beginning to show. She's got these bald spots. So far I've been able to keep them filled in with eyebrow pencil, but I'm afraid her father will notice the next time he's home. I don't know which he'll think is worse, putting eyebrow pencil on an eight-year-old, or letting Emma go around with bald spots in her eyebrows."

"Is Emma's dad away often?"

"Yes, he's home mostly on weekends. The house we live in has been in his family for generations, and he wants us to live in it. It *is* a very nice house, and it's on some land, but since he's a lawyer and his office is in Tucson, he's away a lot. So you can imagine that when he is home, he likes everything to be peaceful and happy."

"Yes, I can imagine that."

"Of course, Emma just adores her daddy. He calls her his perfect little princess."

Jess nodded. "So, is there anything besides the eyebrow plucking that concerns you about Emma?"

Mrs. Anderson twisted her hands and frowned. Jess waited. There was something else.

Finally, she swallowed, and tears filled her eyes. "She beats her dolls! She takes a ruler and just beats them. She yells at them and slams them into a corner, and then she yanks them out and beats them again. It just terrifies me."

*Well, yeah, I can see how you'd find that upsetting.* Jess made an effort to keep her expression and her voice calm and neutral. "Mrs. Anderson, I need to ask you this. Do either you or Mr. Anderson ever spank Emma?"

"No! She's never had a hand raised to her in her life! I don't know where this comes from."

"Okay." If Jess hadn't examined Emma herself and found no evidence of physical abuse, she might have been a little more skeptical. "But it's pretty clear to me that Emma has a lot of anger going on. I'm sure it's clear to you too. But knowing it's there and knowing how to help her with it are two different things. I think it would benefit Emma to talk to a child psychologist, and I strongly recommend you make an appointment sooner rather than later. I could do some research and get some recommendations for you, if you like."

"No. Absolutely not. Emma does not need a psychologist. Besides, there's no way her father wouldn't find out if she was going to a psychologist."

"And why would that be a problem?"

Sue Anderson gathered her purse and stood up. "You know, I came here really hoping you could help me. It looks like I was wrong. Thank you for your time."

As she reached for the door, Jess put a hand on her arm. "Mrs. Anderson, I really hope you reconsider. I'll tell you what I'll do. I'm going to research those psychologists anyway. I'll put my recommendations in an envelope and keep it in my desk drawer. If you change your mind, just stop by the office and tell Eva that I have an envelope for you. That's all you need to do."

Mrs. Anderson just looked at Jess's hand on her arm, and when Jess removed it, she opened the door and swept down the hall to the waiting room. Jess could hear her talking to Eva.

"I'll be paying cash for this appointment. How much do I owe?"

# 16

Jess was on her computer researching child psychologists when Eva stuck her head in the door. "Marta Quintana is here. She says she has an appointment, but there's nothing on the books."

After making one last note, Jess closed her computer and looked up. "Ask her to come on back, would you please?"

Eva hesitated. "If you're just going to be talking, would it be okay if I close up and go on home? I'd like to be back in San Ramon before the rush hour traffic starts."

"Go." Jess waved her away. "I don't need you anymore today." *Rush hour in San Ramon? Who knew?*

When the door opened again and Eva ushered Marta Quintana in, Jess got up, met her halfway across the room, and shook her hand. "Marta! I'm so glad you could come. Please have a seat."

Marta lowered herself to the edge of the chair. Worry lines deepened on her forehead. "Is everything all right? Is there something wrong with Gabe?"

"Gabe is fine. I told him this wasn't about him. Didn't he tell you?"

"He told me, but I started thinking that if something really was wrong, of course you wouldn't tell him before you told me."

Jess had gone back to her desk, but she reached a hand out toward Marta. "Oh, Marta, I'm so sorry you've been worried, and just so you know? If ever I have something to tell you about any of your kids, I'll call you straightaway. I won't send a secondhand message home. Okay?"

"Okay." Marta nodded, but those worry lines were still there.

"So, the reason I asked you to come in." Jess took a deep breath. She hadn't ever done this before, and it was turning out to be a little harder than she thought. "How happy are you at San Ramon General?"

"Happy?" Poor Marta still did not know what was going on, and Jess looked for the quickest way possible to put her out of her misery.

"Okay, here's the deal. I'm looking for a full-time office manager and medical assistant, and I'd like you to think about the job. It's going to be a two-person office here for the foreseeable future, so I need someone who'll be more of a teammate than an employee. And I think we'd be a good team. At least I'd like to talk about it."

"What about Eva? Is she leaving?"

Jess laughed. "As far as Eva is concerned, she is already gone. It was always understood that she was on loan from the San Ramon office, and she is counting the days until she's back there for good. I guess she's just a bright lights and big city kind of girl."

Marta did not smile at Jess's little joke. She just raised her eyebrows and shrugged. "Well, she's young. It's to be expected."

Jess didn't say anything.

After a few seconds of thoughtful silence, Marta spoke again. "You know, this might be an answer to prayer. I've been wondering what I was going to do when Gabe left for college. I wouldn't have been able to do what I've had to do without him. I couldn't have worked the night shift, that's for sure. And he was always around to help with the kids. It would be good to work here in Last Chance and be home nights."

"Well then, could you get me a résumé? I think that would be the next step. We can talk again after that."

"Sure, I can do that." Marta got to her feet, and Jess was pleased to see that the worry lines, while still there, did not seem as deep. "Oh, and I want to thank you for taking so much time with Gabe. We've always talked about him going to college, but now he really sees a way to get there, and it's given him such purpose. And for the first time, I know how it's going to happen too. I can't tell you what a heavy load that has been. Gabe is so smart. It would have killed me if he didn't get to college. He'll get over having to quit football. He knows it's for the best."

"Gabe's a pretty amazing young man, but then, you knew that long before I met him." Jess walked Marta to the front door and let her out.

On the way back to her office, a little niggling finger of accusation poked her in a tender spot under her ribs. Encouraging Gabe when he decided to quit the team wasn't a cruel thing to do. In fact, it was the best decision possible, under the circumstances. She knew it, his mom knew it, and even Gabe knew it. But she couldn't shake the feeling that she had taken something important from someone who valued it and tossed it away.

The lights were on at Jess's house when Andy drove down her street on his way home. Earlier he had thought he might be ready to stop by and talk to her, but nope, he was still too mad. He drove on by. Maybe he needed to rethink this whole thing with Jess, anyway. Yes, she was beautiful, and smart, and funny, and he loved being with her, but she didn't like football. At all. Not even after watching the game last Sunday and listening while he explained the basic rudiments of the game did she show any great interest. And why did he think he had to force it on her, anyway? What fun would it be to be with someone who he had taught to tolerate that which he loved?

*You know what, Ryan? I think you're the problem, not Jess. And as soon as you can figure out a gentlemanly way to do it, you need to let her off the hook for homecoming.*

With a shrug of resignation, Andy turned off Jess's street onto the long dirt road that led to his house. Well, everything didn't always work out the way you wanted it to; he should have learned that by now.

Still lost in thought, Andy stopped his truck in its usual spot under the cottonwood, got out, and headed for the front porch. He had one foot on the bottom step before he noticed the light in the back of the house. He hadn't left a light on; he was almost sure of it. Stepping back, Andy looked around his yard and for the first time spotted the old pickup with the Kansas plates nearly hidden in the brush, with easy access to the back door, and an old chest and a rocker that had been his grandmother's already in the bed.

Walking back to his truck, Andy reached behind the seat for his tire iron. As silently as possible, he mounted the creaky old steps and let himself into the house. Someone was already there. He could hear them moving around in the back bedroom. Thankful he was wearing tennis shoes instead of boots and that he had already oiled the hinges, Andy pushed the door open. Someone was there, all right, kneeling in front of an open dresser drawer and pawing through the contents. Raising the tire iron, he slowly moved forward and stepped on a creaky board.

Instantly, the man's head whipped around, and he raised his arm in front of his face to protect himself. "Shoot fire, Andy, what are you doing with that thing? Put it down before you hurt somebody."

Andy stared hard at the wizened old man kneeling before him. "Dad?"

"Who'd you think it was? Santy Claus?"

"What are you doing here?"

"What am I doing here? This is my house. That's what I'm doing here."

"No, Dad, it's my house." Andy lowered the tire iron, but he didn't put it down. "You just walked off and left it. I bought it for taxes years ago."

"Well, I can't say you took very good care of it. This place is a mess."

"I'll ask you again, Dad. What are you doing here? And what are you looking for in that chest? Nothing there belongs to you."

The old man grabbed the top of the dresser and hauled himself to his feet. "Well, I picked up this old magazine in the barbershop, and it had an article in it about you. Yes it did. Said the NFL didn't want you anymore and you had scooted back to this little wide spot to coach a bunch of snot-nosed kids. They get that right?"

"You still haven't told me why you're here." Andy shifted the tire iron to his other hand. The fingers of the one he had been holding it with were starting to cramp, he was gripping it so tightly.

"Oh, lighten up, Andy. I was just funnin' with you a little. But you brought it on yourself, you know, acting so high and mighty before. And what I was doing in that chest is none of your business."

Andy was tired of asking. He just stood and looked at his dad, until finally the old man muttered something under his breath that Andy couldn't quite hear and looked away. "To tell the truth, I need a place to stay for a while. I've had a run of bad luck and need a place to get back on my feet. Shoot, you're the one who threw me out of my own house, and then stole it out from under me. I think you owe me."

"Owe you. Right." Andy clenched and unclenched his fist. "You still drinking?"

"Naw. Haven't had a drop in years. Swear to it."

Andy dropped his head. When he looked up again, his dad was watching him, naked pleading in his eyes.

"Come on in the kitchen, Dad. We'll get something to eat and talk."

Immediately his dad perked up and followed him to the kitchen. "You don't have much in there, and that's a fact. Hope you don't mind if I ate that leftover chicken. I was pretty hungry when I got here."

Andy opened the refrigerator without saying anything, and his dad perched on a stool, the very stool where Jess had sat while he fixed her dinner on a much happier occasion. When was that? It seemed like a lifetime ago.

"How's your mother?" The question seemed to come from nowhere.

"She's fine." Andy was not inclined to discuss his mother with the man he had to protect her from when he was just in high school.

"Where's she at?"

"She's happy."

His dad laughed. "Not going to tell me, huh? Well, you don't have to. That meddling sister of hers was always trying to get her to leave me and come live with her. I bet your mom high-tailed it up there the minute she thought I was gone. Betcha if I went on up to Oklahoma and knocked on that front door right now, she'd be the one to open it. That'd be a kick, wouldn't it?"

Andy turned and leveled his gaze on his dad. "I wouldn't advise that."

"So what are you going to do? Call the law on me again?"

Leaning against the counter, Andy folded his arms and looked around the room. When he spoke, his every word was cold and measured. "I've been working pretty hard on the house, Dad. What do you think of my work?"

His dad shrugged. "I told you I thought the place was a mess. What'd you do?"

"See those rough patches on the wall there, and there, and there? That's where I patched holes you punched in the wall. They're a little rough yet, but I'm not finished. And see that doorjamb over there? The unpainted one? Well, I've replaced that one because it was out of line after you kicked the door in. I fixed the one in Mom's bedroom too. So, yeah, when I say leave Mom alone, you can bet I mean it."

"Well, here's a surprise for you, buddy. I'm not any more interested in seeing that old bat than she is in seeing me. So don't worry about it."

The muscles in Andy's neck and shoulders ached, they were so tight, and he rolled his shoulders to loosen them. "Look, Dad, we've got to call a truce. You've said you need a place to get on your feet, and I've said you can stay awhile, so we've got to find a way to do that without killing each other. There's plenty of room. It's a big house, but it's my house, and that includes the furniture you've got out in your truck. We need to get that back in here."

"Shoot, boy, I'm all for a truce. I'm the easiest man in the world to get along with now, you just try me."

"Glad to hear it. But everything rests on you not drinking. The minute you start drinking again, you're gone. And if that means calling the law again, don't think I won't do it."

"I told you, son. I'm not drinking."

"Then we're good." He turned back to the stove. "I'm just going to fix sausage and scrambled eggs. And I think I've got a roll of those canned biscuits. That sound good to you?"

"Sounds more'n good. Especially if you've got some green chile to go with it."

"I've got green chile."

"Oh, man. Home again and eating real green chile. I have died and gone to heaven."

Andy pulled a package of sausage from the refrigerator and began making patties. "Well, as close as you're likely to get, anyway."

Later, after dinner, and after Andy had cleaned the kitchen, he wandered into the living room and flipped on the TV before settling into his chair. His scrambled eggs and sausage sat like a fist in his stomach. All his life, his dad had found some excuse or another to go off by himself, and when he did, the man who returned was a different man completely—swaggering, obnoxious, and downright mean. Tonight, as soon as his dad had taken his last bite of scrambled egg, he leaned back in his chair, stretched, and said he might as well go get himself settled in. Since then, only silence had come from behind the closed door. Was he drinking? Andy told himself he couldn't care less one way or the other. If he wasn't, that was fine, he could stay a little longer; if he was drinking, he was gone tonight. Simple as that. But the old sick feeling in his stomach said it wasn't quite so simple. So did the slight trembling in his hands. When does your dad stop being your dad? And how long does it take to stop being the kid who loves and fears and hates him all at the same time?

"Son?"

Andy jumped.

"Son, I have a couple things I need to say, and I'd like to get 'em said before I go to bed."

"Okay." Andy looked closely at his dad. He seemed okay so far.

"First of all, I want to say I'm sorry about what I said about that magazine in the barbershop. You just surprised me coming up behind me like that, waving that tire iron all around, and I guess I got a little ticked off. There was an article about you in there, but it wasn't ugly like I made it sound. It was just about how you were going back to coach your old team, and the Glory Days, and so forth. I just want you to know that."

"Thanks. I appreciate you telling me that."

"And the other thing, well, I had no need to call your mom an old bat. She's a good woman, and I'm glad to hear she's happy. She deserves a little happiness. That's all I wanted to say. G'night, now. I'm going to turn in." He gave a half wave of his hand and ambled back where he came from.

For a moment, Andy sat frozen in his chair as a wave of rage began in his middle and spread through his body to his fingers, causing them to grip the arms of his chair until his knuckles turned white. Who did his dad think he was? Turning up after how many years? Thirteen? And waltzing in here like nothing had happened, calling him son? Conceding that his mother was a good woman and deserved happiness like he wasn't the cause of all her pain? And acting like just because he wasn't drinking anymore—if he actually *wasn't* drinking anymore—everything was just fine and all should be forgiven? *Well, life doesn't work that way, Dad.*

Andy jumped up; there was no way he could sit still. His hands closed and the desire to crash his fist into something was almost overwhelming. One look at his living room wall with its still-rough patches convinced him that couldn't be an option. This room had seen far too much punching; there would be no more.

Grabbing a windbreaker off a hook, Andy opened the door and set off running across the porch, down the front steps, and down the road. The moon hadn't come up yet, and the road was so dark he couldn't see his feet rise and fall. But he could hear their rhythmic pounding, and he had run this road a thousand times and knew every rut and curve. Finally, up ahead, he saw the gentle glow of porch lights and his feet touched pavement. Still he ran, even faster now that asphalt was under his feet instead of rough dirt.

"Andy? Is that you?"

Andy realized he had been aware all along that he was approaching Jess's house, and hearing her voice came as no surprise, even though other than the two of them, the street was deserted.

"Are you out running in the dark? Why don't you have a light or some reflective gear on, or something? People won't be able to see you."

Andy stood bent over, hands on his knees, trying to pull air into his starving lungs. With one arm, and because he had no air to speak with anyway, he gestured toward the empty street.

"Well, I guess you're right. It's not exactly a freeway out here tonight, is it? Come on, you need to walk to cool down. I'll walk with you. Let me run in and grab my jacket. I just came out to drop a birthday card to my mom in my mailbox."

He had already started walking when she came back, but it didn't take more than a few quick steps for her to catch up. Matching her steps to his, she walked with him in silence down to the end of the block and back. Finally, as they approached her house again, she spoke.

"You were really moving when I saw you coming. Either something really was after you, like Les always says, or you were trying to work something out. I'm guessing option two. Am I right?"

He didn't look at her but pulled another deep breath into his lungs. "It has not been a good day."

"I'm sorry about that, especially since I think I know why it was so bad." She stopped at the walk that led through her front yard to her porch. "Why don't you come on in, and I'll make us some cocoa, or tea, or coffee if that's what you want. We can talk. We probably need to talk, don't you think?"

Andy hesitated. He wasn't at all sure he was ready to talk to Jess, but if he didn't go in, he'd just have to go home again where his dad was, or maybe just keep on running, and truthfully, he didn't think he could do that.

"Come on." She held out her hand. "I've got a nice fire going, and I make the best cocoa. I think you want to yell at me, and I need to tell you why I think I did the right thing. We can have a fine old time."

She was little more than a shadow standing there at the end of her walk with the dim glow coming from the porch backlighting her hair, but he could see that she was smiling for all the world as if they had just had a little tiff that a cup of cocoa could set straight. Maybe he did need to talk to her tonight, after all. He'd start by telling her about his dad and see where that led. Pretending not to see the hand she offered and shoving his hands in his pockets, he walked beside her to her front door.

"Seriously? Not a word for thirteen years and then he just turns up?" Jess sat with her feet tucked under her, cradling her mug of cocoa in both hands.

In the fireplace, a piñon log crumbled to glowing coals, and Andy got up to add another log. "Yup. That's about it."

"But why now?"

"I think he's just out of options and wants to come home. Despite the fact that he sold every inch of land we once had and did his level best to destroy the house, it's home. He grew up there, just like I did. Just like *his* father did."

"But he said he only wants to stay for a little while, didn't he? Till he gets his feet on the ground?"

Andy gave a wry chuckle. "Did you ever hear the story about the camel who just wanted to get his nose in the tent? Before anyone knew it, the camel was in the tent and everyone else was outside. That's Dad. He's not going anywhere unless . . ." His voice trailed away.

"Unless what?"

"I told him if he started drinking again, he was gone. I meant it too."

"What do you think the chances of that happening are?"

"To tell the truth, I haven't the slightest idea. I don't even know when he stopped drinking. Ten years ago? Tonight when I told him he couldn't stay if he was still drinking? I don't even know if, when I go home tonight, he'll be asleep or busy trying to set the house on fire. He doesn't look good, though. If I saw him on the street, I'd guess him to be about ten years older than I know him to be. He's had a rough life."

The room fell silent except for the pop and crackle of the fire. Andy looked down into his cooling cocoa. After a long moment, he spoke.

"Gabe Quintana came in to see me today. That's some scar he's got."

"It'll nearly disappear by the time all is said and done. He'll be able to make up all sorts of stories about how he got it." She grinned at Andy, but he was staring into the fire and didn't see.

"Saying he got it playing football is a pretty good story in itself."

"So he did tell you."

"He did." Andy still didn't look at her.

"Andy, you've got to see it's the best thing for Gabe. He has got so much potential, and football, right now, is just getting in the way of him fulfilling that potential. Do you know he wants to be a doctor? He's certainly smart enough, but if you really want to be a doctor, you can't want anything more, or it's not going to happen. Believe me, I know."

This time, Andy did look at her, and to tell the truth, she found herself wishing he wouldn't.

"Okay, for the moment, I'm not going into your just deciding to take over my job."

Jess set her mug on the coffee table with a thump. "I never—"

Andy stopped her with a raised hand. "Let me finish. But there's something that you don't know, and Gabe does. Leaving the team in the middle of the season just because you change your mind is a character issue. It marks you as a quitter, someone who can't be depended on."

"Gabe, someone who can't be depended on? That's crazy, and you know it. And the last thing anyone could ever call Gabe is a quitter. Sometimes things just come up. Surely the team can understand that. And if they can't, well, Gabe is going to have to learn that he can't let other people's opinions dictate what he does."

"You still don't understand, do you? I said it's a character issue. It's not how the team will view Gabe, it's how he'll see himself, and no matter what else he does, a part of him will always believe he let the team down."

Jess looked away for a long moment before turning back to Andy. "This is all just too preposterous. Football is a game, for pity's sake, not holy orders."

Andy just looked at her in silence for a long moment while she wished she could snatch the words she had just spoken from the air. When he did speak, his voice was low and tightly controlled. "You're right. Football is just a game. But it's a game Gabe loves, and one he's good at. Maybe he's not scholarship material, but so what? Does everything you do have to have some kind of material value? Can't you do something for the sheer joy it gives you? Look, you've said he should sit out this Friday's game, and maybe next week's as well. Okay. You're his doctor, and I respect that. But after that? That's between me and Gabe. Do you get that? It just doesn't concern you. There'll be a grand total of three games left when Gabe can play again. Are three games really going to make the difference between medical school and sweeping up after folks? Really?"

"Maybe not for most kids, but for Gabe? Who knows?" Jess wanted to shake Andy. Why couldn't he understand that this wasn't just about football? It was about Gabe and his future. "Do you know how thin he's stretched? He doesn't have five unscheduled minutes in a day. He's worried about letting his mom down; he's worried about letting you down. But what about Gabe? When does he get to think about what's good for him?"

"Are you even listening to me, or are you really that convinced that nobody but you knows anything?" Andy's voice was still low, but Jess had never heard it sound so cold. "There will be three games when Gabe comes back. Three. If he plays, he will prove to himself one more time that he can finish whatever he starts, even if it's hard. And that just might be more valuable to him in the long run than three weeks sitting in your office with his books while his team beats their brains out on the field."

Jess felt heat flood through her body and reach her fingertips. Her hands trembled slightly as she glanced at her watch and stood up.

"It's getting late. I've got to make an early start, and I'm sure you do too. Besides, I know you want to get back to see how your dad is getting along."

Andy sat where he was a moment looking up at her before he too got to his feet. He looked as if he had so much more to say, but he just nodded as he leaned over and placed his mug next to Jess's on the coffee table. "Right. It's late. We can talk more later."

Jess walked to the door and opened it. *Oh, I think we've said enough on the subject.* "Wait." She stopped Andy as he crossed the threshold. "About homecoming? I'm afraid you'd probably better count me out. I don't think I'd be very good company, now that I think about it."

He just looked at her for a long moment before he nodded. "Right."

Turning away, he crossed her porch and broke into a slow run as he moved down her walk. Jess closed the door before he reached the street.

Leaning against the door, Jess took deep breaths, trying to calm herself. How dare Andy challenge her like that? She didn't just arbitrarily snatch people off the street and start rearranging their lives. Gabe was a special kid. He had so much going for him, and if she could help him reach some goals, what was wrong with that? She was supposed to feel bad because she was encouraging Gabe to use his brain instead of getting it beat out—Andy's own words—on the football field? Not hardly!

Blowing out a long breath, Jess crossed the room and picked up the mugs to carry to the kitchen. Maybe she shouldn't have tried so hard to calm down, because now that she wasn't quite so mad, Andy's question floated in her mind demanding an answer: What difference, really, would three weeks make in the grand scheme of things?

# 17

Kaitlyn?" Jess stretched her legs out under her desk and kicked off her shoes. Her confidence had felt a bit wobbly since her confrontation with Andy last week, but this conversation with Kaitlyn Reed was one she had been looking forward to. "It's Jess MacLeod. I just got the results from your tests, and they all came back clear. I thought you'd like to know as soon as possible."

A beat or two of silence, and then Kaitlyn's voice came almost as a whisper. "Seriously?"

"Seriously. You sound surprised."

"No, no, not really surprised, but very thankful. My life before I came to Last Chance was pretty wild. I took all kinds of chances without even thinking about it."

"Well, it looks like you were lucky. Everything is fine."

"Oh, thank you. I can't tell you how grateful I am." Kaitlyn paused for a moment. "Do you know Elizabeth Cooley?"

"I love Elizabeth Cooley. Everyone does. She's a walking buddy of mine. Why?"

"She just came to mind when you said I was lucky." Kaitlyn gave a little laugh. "She doesn't believe in it. She always says, 'Luck doesn't have anything to do with it, and you know that as well as I do.' It's to the point where every time I hear the word, or even think it, I can hear her voice in my ear."

"I guess I don't really believe in luck either, not in the sense that you either have it or you don't. I just use it as shorthand to describe a random series of events with a determined outcome. Lucky if you have the outcome you're looking for, unlucky if you don't. That's all. What does Elizabeth think it is, if not luck?"

"Elizabeth doesn't think, she *knows*, that it's God."

"Okay then." *What do you do with a comment like that?* "Well, I just wanted to get these results to you and put your mind at ease. I know you were concerned."

"Thank you *so* much." The relief in Kaitlyn's voice was so profound that Jess wanted to reach through the phone and hug her.

"Talk to you soon." Jess was about to hang up when she hesitated. "Kaitlyn, can I ask you something?"

"Sure."

"Do you think your results came back the way they did because God likes you better than he might like someone else, maybe because you go to church more or something?"

"No, of course not. I have no idea why I got the results I did. It certainly wasn't because I deserved it. It was just part of the plan God has for my life. And if the results had come back the way I was afraid they might, well, that would have been part of God's plan for my life too. Not as punishment, or judgment, but as a natural consequence of my actions. And he would have had a plan for my life that included that too. And you know what? It would have been a good plan."

Jess didn't say anything for a moment.

"Well, Kaitlyn, I hear the things you're saying, but I just don't get it."

"I don't get it either. I just know it's true. But talk to Elizabeth. She believes it *and* she gets it. And she'll be real happy to explain it to you. All you have to do is say something like, 'Boy, it's lucky I ran into you today.'"

Jess laughed. “That would be an interesting conversation, and I might just do that. I’ve been meaning to get by to see her, anyway.”

After hanging up, Jess leaned back in her chair and thought about her conversation with Kaitlyn. It wasn’t that she didn’t believe in God; she did. She had just always thought of him as being too busy running the universe to get involved in the results of a blood test. And she supposed that if you were braced for bad news, like Kaitlyn was, and got good news instead, you might think God had done that, as a reward, maybe, for being a good person. But Jess knew that good people got sick sometimes, just like bad people stayed well, and how that all added up to being part of God’s plan was the thing that didn’t make sense.

A tap on her office door interrupted her musing, and she felt for her shoes with her toes and slipped them on. “Come in.”

Gabe Quintana, with a backpack slung over one shoulder, opened the door. “Hi, Dr. MacLeod. I came. Is it still okay?”

“Of course. I was expecting you. Why don’t you get set up at that table? I’ve got a patient coming in in a few minutes, but I think I’ve got time to see what you’re doing and where you are.”

“Oh, here. My mom wanted me to give you this.” He handed her a manila envelope on his way to the table.

“Thanks.” She took a peek inside before tossing it on her desk. “Perfect. Just what I was looking for.”

“Everything okay?” Gabe gestured toward the envelope with his chin as he sat down and pulled books and notebooks from his backpack.

“Everything’s fine. Didn’t I tell you that everything isn’t about you?” Jess grinned as she pulled a chair over next to him. “Now, show me what you’ve got here.”

Fifteen minutes later, Eva stuck her head in to tell her that her next patient was ready for her, and Jess got to her feet. “Okay, I think you're good to go with this. I'll pop in to see how you're doing from time to time, but other than that, you're on your own. Are you okay with that?"

"Yeah, sure. Thanks." He positioned his book in front of him and flipped open his notebook, and by the time Jess reached the door and looked back, he was already scribbling in his notebook. He was going to be fine. She had no doubt of it.

Not till the last patient and Eva left almost simultaneously did Jess get back to her office, and she found Gabe pretty much where she had left him, except there were a few wadded-up sheets of paper around, and a couple other notebooks were open on the table.

"Hey there, how's it going?"

"Good." He didn't look up.

"Any questions so far?"

"Nope."

"Want something to drink? Some water?"

"I'm good, thanks."

Jess smiled and shook her head. Whatever might keep Gabe from achieving his dreams, it would not be inability to focus, that she could see.

Sitting at her desk and slipping off her shoes, she opened the manila envelope and pulled out Marta's résumé. The more she read, the more delighted she became. If she had written Marta's résumé to her own specifications, it couldn't have been more perfect. Marta had even taken a course or two in billing and office management.

"Gabe, what time does your mom get up? Gabe? Gabe!"

He finally looked up, almost as if he wondered where he was. "What?"

"What time does your mom leave for work?"

"Around 4:30. Why?"

Jess looked at her watch. "Shoot, it's nearly 5:30. She's long gone."

"5:30?" Gabe started slamming his notebooks closed and shoving everything into his backpack. "Man. I've got to go get the kids from the neighbor's and make them their dinner."

"Okay." Jess was glad she wasn't between him and the door. It seemed like a good way to get run down. "It looks like you're doing just fine. When's your next test?"

"I've got a chemistry test Wednesday, and we have a calculus quiz every Friday." Gabe slipped one arm through a backpack strap.

"Remember, you have to get A's on both, so let me know if there's anything in either that you don't understand."

"Got it. Thanks." He was already out the door.

By the time Jess got to the front door to lock it, Gabe was backing his old truck around so he could exit the parking lot. Checking each room as she went, Jess headed back to her office. She still had perhaps an hour of work before she could leave. Marta Quintana's résumé, still in the center of her desk, caught her eye, causing her to break into a wide smile. Tomorrow she'd give Marta a call, and tomorrow she'd tell Eva that her days of exile might be coming to an end. And if everything went well, within a couple weeks, she'd have Marta working right here with her.

"Your mom called."

Andy hung his jacket and his hat on the hook by the front door. This really wasn't the first thing he wanted to hear when he walked in the front door, but that's what he got for forgetting his phone this morning. "Did you talk to her?"

"Not for long, I didn't. I said, 'Hello.' She said, 'Who's this?' I said, 'This is Tim Ryan, who's this?' She said, 'Tim?' And the next thing you know there's this ruckus on the other end and that sister of hers comes on and says, 'How dare you try to talk to her? Don't you ever call this number again.' Then she slams the phone down. The thing is, o' course, is that I never did call her. She called me."

"I'll call her and make sure she's okay." Andy walked down the hall to his room with his phone pressed to his ear. His call went to voice mail. "Hi Mom. Sorry about the call. I went off and left my phone on the charger this morning. But if you want to call back, I'm home now."

Within a minute, his phone rang, and the screen said "Mom." He hit Accept.

"Hi Mom."

"Would you tell me what in this world that man is doing with your phone?"

So much for preliminary pleasantries.

"I told you. I left my phone on the charger this morning, so when you called, he just answered it."

"I think you know I'm not interested in whether your phone is all charged up or not. Hang on. Aunt Barb wants to talk to you."

Andy rolled his head in a circle. The knot between his shoulders felt like it was the size of his fist.

"Andrew Ryan, is that you?"

"Hi Aunt Barb."

"Andy, would you please tell me why you opened the door to that man after all he's done to your mother? And to you, for that matter."

"Well, I didn't open the door to him. He opened it before I got home. He just needs someplace to stay awhile."

There was a moment of silence. Aunt Barb was probably re-loading.

"Well, let me tell you this, young man. Your mother has been planning for your Christmas visit since the day you told her you were coming. Just last Sunday in church when they said they needed folks to sign up for the Christmas program, the first words out of her mouth were, 'Oh, I hope Andy's here for that.' But I'm telling you right now, if that man comes with you, I'll leave you both standing on the front porch, and don't think I won't. Even if it does break your mother's heart."

"Aunt Barb, it's only October. We'll get this worked out. I will be there for Christmas, and I'll come by myself."

"Okay, then. Well, you take care, honey. Here's your mom. Love you."

By the time Andy was able to get off the phone and head back to the kitchen, his head throbbed. He had forgotten to ask why his mother had called in the first place, and she hadn't mentioned it herself, but the fact that his dad was not invited for Christmas had been made abundantly clear.

"Everything okay?" Tim was standing in front of the stove. "I found some pork chops in your freezer. Thought I'd fry 'em up, if that sounds good."

"Fine." Andy rummaged in the cupboard for aspirin. "Dad, why did you answer the phone? You knew it would only upset her."

"Well, how was I supposed to know who was on the phone? Think I'm a mind reader?"

"How about the fact that it said 'Mom' in big letters across the screen? How many moms do you think I have?"

Tim turned around and poked the sizzling pork chops with a fork. "Countin' that sister of hers, I'd say about one too many."

"Anyway, she's upset, Aunt Barb's upset, and the only thing that really got settled was that you're not invited for Christmas."

"I wouldn't go there for Christmas in a one-horse open sleigh. And you can tell 'em I said so, next time you talk to 'em."

"So, you haven't told me, Dad. Why did you answer the phone? You had to know it wasn't going to end well."

"I don't know." Tim flipped the pork chops over in the skillet. "When the phone rang and I saw it said 'Mom,' I realized what a long time it has been since I heard her voice. Not since the night, well, you know what happened. I just wondered if she sounded the same."

"And did she?"

"Pretty much the same, at least as far as I could tell before that sister of hers got the phone away from her. You know, I don't want to mess with your mom's life. When I told you I was glad she was happy, I meant it. And I'm as sorry as I can be that things turned out the way they did. That wasn't what we thought was going to happen when we started out. Someday I hope I can tell her that."

"That might be awhile, Dad. You burned a lot of bridges."

"I know I did." He turned off the fire under the skillet and looked in. "I didn't think to make anything to go with these pork chops."

"That's okay. We can heat some corn real quick. I think we can get by with a little skimpiness for one meal."

Andy watched his dad while they ate. He still had that hair-trigger temper, but he didn't seem to have the violence that used to accompany it. His eyes had bags under them and were heavy-lidded, but they weren't red and watery like they used to be. And his hands didn't shake.

"Dad, the other night you told me you weren't drinking anymore. How long has it been?"

Tim rested his elbow on the table and rubbed his chin. "Pretty close to four years. Four years next month, come to think of it. I got real sick. My heart about give out on me. The doctor said the booze was killing me and if I didn't stop, I'd wind up as dead as Jacob's mule. So I stopped. I still had some things I wanted to do."

"You stopped? Just like that?" Andy felt anger begin to course through him again. If it was that easy, why had it taken so long? And if destroying his family wasn't a big enough reason to quit, then what was?

"Well, maybe not just like that. I got myself checked into the county loony bin and fought it out, but I beat that sucker. And I fight it again every day, but so far, so good."

"And the things you wanted to do? Have you got 'em done yet?" Andy still wasn't quite ready to give up the hurt he had carried with him for way too many years.

"Some. I saw the Carlsbad Caverns on my way down here."

*The Carlsbad Caverns.*

"Well, good. Glad that stay in the county loony bin wasn't wasted."

Tim put down his fork. "Son, I can tell you're still awful mad at me. I guess you've got something to be mad about. But I thought you'd know without my having to tell you: I wanted to come home to Last Chance. And when I read that article in the barbershop and knew you were here, well, that's all I needed to know."

Andy shoved his chair back from the table so hard that he almost tipped it over. "What do you want from me, Dad? You want me to get all weepy and tell you that as long as we're together everything is just peachy? Well, I can't. I'm sorry. I just can't. Thanks for cooking dinner. I'm going for a walk."

He got up from the table, put his jacket on, and left the house. He had no choice but to walk by Jess's house, but this time he walked on the other side of the street with his hat pulled low over his eyes. He didn't think there was much chance that she'd be putting a birthday card in the mail again, but he didn't want to take any chances. Truthfully, he didn't imagine she wanted to see him any more than he wanted to run into her. But even if last night hadn't ended like it did, he had a lot to think over, and tonight he wanted to be alone.

When he got back, the dishes had been done, and the door to his dad's bedroom was closed. He was glad to see that. The walk had done its job, and he felt much quieter, but the best way for him to stay that way would be if he didn't have to deal with his dad at least till morning.

He went into the kitchen to turn out the lights, and as he did so, several little piles of white dust along the baseboard caught his eye. *Oh, no. Not termites. I think what I need to do is put the boards back on the windows of this place and just walk away.* He knelt and rubbed the dust between his fingers and thumb. Not termites. The dust was far too fine. Looking up, he noticed that each pile of dust was below one of his patches, and each patch had been sanded smooth.

Just before the lunch bell rang the next day, Andy walked out of his office and got in his truck. Most days he ate his lunch at his desk, but not today. With his dad there at home, his mom and aunt still furious at him in Oklahoma, and pressure building from all sides at school to keep that two-game win streak going, he needed to get away from school, if only for an hour.

"Well, look who's here! The man of the hour!" Juanita Sheppard greeted him when he walked into the Dip 'n' Dine. "What do you think, Coach? Are we going to pound them into the ground like a tent stake again this week?"

"Well, we're facing a strong team this week. We need to make sure we want it more than they do."

"Oh, pshaw, Andy, do you know how many times I've heard those exact same words? Every time a coach gets in front of a microphone, he says the exact same thing: we're up against a strong team and need to see who wants it most. I think they must make you memorize that in coach's school or something."

"It works pretty well, don't you think?" Andy took a seat in a booth by the window. "Strikes just the right tone between humble and confident."

"I don't want humble. I want you to march in here yelling, 'We're going to smash 'em to smithereens.'" She handed Andy a menu.

"You know, Juanita, I think they hired the wrong person for coach. You were here all along, and they went and looked elsewhere, and with Russ on the selection committee too."

"Don't you think I couldn't have done a good job either. But I can only do so much, and my work is here. I don't know what Chris would do without me, and he doesn't either, do you, Chris?"

"I'd be the last to hold you back, Juanita. If your destiny calls, we'll just have to muddle through somehow." Chris, who had just come out of the kitchen, walked over to shake Andy's hand. "Hey, Coach, good to see you. So you're thinking of hiring Juanita, are you? What can I do to sweeten the pot?"

"In case you hadn't noticed, Chris, the position of coach has been filled, and you're looking at the one who filled it. And it would serve you right if I walked right out of here, after you making a comment like that. This place wouldn't last two weeks without me here, and you know it. I'll be right back with your water, Andy."

It wasn't always easy to know if Juanita was really offended, since she couldn't say good morning without sounding as if the whole process was a personal affront to her, but she sure didn't sound happy. Andy looked up at Chris. "I was just teasing her a little bit. Think we went too far?"

"Nah. If Juanita didn't threaten to quit at least once a day, I'd be worried about her. Besides, you just told her they should have hired her instead of you. I'm sure she agrees with you completely."

Chris shook his hand again and wished him well on the game Friday before heading back to the kitchen. Juanita put his water on the table, pulled her pad out of her pocket, and gazed out the window while Andy looked at the menu.

"Well, look at that. Here comes the doctor. This place is just filling up with VIPs."

Andy looked up as Jess came through the front door. She quickly looked away and tucked the brown paper bag she carried behind her purse as she slipped into a booth at the other end of the diner.

"Hhmph. I thought for sure Jess'd want to come sit with you. You two have a tiff or something?"

Andy ignored the question and handed her his menu. "I'll have a bowl of green chile stew and an extra tortilla. Oh, and some iced tea."

"Well, looks like you just answered my question for me." Juanita patted his shoulder as she took his menu. "Well, don't worry. I'm sure everything will work itself out. It always does."

Andy gazed out the window as Juanita moved on down to talk to Jess.

*Please, just for once in your life, mind your own business and don't start talking about tiffs.*

Thankfully, she didn't, but since Juanita never spoke in a voice that couldn't carry through three counties, Andy as well as every other diner in the place heard everything she had to say.

"I see you've been to the bookstore. What did you get?"

"Oh, nothing, really. I just stopped in real quick on my way home from the hospital." Jess was clearly trying to sound breezy, but Andy caught the annoyed edge to her voice. Sounded like she might still be mad.

"Well, that would be a trick since the bookstore is on the opposite side of town from the hospital and nowhere near the Last Chance Highway." Once Juanita's curiosity got up, you almost had to hit her with a stick to get her to drop the subject. "What are you reading that you don't want us to know about?"

"Nothing!"

It was clear to Andy that Jess did not want to talk any further about her trip to the bookstore, and it must have been clear to Chris as well, as he appeared in the window to the kitchen and hit the bell with the palm of his hand.

Juanita rolled her eyes and huffed a loud sigh. "Good night, nurse, Chris. What now? I'm just handing the doctor a menu. Is that allowed? And I know that she doesn't have to explain her reading selections to anyone. She's over twenty-one."

By now everyone in the diner was following the conversation with undisguised interest. Andy almost felt sorry for Jess, whose cheeks were beginning to match the color of her hair.

"You know, I don't think I'll have time for lunch after all." Jess got up to go, and as she fumbled with her purse, the bag fell to the floor and her book slid out.

"Good night, is that what you were all mysterious about?" Juanita picked it up and handed it to her. "Here I thought you had picked up some X-rated romance novel, and all you got was *Football for the Clueless*."

# 18

When Eva brought Marta Quintana back to talk to Jess, she was as pleasant and proficient as Jess had ever seen her. In fact, since Jess had told her that Marta would be coming in today and why, Eva had been practically singing, and Jess was beginning to remember why she had asked for Eva in the first place.

"Dr. MacLeod, Marta Quintana is here to see you." Eva stood in the doorway after ushering Marta into Jess's office. "And since we don't have any more patients today, is it all right if I close up and go home?"

"Sure. Go ahead." The question and the reply had become automatic with daily use, and Jess barely glanced Eva's way as she rose from her desk to greet Marta Quintana.

The door closed behind Eva but promptly opened again as she stuck her head back in. "Good luck, Marta!"

This time Jess did frown at her, but if Eva noticed her annoyance, she gave no sign. She just wiggled her fingers in a wave, smiled, and closed the door again.

Jess gestured to the chair in front of her desk as she sat down again. "As you can probably guess, Eva has high hopes for this interview."

"Eva is a nice girl." Marta's smile was warm and kind. "I know her mother. She dated my older brother a long time ago."

*Of course she did.* Jess had the distinct impression that if she started tugging on the string intertwined through Last Chance families, she'd find a continuous thread that bound everyone to everyone else.

"I was really impressed with your résumé, Marta." Jess tapped the document in front of her. "What made you go into nursing?"

"I don't know if Gabe told you or not, but my husband is serving a life term in the state penitentiary." Marta's voice was as serene as if she were discussing the weather. "When I understood that I was going to be the sole provider for our family, I knew I had to prepare for that, and since I had always wanted to be a doctor—just like Gabe—I packed up the kids and we all went to El Paso so I could go to school."

"El Paso?" Jess tried to keep her voice and her expression free from astonishment.

"My parents had moved to El Paso, so we all piled in on them." Marta laughed a little. "Of course, there was no way I could have become a doctor, not at this point, and not with five kids I needed to take care of. So I went into nursing and became an LPN. It was a good decision."

It didn't take more than a few more questions for Jess to realize that her original instincts had been right: she really did want Marta working with her here at the Last Chance office. She went ahead with every question on the list she had made for herself anyway, making notes as she did. Marta was the first person she had ever interviewed and would be her first employee. It was important that she get this right, and if Marta never got a clue that Jess didn't do this every day, well, that would be okay too.

When Marta left a half hour later with the promise that a written offer would follow the verbal one, it took a little doing for Jess to merely walk Marta to the door in a dignified, professional manner and not click her heels and offer a high five. First of all, she was hiring what appeared to be an outstanding office assistant with deep ties to Last Chance. Second, it was gratifying to see Marta so pleased to be able to work for *her*, in the daytime and near her kids. And finally, though it paled in importance compared to reasons one and two, Jess was not going to have to tell Eva that her escape from Last Chance had been delayed.

Marta stopped at the door and squeezed Jess's hand. "Thank you again for helping Gabe. Do you really think he can become a doctor?"

"I know he can. No question." Jess chose her words carefully. "He's smart enough, focused enough, and I don't need to tell you what a hard worker he is. But I know I also don't need to tell you, of all people, that it's not going to be easy. He's got a long journey ahead, and there are so many things that could derail his plans along the way."

"Not with me for his mother." Marta lifted her chin. "I can't make it easier for him to get there, but I can make it impossible for him to give up."

After seeing her out, Jess turned out the lights in the waiting room and smiled to herself as she headed back down the hall. She knew Gabe was headed for medical school. Anything else was just not an option.

It wasn't late but was already nearly dark when Jess let herself out the back door of her office. The wind that had rattled the windows all afternoon had died down, leaving the evening cold and still. Jess pulled her coat tighter as she got in her car. It was a good night for a fire.

She had just touched match to kindling and sat back on her

heels to watch the flames lick at the piñon logs stacked there when her phone rang.

"Hey there, are you home yet?" Sarah always sounded like she had something exciting going on.

"Just walked in a minute ago."

"Good. I didn't want to bother you at work. What are you doing Friday night?"

"I don't have any plans. Why? Has *The House Down the Road 5* come out?" Jess sat cross-legged on her couch and tucked a cushion behind her back.

"No, that doesn't come out till next spring. Anyway, that's not why I called. There's a home game this week, and we're meeting Lainie and Ray at halftime. Come with us."

Jess let her head drop back and gazed up at the ceiling. *People should not begin conversations by saying, "What are you doing this weekend?" They should tell you what they have in mind straight off the bat so you can say, "Oh, I'd love to, but I'm having a migraine that day."*

"Oh, I don't know, Sarah. It's going to be cold and windy and dark. And I won't know what's going on."

"Then read your book. You have plenty of time before Friday to at least get a general idea."

"My book." Jess had been cringing with embarrassment every time she thought of her noontime encounter with Juanita. Of course, Andy had been there to witness it. She felt her face flaming again.

"Chris told me all about it. If it will make you feel any better, Chris really raked Juanita over the coals this time, and Juanita actually feels bad that you left. I know this for a fact because I asked Chris if she threatened to quit, and he said no. She just hopes you come back so she can say she's sorry. And I have never heard Juanita say she's sorry for anything."

Jess closed her eyes. One of two things was going to happen, and happen soon. She was going to understand, and even embrace, the fact that there were no secrets in Last Chance, or she was going to call her mother's friend Moira Conner and talk to her about coming back to Mill Valley.

"Jess? Are you there? Are you okay?"

"I'm here." Jess sighed. "Just trying to get used to running down Main Street naked, that's all."

"Really? Oh, girl, that was nothing—other than it made Chris really mad. No one but you even remembers it."

"You did."

"Mainly what I remembered was that you had a book on football. If I had thought about the rest, I may not have mentioned it. Now, can you come with us to the game?"

"Okay. Sure. I'll go." Jess realized she had spoken mostly to change the subject, but the damage had been done. She had agreed to go to a football game—and sit in the cold and the dark and the wind, watching a bunch of high school kids run into each other and fall down, while she tried not to notice the coach.

"Oh, good. Since Chris and I can't get there till halftime, Ray and Lainie will pick you up. You'll have a much better time knowing what's going on if you watch it from the beginning. And then afterward, we're all going over to Gran's for coffee. She can't go to the games anymore, but she still likes a play-by-play account as soon as she can get one."

"Seriously?" Jess shook her head. "I can't get over the fact that Elizabeth, of all people, is a football fan."

"Gran? Oh, yes. She never used to miss. Of course, most years she had a family member on the team, starting with my dad and uncle and moving on to my brother and my cousins. Now I've got some nephews headed that direction, but I think Gran's days of going herself are over now. That's why she looks forward to us rehashing the game with her."

"You know? That actually sounds like the best part. At least we'll be inside and warm."

After Sarah hung up, Jess pulled a throw over herself and snuggled down on the sofa to watch the flames crackling in the fireplace. It looked like she was going to a football game on Friday, in spite of herself. It wasn't that she hated football—how could she? She'd never even been to a game. It was simply that she'd never wanted to. There were always too many other things that she'd rather be doing. But Last Chance didn't seem to understand that. And the more she tried to explain that she just didn't care about the game, the more everyone seemed bent on getting her to one, until what began as mild disinterest had mushroomed into common knowledge shared by all of Last Chance: Dr. Jess MacLeod *hates* football.

"How did you do on your chem test?" Jess popped into her office, where Gabe was already studying, between patients the next day.

"Aced it." He looked up with a grin.

"Hey!" Jess held up her hand for a high five. "That's what I want to hear. And do you feel good about the calculus quiz coming up tomorrow?"

He shrugged. "Yeah. Sure. Calculus is my favorite subject."

"Seriously? It was mine too, when I was in high school. In fact, I was a real math geek. I used to joke about making a sign that said 'Will solve math problems for food' and taking it on the road. Fortunately for both of us, math aptitude is a good thing to have if you're going to medical school."

"Good." He nodded absently and went back to his book. The boy was not easily distracted, perhaps the result of having to study while caring for four younger siblings.

"Gabe, I need to talk to you a minute. I won't keep you from your studies long." Jess sat down in the chair next to his. After a second or two, he looked up, a frown of concentration still furrowing his eyebrows. "First let me take a look at your cut." She took his chin between her thumb and forefinger and turned it so she could better examine him. "That's healing well. Good." She rested one elbow on the table and propped her chin on it. "I had a talk with Coach Ryan the other day."

Now she did have his attention. He put down his pencil.

"He told me that quitting the team in the middle of the season is a really big deal. That it's not something you do just because you feel like it."

He ducked his head. "I didn't do it because I just felt like it. I did it because I need to make straight A's, like you said."

"I know that, and believe it or not, Coach Ryan knows that too. But he posed an interesting question."

Gabe looked up and fastened his gaze on Jess's face.

She took a deep breath. "He asked me if playing three or four more football games during your senior year in high school was really going to make the difference between your going to medical school or doing something else with your life. After thinking about it, I have to say no, or at least, it doesn't have to. What do you think? We're talking about a month here. Do you think you can play and still make your A's?"

"Yes." His answer came immediately. "Yes, I can. I know I can."

Jess leaned back and folded her arms. "Then it's your decision, Gabe. You know what you can do. And from what I've seen since we first talked, it's pretty much anything you set your mind to. But you still need to wait at least a week before you go back to practice. Are we clear on that?"

"We're clear."

Gabe picked up his pencil and went back to his books. Within moments, his concentration appeared as deep as if she had never spoken. Jess watched him for a moment before quietly letting herself out of the office. No problems there. She could help him with his college applications, perhaps, and she did know about scholarships and loans, but now that Gabe knew what was required to get those scholarships, she had no doubt that he would come through.

Friday was a shirtsleeve day: warm, sunny, and spicy with the scent of chile, even though the harvest was over. Whether it was the mellow warmth of the day or the anticipation of spending an evening out with friends—even if it was at a football game—Jess found she was singing to herself and glancing at her watch almost as much as Eva looked at hers.

Even though the sun had gone down by the time she drove into her own driveway, the warmth of the day still lingered just beneath the cool breeze that gusted through the trees on her street and ruffled her hair when she got out of her car. Checking her watch yet again, Jess trotted into the house and down the hall to her room, where she started digging around in her closet. She had fifteen minutes to get ready before Ray and Lainie came to pick her up, and this beautiful day didn't fool her one bit. She was going to dress warm.

She was sitting on a front porch chair with one foot tucked up when Ray's pickup slowed to a stop in front of her house.

"Did you see the sunset tonight?" Lainie scooted over to the middle of the seat to make room for Jess. "It was absolutely breathtaking. I've been here for over two years now and I cannot get used to them. I don't think Ray even sees them anymore."

"You cut me to the quick, woman." Ray turned onto Main Street and headed south, where the glow of stadium lights lit the sky. "I paint landscapes, in case you hadn't noticed. And you might find a sunset or two among them, if you look real carefully."

"Oh. Yeah. I forgot." Lainie didn't sound the slightest bit embarrassed. "I guess you have to look at them to paint them, don't you? But what I mean is, do you ever just sit and take it all in? Just let all those rich colors feed your soul?"

"Nah. I just throw a little red paint on, a little yellow and pink. It all pretty much looks the same."

Lainie nudged Jess. "I think I'd better quit while I'm ahead."

"Too late. The last you were ahead was when you said the sunset tonight was pretty. It's pretty much been all downhill from then." Ray kept his eyes on the road.

"Oh, but you're not going to be mad, are you?" Lainie leaned her head on his shoulder and looked up at him. "I'm too cute to be mad at, and besides, I'm the mother of your child."

Ray glanced down at her. "Boy, you play rough, don't you? You think just because you're cute and you're going to be a mother, I can't be mad?"

"That's right." She looked up at him and batted her eyes.

"Well, I guess you have a point."

He turned past a bronze statue of a snarling puma mounted on a six-foot pedestal and a marquee announcing the dates of homecoming and drove down a long asphalt driveway, toward the banks of lights that towered over the school and the stadium behind it. The dirt parking lot was already nearly full, but Ray found a spot to park, and the three of them, with Ray in the lead, headed into the stadium.

Jess stopped and stared. No wonder everyone always sounded surprised when she said she wasn't going to the game. The stands were filled. Jess had no idea there were that many people in Last Chance and that every last one of them would be at the game.

"I don't know how Chris and Sarah will ever find us." Jess couldn't take her eyes off the crowd. The population sign on the edge of town said seven hundred something, but there were way more than that in the stands. "I guess they can call from the parking lot and one of us can go get them."

"Oh, they'll know where to look." Ray took Lainie's arm as they began to climb the stands. "It's like church; everyone has their own spot. And the Cooleys have been sitting about a third of the way up on the scoreboard forty since before my time."

"Scoreboard forty?" Jess muttered under her breath to Lainie.

"The forty yard line. See the white markings? And on the side of the fifty that has the scoreboard. See? That's the scoreboard, so we sit about a third of the way up right here."

Jess followed them both up the concrete steps to the row a third of the way up that was indeed empty, or nearly so, as if it had been awaiting their arrival.

"Oh my goodness! Look who's here!" Lainie entered the row and threw her arms around a tall blond man standing next to Kaitlyn. "When did you get in?"

Jess hadn't seen Kaitlyn until Lainie spoke, since she had been walking behind Lainie and Ray, but even without an introduction, she was willing to take a wild guess and say that this was Steven.

"And why didn't you tell us you were coming?" Ray reached across Lainie to hug his brother.

"Taking your questions in order. I got in around noon, and I didn't say anything because I wanted to see Kaitlyn for a little while before anyone knew I was home."

"And me. You wanted to see me too." The little girl sitting on the other side of Kaitlyn, who Jess remembered as Olivia, got up and traded places with her mother, placing herself between Steven and Kaitlyn.

"Yes, I wanted to see Livvy too." Steven lifted her so she could stand on the seat and put his arm around her, giving her a squeeze.

Steven had been flicking his glance toward Jess all the time they had been talking, and after they all sat down again, Jess reached across Ray and Lainie to offer her hand. "Hi, I'm Jess MacLeod."

"Oh, I'm sorry, Jess. I was just so surprised to see Steven that I forgot my manners. Steven, this is our new doctor, Jess MacLeod. She has an office right there on Main Street. And Jess, this is Steven, Ray's brother and Kaitlyn's . . ." While Lainie hesitated, clearly looking for a word, Kaitlyn casually extended her left hand. "Fiancé?" Lainie grabbed her hand. "You're engaged? When did this happen?"

"This afternoon." Kaitlyn's face was shining. "We went for a long drive, and Steven stopped at a spot that overlooks the whole valley, and then he pulled the ring box out of his pocket."

"Congratulations, bro." Ray leaned across Lainie to shake his brother's hand. "I couldn't be happier for you. And Kaitlyn, I owe you a kiss. Maybe at halftime."

"And then what?" Clearly, Lainie was not ready to let the story end.

"Well, then we went and picked Livvy up from school."

"And then he asked me if he could be my dad." Olivia picked up the story. "And I said yes, and he gave me this necklace." She leaned over so Lainie could see the little gold heart with the tiny diamond in its center.

"Oh my goodness, you're going to make me cry." Lainie gave Steven another hug. "Have you told Gran?"

"No, I thought we'd surprise her."

"But she does know you're in town?"

"No, that's going to be a surprise too."

"For Pete's sake, Steven, Gran's nearly ninety years old. She can only take so many more shocks." Lainie bumped his shoulder. "At least call and tell her you're in town and that you and Kaitlyn want to come by and see her."

"But that will spoil the surprise. She'll probably guess."

"Of course she will," Kaitlyn put her hand on his arm and smiled at him. "But think of how much pleasure she'll have waiting for us to come. That's not so bad, is it?"

"Maybe not." Steven smiled back at her.

Lainie and Ray exchanged glances, and Lainie shrugged.

Watching everything unfold from her place on the end, Jess couldn't help feel the outsider she was. But when the crowd around her erupted in a deafening roar, she looked to the field where a team wearing black and gold and led by a kid in a puma costume took the field. Following behind was Gabe, wearing his letterman's jacket and walking with a dark-haired man not much taller than Gabe. Bringing up the rear was Andy, wearing a dark sports jacket and a tie and carrying a clipboard. And even though she had promised herself to concentrate on the game and not the coach, Jess found her attention drawn again and again to the man with the clipboard who paced the sideline.

# 19

"So, do you understand what's going on?"

By the time everybody got settled and seated and the attention had turned from Kaitlyn and Steven's engagement to the game on the field, Jess was sitting next to Lainie on the end.

"Nope, not really." Lainie propped her feet up on the back edge of the bleacher in front of her. "My high school years, brief as they were, didn't include pep rallies and football games. The first football game I ever saw, I was sitting right where I am now. To tell the truth, I don't know a whole lot more now than I did then. And that's okay with me. It just takes a few hours, it makes Ray happy, and at least I get to sit down."

Jess looked back at the field. Yep, they were all running into each other and falling down. "I was hoping by watching a game, I could learn something about it, but it's not happening."

"Wait till Sarah and Chris get here, and make sure Sarah sits by you. She could write a book. Meanwhile, I can give you the basics, if you want."

"Sure. Anything would help."

"Okay. See the guys in black and gold? They're our team, and we cheer for them. When they get the football past all those guys in red and gray and clear to the end of the field, we score. They post the score up there on the scoreboard so you can keep track of who's ahead."

"I've got that part down. It's the middle part I don't get. If everyone's just running around bumping into each other, how do you know when to cheer?"

Suddenly, everyone around them jumped to their feet with a roar that had to be rattling the windows at Elizabeth's house. Lainie leaned in so Jess could hear her. "That's how you know when to cheer."

"But what happened?"

Lainie leaned to her other side to ask Ray, "What happened?"

"Interception."

Lainie leaned back. "Interception."

Jess opened her mouth to ask what that was but closed it again. What was the point? Lainie would just ask Ray, and he was trying to watch the game. If they kept that up very long, he was bound to get annoyed eventually, even if he was too polite to show it. Reaching into her bag, she pulled out the small pad and pencil she always carried and flipped to a clean page. She wrote "Interception" at the top.

When the crowd went wild again a few minutes later, Jess had no trouble figuring out what had happened. One of the boys wearing black and gold had the football and had somehow gotten around all the boys wearing red and gray and was running for the goal line as fast as he could go, with everybody else chasing him down the field. When he crossed the goal line, Jess found she was screaming just like everyone else and looking around for strangers to exchange high fives with.

While Jess was watching the first score of the game going up on the Last Chance side of the scoreboard, someone kicked the ball over the goalpost, and another point got added to the score. It now stood 7–0, Last Chance.

She turned to Lainie. "What was that?"

"The extra point. After they make a touchdown, they get to try to kick it over the goalpost for an extra point."

"Why do they do that?"

Lainie shrugged, and Jess got out her little pad and wrote "Extra point" under "Interception."

By the time the halftime whistle blew, the score stood 21–3, and Jess's list had grown to include punt, fair catch, and field goal. As the team trotted off the field, followed by the coaches, and the marching band marched on to the quick beat of the drum, Jess tucked her list in her bag. Lainie had assured her that Ray would be happy to answer any question she had during halftime, but she always learned best from books, and anyway, if they ever got back on speaking terms, she'd like to ask Andy. She had either mocked his vocation or dismissed it as trivial almost from the day they had met, and except for the Gabe issue, he had just let it roll off his back. She still didn't get football, but, even if they'd never be more than friends, she wanted him to know that she was sorry she had so summarily dismissed it.

"Here you are. Did you save us any room?" Sarah, followed by Chris, came up the steps. "That's some score. I hope the second half is as exciting."

"You don't know the half of it." Lainie leaned back to give Sarah and Chris a better view of Steven and Kaitlyn. "Look who turned up. Show them your hand, Kaitlyn."

Kaitlyn extended her hand again, and Sarah smiled. "It really is gorgeous. I didn't know you had that kind of taste, Steven."

It took a second for the truth to dawn on Lainie. "You already knew! When did you find out?"

"They stopped in the Dip 'n' Dine on their way here to tell Chris. I just happened to be in the right place at the right time. So I got to hear about it too." Sarah blew a little kiss down the row to Kaitlyn.

"I had to share my happy news with my brother as soon as possible. I couldn't just spring it on him at a football game."

Ray glared at Steven. "You sure didn't have any problem with that."

Steven held up his hands in mock surrender. "Hey, I'm just doing what you said I should do when you gave me all that advice before I left for the academy. You said, 'If it comes to that, just keep your mouth shut and do whatever she wants. All you really need to do to keep the peace is put on a tie and show up.'"

"*Seriously?*" Lainie was the one who spoke, but Sarah and Kaitlyn both turned to stare at Ray too. Even Jess was curious as to what Ray would say about that.

"Wait a minute, don't get mad at Ray. I was just paraphrasing." Steven couldn't have looked more innocent. "What he really said was, 'Your lovely bride deserves to have the wedding of her dreams, and it is your job to move heaven and earth, if need be, to see that everything happens just the way she wants it.' That's pretty much what you said, right, bro?"

Jess had only met Ray a few times, but if he had ever in his life said anything remotely like this, Jess was immensely sorry she hadn't been there to hear it.

Ray just shook his head. "You are on your own on this one, Steven. You have us both dug in so deep we'll never see daylight again."

"While you all are sorting this out, I think Olivia and I will make another visit to the restroom, and we might stop at the concession stand on our way back. Anyone want anything?" Kaitlyn took Olivia's hand and edged past everyone on their way to the aisle.

Ray winced when Olivia squeezed by him. He watched them head down the stairs before turning to Steven. "I think we need to move things around a little bit. You and Kaitlyn and Livvy need to sit on the end. I know it's got to be hard for a little kid to sit still very long, but she must have made four trips during the first half, and she managed to step on both my feet every time she went by, going and coming."

"When did your toes get so sensitive? She probably doesn't weigh fifty pounds." Steven bristled at the very implication of criticism of Livvy.

Jess smiled to herself at how protective Steven was of his little family. It looked like Kaitlyn and her daughter were in good hands. And from everything Kaitlyn had told her, they had it coming.

By the time Kaitlyn and Livvy came back, Steven had moved them to the end of the bleacher, though he was still glowering a bit.

"Well, this is smart." Kaitlyn kissed his cheek. "I don't know why we didn't do this earlier. Thanks for thinking of it."

"Well, no point in you having to climb all over everybody." Steven slid his arm around her shoulders.

Lainie and Ray exchanged glances, and Lainie grinned as the Last Chance Pumas took the field again while the crowd cheered.

The second half of the game was as satisfying as the first, if not quite as exciting. Each team scored another touchdown with its extra point, and when the final whistle blew, the score was 28–10, Last Chance.

As they all made their way down the steps of the stands, Steven grabbed Ray's shoulder.

"Look, down there at the bottom, just now walking in front of the first bleacher at the thirty yard line. Who is that?"

Ray looked. "I don't know. Some old guy. I don't know that I've ever seen him before."

"Something about him . . ." Steven's eyes narrowed in an effort to focus better. "If I didn't know better, I'd swear that was Andy's dad."

Ray looked again. "Nah, can't be. If he was back, someone

would have said something. Besides, that old boy looks about ten, fifteen years older than Andy's dad would be."

Steven gave another hard look before shrugging and looking away. "I guess, but I don't know, something about him . . ."

*So that's Andy's dad.* Jess, on the stadium stair just above Steven, said nothing. This was Andy's business, and if he wanted to say his dad was back in town, he would. She watched the old man shuffle along, one hand deep in the pocket of his denim jacket, the other lightly running along the top rail of the fence that separated stands from field, and couldn't help wondering if Andy knew his dad had finally come to a game.

"You don't have to tell me who won the game. I've been listening to those horns honk for the last fifteen minutes." Elizabeth opened the front door before they reached the porch. "Come in. Steven and Kaitlyn, you come over and give me a big hug and tell what all this mystery is about."

Olivia ran past them all and tackled Elizabeth with a hug around the waist.

"Careful!" The adults all spoke in unison, but Olivia didn't even seem to notice.

"Look!" She held up her locket for Elizabeth's inspection. "Steven asked me if he could be my dad, and I said yes, and he gave me this."

"My goodness, Livvy, I do believe that is the most beautiful necklace I've ever seen. So this is the reason your mom said you wouldn't be coming over this afternoon!" She looked up and over Olivia's head, and tears had already begun to find their way down her lined face. She reached in her pocket for a handkerchief. "I had a feeling, of course, that you were going to bring me this happy news when you called earlier. I just had no idea that it was going to affect me this way. Livvy, honey, help me get to my chair before I trip over the cat again or something. I'm not seeing real well right now."

With Livvy on one side, complaining that she could help Elizabeth all by herself, and Steven on the other, they helped her back to her recliner. When they got her settled, Steven knelt at her side.

"What's up, Gran? I expected a few happy tears, maybe, but folks usually smile when they're crying happy tears, and you're carrying on like someone burned your house down and ran off with the dog, or the cat, in this case. What's wrong?"

"Wrong? How can you possibly think anything's wrong? I'm as happy this minute as I've ever been in my life." Elizabeth took a deep breath and swiped at her nose with her handkerchief before resting her hand on his arm. "You know, honey, I pretty much talk to the Lord all day long. The first thing I do every morning is to thank the Lord for waking me, and I'm still talking to him when I turn out the light at night. Then there are other things that come up that need special attention, like someone getting sick or going on a trip. But in my long life, there have been a few—surprisingly just a few—things that I have taken before the throne of God and left them there, so brokenhearted that I had to let the Holy Spirit do my praying for me. We almost lost the ranch in the early days, due to drought and the bottom falling out of the cattle market, and we almost lost your Uncle Joe Jr. to pneumonia when he was about six months old. In both cases, the Lord gave me what I prayed for." She paused to draw a shaky breath. "But there were other times, like when I prayed for your mama to get well, and for your Uncle Jerry, who you never knew, to come home safe from Vietnam, when I had to accept that what I was asking for wasn't part of his plan. And I have been at peace with the way God answered my prayers all this time. But there was one thing left, and that was you. Oh, honey. The hours I've spent praying for you, I'm surprised the carpet where I've knelt by my bed isn't worn through. If you added them all together, I imagine it would be years."

"Years? Really?" Steven looked a little disconcerted.

"I've had nearly ninety. I can spare you one or two." Elizabeth's face was still pink and a little damp, but she was smiling now. "But anyway, here you are now, a handsome state police officer, bringing me a beautiful and godly new granddaughter and a precious great-granddaughter. My heart overflows."

Jess tried to understand what Elizabeth meant when she talked about being at peace no matter how God answered her prayers. It sounded a lot like the conversation she'd had with Kaitlyn about why Elizabeth rejected the concept of luck. It all came down to believing that God was in control and knowing that meant all was well. She smiled to herself as she remembered Sarah saying that family was only Elizabeth's second favorite topic of conversation. At the time Jess couldn't imagine what number one could be. Now she knew.

"Can I call you Gran now?" Olivia, at the first sign of tears, had attached herself to the other arm of Elizabeth's recliner, her face screwed into a worried frown.

"Of course you may call me Gran." Elizabeth held Olivia's hand to her face and kissed it. "You too, Kaitlyn. Now come give me a kiss and show me that beautiful ring you're wearing."

"The coffee's about ready." Lainie came in from the kitchen. "And who wants cake? It's Gran's applesauce cake."

The room, which had been a frozen tableau while Elizabeth spoke to Steven, dissolved again into the slightly chaotic family Jess had spent the evening with.

"None for me, thanks." Chris reached for the door. "I need to get home and get to bed. The Dip 'n' Dine opens at 6:00, and that alarm goes off awfully early in the morning."

"See you at home, honey. I won't be late." Sarah gave him a hug before turning to Lainie. "Let me help you with the cake."

Steven pulled Kaitlyn down on the sofa next to him, and the two bent their heads in conversation while Olivia still leaned on Elizabeth's chair. Jess was about to get up and go see if Sarah and Lainie needed any help when the front door opened and Andy stuck his head in.

"Knock-knock. I saw Chris outside and he told me to come on in. Hope it's okay."

Jess froze.

"Certainly! If you don't mind my not getting up, I surely don't mind you coming in—even if you hadn't run into Chris outside." Elizabeth smiled from her recliner. "And congratulations on the game. I know you won, but we haven't quite gotten around to the score yet. We've had a little excitement of our own here tonight."

"Oh?" He looked around for further explanation, his glance resting briefly on Jess before he came to Kaitlyn, who was holding out her hand. "You're kidding! Well, congratulations, and welcome home, Steven. It's great to see you." Andy crossed to the sofa, where he shook Steven's hand and bent down to kiss Kaitlyn's cheek. "So, when's the big day?"

"Oh, we haven't begun to think about that. Sometime this spring, I imagine." Kaitlyn smiled up from the shelter of Steven's arm.

"Well, hey, that's great. Congratulations again."

Andy had clearly run out of things to say and looked as uncomfortable as Jess felt.

"That was a great game, Andy, although that turnover on our own twenty-three with 1:03 left in the fourth could have been bad." There was no point in Jess pretending she didn't see Andy, and if she sat there without saying anything at all, someone was bound to notice.

He stared at her. "Say what?"

Jess tried to look interested yet nonchalant. "I sat next to Sarah during the second half. She's a treasure trove of information."

"Sarah's what?" Sarah came in carrying plates of applesauce cake, followed by Lainie carrying more. "Oh, hi, Andy. Want some cake?"

"A treasure trove of football knowledge. I was telling Andy how much I learned sitting next to you."

"Well, if Sarah thought we were in danger of giving up an eighteen-point lead with a minute and three seconds left in the game, I think there are a few rocks in her trove." Andy accepted the plate Sarah offered him. "Thanks."

"What are you talking about? I never said that." Sarah handed a plate to Elizabeth.

"That was me, I'm afraid." Jess felt her cheeks reddening. *Nice try. Next time, don't.* "I was trying to sound like I knew something by stringing together a bunch of words I heard you say. I don't think Andy's all that impressed."

"Oh, I was impressed, all right." Andy straddled the piano bench and forked in a bite of cake.

"Well, I know now that you had at least an eighteen-point lead." Elizabeth scooted over to make room for Olivia, who was trying to climb in the chair with her. "So what was the final score? And who did you play? Tell me all about it."

Andy had already taken off his sports coat, but he loosened his tie and leaned forward to rest his forearms on his knees, clasping his hands between them. As he told Elizabeth all about the game, with Ray and Steven chiming in every now and then, Jess could tell by her rapt expression that Elizabeth saw it all unfold before her. How many games, Jess wondered, had Elizabeth seen while sitting in the bleachers of Last Chance High? Her sons had played, and her grandsons, and for all Jess knew, she had gone to games before that. Certainly her interest in the game was real and her knowledge was phenomenal. If Sarah could write a book, Jess had no doubt that Elizabeth could write an encyclopedia.

"That's pretty much it," Andy finished up. "There was that turnover with a minute left in the fourth, but despite what you may have been led to believe, it didn't pose that much of a threat."

"And on that note, I should go." Kaitlyn got to her feet. "Livvy's squashing you flat, Elizabeth, and I need to get her home to bed."

Olivia had almost immediately fallen asleep and was indeed sprawled all over Elizabeth and snoring gently. Steven carefully removed her and draped her over his shoulder. "I'll be back later, if that's okay. I haven't figured out where I'm going to stay yet, but Lainie said she thought it would be okay if I slept in your sewing room for a while. Sorry I didn't ask you, but you didn't know I was in town yet."

"Of course it's okay. I'll put the bedding out and leave a light on if I decide to go on to bed. Congratulations again, my very dear ones. I am as happy and as at peace as I've been in a long, long time. And I do hope you can call me Gran, Kaitlyn. I feel like you're one of my own, even if you weren't marrying my grandson."

"I'll try." Kaitlyn threw a kiss Elizabeth's way and opened the door for Steven and Olivia.

"I'll walk out with you. I need to get home too." Sarah got to her feet. "Good night, all."

When the door closed behind the four of them. Elizabeth sighed. "You know, when Steven scooped that sweet child off my lap and carried her out over his shoulder, I thought I had received every blessing that the Lord might ever have had for me—my grandchildren all walking with the Lord and starting families of their own. But then I looked over at you, Lainie, and thought of that little one you're carrying, and I realize there is just no end to God's blessings. Just when you think you've seen everything, why, he just shows you some more."

"Mmmhmm." Lainie's eyes drooped and she stifled a yawn. "We are blessed, all right."

Ray stood up and pulled her to her feet. "You need to go to bed. Chris is not the only one who needs to be at that diner in the morning."

Andy and Jess took Ray's comment as a cue and began to gather their things, but Ray turned to them and waved them back in their seats. "No, don't go, you guys. Gran's a real night owl, and she's really been looking forward to having company this evening. Please stay."

"Yes. Please stay." Elizabeth chimed in. "We always send Lainie to bed early since she insists on working, but it's still early. Don't go."

Jess glanced at her watch. Maybe 11:20 wasn't late for Elizabeth, but Jess had been up since 6:00, and it seemed awfully late to her. She stood up.

"Elizabeth, I am sorry, but I do need to get home. It has been so nice to see you, and I'd love to come back real soon and have a good long visit. Maybe some evening when Ray and Lainie go out?" Jess looked up at Ray. "Not that I don't enjoy you two, of course."

"Yeah, Gran's always been the popular one. It doesn't hurt my feelings anymore. Much."

"Oh, you." Elizabeth took a swat at Ray and missed him by two feet.

"I should get home too. My dad's there and I need to make sure he's okay." Andy jingled his keys in his pocket.

"Your dad! So that *was* him at the game tonight. Steven thought it might be your dad, but I thought he looked too . . ." Ray's voice trailed away.

"Old? Beat up? Yeah, you'd be right on both counts. He's had a rough life, not that he didn't choose it."

"How is Tim doing, Andy?" Elizabeth's voice was rich with compassion.

"Oh, fine, I guess. He says he's not drinking now. Says it's been three or four years, and from everything I've seen, he's telling the truth, but it's probably too late to do him any good."

"Give him my best, will you? And bring him to visit me. I'd love to see Tim again."

"I'll do that, Miss Elizabeth. I'm sure it will mean a lot to him." Andy took her hand and bent down to kiss her cheek.

Jess kissed Elizabeth's cheek too, and turned to Ray with a little smile. "I'm afraid I'm going to have to ask for a ride home, Ray. You picked me up, remember?"

"I'll drop you off." Andy picked up his jacket and slung it over his shoulder. "You're right on the way."

Jess looked at Ray, hoping he would say it was no trouble at all, but he actually seemed to think Andy's suggestion was a good one.

"Okay, then. Thanks." Jess passed through the door Andy held open for her, trying to think of something, *anything* she could say that didn't involve football. Every time she tried to meet Andy on his own ground, it seemed to wind up in humiliation. "It sounds like Elizabeth really would like to see your dad. Were they friends back in the day?"

"The Cooleys and the Ryans go way back." Andy opened the door of his pickup for Jess, then walked around to the driver's side and got in. "My great-grandfather was Elizabeth's husband's father's foreman. With me so far?"

Jess nodded. "I think so."

"Okay. Well, the story goes that one day, Elizabeth's husband's father, who went by the name of Johnny, by the way, turned up missing, and my great-grandfather, whose name was Seamus, went looking for him." From the sound of it, Andy was searching for something to fill the silence of the ride home as well. "After about three days, he found Johnny nearly dead under his horse that'd been spooked by something or other and jumped off into an arroyo. So Seamus used his rope to get Johnny's horse off him and then somehow got old Johnny up on his own horse and walked them home again, where they fixed Johnny up, except that he always limped after that. Well, it's too late to make this long story short, but in gratitude, Johnny gave Seamus a little chunk of his ranch so he could start his own herd. And that's the story of the Cooleys and the Ryans." Andy stopped his truck in front of Jess's house. "Aren't you glad you asked?"

"I am, actually. Last Chance is my home now. I love hearing its stories." Jess reached for her door handle. "Thanks for the ride."

"No problem." Just as Jess was about to shut the door, he spoke again. "Surprised to see you at Miss Elizabeth's after the game. Did Gabe talk you into going?"

"No." Jess paused with her hand on the door. "Sarah asked if I had plans for tonight, and before I knew she was talking about going to the game, I said no. I was kind of stuck after that."

"Ah." Andy shifted from Park to Drive. "Well, glad we could win it for you."

"Thanks again for the ride." Jess shut the door of Andy's truck and walked to her front door. Not till she unlocked and opened it did Andy lift his hand in a wave and pull away from her curb. She stood in her doorway and watched until a dust cloud dimming his taillights indicated he had reached the dirt road at the end of her street. Why couldn't she tell him how much she had enjoyed the game?

# 20

Jess was reminded again that things between Andy and her had changed when she drove herself to church Sunday morning. Except for that first Sunday when she drove Elizabeth and last Sunday, Andy had always come by to pick her up. But he hadn't offered, and of course she'd never ask. She found herself driving to a different spot in the parking lot from where Andy usually parked, although she could see that his truck was not in its usual place. Actually, her attempt to avoid running into him made her feel kind of silly. If he were there, she would see him. The church was just too small not to.

"Where's Andy?" Sarah leaned over and whispered as Jess slid in next to her.

Jess shrugged, feeling somewhat annoyed. Sarah had asked the same question last week, and received the same shrug. How was Jess supposed to know where Andy was? Okay, since he had brought her every Sunday, perhaps it did seem likely that she would, but still . . . She picked up a hymnal and faced forward as the choir filed in.

By the time the service was over, that troubling, unsettled feeling that had bothered her since she got up had completely dissipated. Brother Parker had preached on a peace that passes understanding, and for once she completely got it. She felt completely at peace, and she didn't know why. Certainly nothing about her circumstances had changed since she sat down.

"Come have lunch with us." Elizabeth took her hand as they filed out of her pew into the aisle. "There's always room for one more, and we'd love to have you."

"Do come." Lainie chimed in. "We're having a little family celebration in honor of Kaitlyn and Steven's engagement. It would be so nice if you'd join us."

Jess hesitated. Lunch with the Cooleys did sound tempting, but she had made other plans. "Thank you so much, but not today. I need to get on home. I'll send my congratulations home with you, though." She blew a kiss toward Steven and Kaitlyn and headed for her own car. Andy's pickup was still missing from the parking lot.

The rich aroma of the soup she had made yesterday enveloped her when she walked in her front door. It really was too bad that no one was here to join her for lunch. Chicken noodle soup may have been one of the only things she knew how to make, but when you could make a soup like this, you just didn't need a backup plan.

Filling a bowl and putting it on the table next to her spot on the sofa, Jess got ready to watch the Colts play the Panthers. She had a strategy. She got a pen, a legal pad, and her copy of *Football for the Clueless* and set them next to her on the sofa. She would pay particular attention to the broadcasters and try to match their comments with the plays on the field, take notes, and look up things she didn't understand in her book during halftime. Jess was all too aware of what a geeky thing this was to do, but then, she was an unredeemable geek, and always had been.

The second half had just started and Jess was looking up "touchback" when her phone rang. She frowned a little at the screen when she picked it up. Why would Andy be calling? She decided to play it light.

"Hey! Are you watching the game too? I find that I'm rooting for the Panthers. Any reason I should be for the Colts?"

"Jess, I hate to ask it of you, but I'm worried about Dad. Could you possibly come over and look at him to see if I should take him to the emergency room? He keeps saying he's fine, but I don't like the way he looks."

"Sure, I'll come. Is this something that just came up, or has this been going on awhile?"

"Since this morning, anyway. He went back to bed after breakfast saying he didn't feel good, but he got up a little while ago and got dressed. It's just . . . Dad? Dad! Jess, he collapsed."

Jess jumped up and ran to find the shoes she had kicked off when she walked through the door. "Is he breathing?"

"I don't know. I can't tell. I can't hear anything."

"Do you know CPR?"

"Yeah. I'm certified."

"Then lay him out straight on the floor, open his shirt, make sure nothing is obstructing his breathing, and start CPR now. I'll call 9-1-1 and be right there."

Jess called 9-1-1 as she ran for her car. By the time she reached Andy's house, the dispatcher had assured her the EMTs were on the way, even if the best address she could give was "drive past 225 Mescalero to the dirt road at the end of the street and continue a quarter mile or so. It's the only house on the road."

She took her medical bag from where she kept it in the trunk of her car and was pulling a defibrillator from it as she came in the door. Andy was kneeling on the floor next to his dad applying CPR. He didn't look up.

"They're on their way." She knelt on the other side of Tim and placed her fingers on his neck, searching for a pulse. "Any change at all?"

Andy shook his head and kept on.

"Then move back. We need to do this now." She ripped open Tim's shirt and positioned the electropads on his chest. Motioning Andy back even further, she sent the charge through the old man's heart and resumed the CPR. After a few minutes, she sat back on her heels and, as the sound of a siren began in the distance, sent a second shock coursing through Tim's body.

It did not take long for the EMTs to check the old man out, take over the CPR, and put Tim in the ambulance for his trip to San Ramon.

Andy had moved to the sofa, and Jess sat next to him.

"Would you like me to drive you to the hospital?" She lightly rubbed his back between his shoulders.

He shrugged. "I don't know."

"Okay, Andy. Here are some things you should know. First, I'm so sorry to have to tell you, but I didn't find any pulse or heartbeat. They'll make the assessment in the ER, of course, but I think you need to prepare yourself for the probability that your dad is gone."

He nodded. "I know."

"And secondly, as his next of kin, there are some documents you need to sign and some decisions you have to make, so we really do have to go to the hospital."

He didn't move but just stared at the floor where his father had been.

Jess stood and took his hand. "Come on. I'll drive. You be thinking about what kind of arrangements you want to make. I know it seems harsh to talk about this right now, but these are questions they're going to ask you."

Andy folded himself into the front seat of Jess's little car. He shifted to find some room. "How does anyone fit in this thing? And how do you keep from getting crushed on the highway? I'd feel safer in a kiddie car."

"It works." Jess turned the key in the ignition and just let him talk, or not, as he chose. Not everyone who knew her would believe it, but sometimes she knew when to just listen without words.

Hours later, well after dark, she drove Andy back to his front door. Tim Ryan had indeed passed away that afternoon due to a massive heart attack, and from all appearances, he was probably gone before Andy and Jess ended their phone call.

Andy sat a moment without making a move to get out. "Can you come in?"

"Sure. I need to get my things anyway. I'll stay as long as you like."

Andy managed to get himself unfolded from the front seat of Jess's car and headed up the front steps with Jess behind him. He stood in the middle of the living room with his hands in his pockets, watching Jess pack her medical bag.

"So doctors still carry black bags? I thought that was just something you saw in old movies."

"This doctor does." She smiled up at him. "When you live someplace where you might be miles from the nearest medical facility, it seems like a good idea."

"Makes sense." He rocked on his heels and checked his watch. "What time is it in Oklahoma?"

"It's an hour later, isn't it?" Jess stood up and put her bag by the door.

"Yeah, of course. Man, I just can't seem to concentrate. Think it's too late to call? I really should tell my mom, even though she hasn't seen him in over ten years."

"That would be a considerate thing to do. I'm sure she'd want to know, if only for your sake."

Andy took his phone out and looked at it like he was trying to remember how it worked.

Jess put her hand on his. "Look, don't call her tonight. There will be time enough tomorrow. Come sit here on the sofa. I'm going to go put on a pot of coffee, and then I'd like you to tell me about your dad. I know he let you down in some major ways, and if you want to talk about it, I'll listen. But I'll bet you have some good memories, if only a few, maybe from way back when you were little? I'd like to hear about them too—that is, if you'd like to talk about them."

When Jess came back with a couple mugs of coffee, Andy was going through a scrapbook. "My mom put these together. When she left, she said she couldn't look at them anymore, so they've spent all this time in a bottom drawer in the back bedroom. Look at this. They look so young."

Jess leaned over. "And that's you?"

"Yep. Cute little dude, wasn't I?"

"You sure were. And that picture of your dad could be a picture of you today, if you wore a mullet."

"Yeah, Dad was quite the looker. I'm trying to remember if he still had that mullet when he left. It may have been gone by then."

"Your mom was sure pretty. I love the big hair."

"Yeah, she was. Back before she married Dad, if there was a Miss Something, or a Something Queen, you can bet Mom was right in the middle of it."

"You look like such a happy family in this picture. You're even holding a football. How old were you?"

Andy took a closer look. "That may have been my fourth birthday. I don't remember hearing it, but somehow I've always known that Dad bought me my first football for my fourth birthday."

"When did it start to go wrong, Andy? That young couple and their little boy look like they don't have a worry in the world. I'd bet on their success."

Andy shrugged. "I don't know. When I was a kid, he was just a happy redneck, working hard all week, going out with his buddies on Friday night, and sleeping till noon on Saturday. But gradually, the drinking started taking over, and he started losing jobs over it. And when that started happening, he turned into a mean drunk. Then one night in my junior year, he backhanded my mother to the floor, and I literally threw him out that front door. I was bigger than him by then. Then I locked the door and called the sheriff. The last sight I had of my dad from that night to the night I came home to find him here in the house was watching from the window as Ben Apodaca put the cuffs on him and put him in the back of his patrol car."

"Wow. That's a huge thing for a high school kid to have to do."

"Well, now you know why we weren't exactly close." Andy flipped through the rest of the pages of the scrapbook. "See, Dad isn't in most of the later pictures, and since Mom was the one taking the pictures, most of what you have here is me. Me in my football uniform, me in my baseball uniform, me ready for church on Easter morning. It got so I'd cut and run every time she reached for the camera." He closed the scrapbook and reached for the other one he had brought with him from the bedroom. Flipping it open, he frowned at the first page. "I don't think I've seen these. Someone must have taken these and given them to Mom. They look like they were taken from the next county."

"What are they?"

"Football pictures. See that tiny little speck there? That's me."

Jess looked closer. "How do you know?"

"I just do. I recognize the play formation, and if you look real close, you can see my number, 14." He turned another page and shook his head. "I don't know why Mom even kept these. They're terrible." He flipped a few more pages and stopped. The uniforms had changed and the pictures looked like they had been taken inside a much larger stadium. "This is the University of Arizona. See, that's me there."

Andy scowled a little and turned page after page without saying a word. The snapshots of college football games gave way to clippings and articles. "Andy Ryan drafted by the Denver Broncos," "Andy Ryan throws winning touchdown pass late in the fourth quarter," and on the last page, looking as if it had been torn from a magazine, "Glory Days 2.0? Former Denver Bronco Andy Ryan returns to Last Chance, New Mexico, to coach his own once-renowned high school football team."

Andy bent his head over the battered scrapbook, and as the first tears he'd shed in thirteen years dropped on the pages, he felt Jess's hand steal across his back and gently hold his shoulder.

# 21

"They're ready for you, Coach." At Andy's distracted nod, Kev turned to go, but he hesitated in the doorway. "I was sorry to hear about your dad. I didn't even know he was in town."

"Not too many people did, Kev. He wasn't here long, and he was pretty sick when he got here."

"You know, it would have been okay if you had taken some time off. Everyone would have understood, and I could have handled practice just fine."

"I have no doubt that you could. And if I had needed some time off, I would have turned the team over to you without a second thought, but I think what I needed most was to be here. I'd have gone nuts if I'd stayed home." Andy got up and slapped Kev on the shoulder. "Let's go. I have some things I want to say to the team before they head out to the field."

They crossed the short hall to the locker room where the team, in practice uniforms, sprawled on benches, did stretches on the floor, and leaned against the lockers as they waited.

"Guys, I have just a few things I want to go over with you. First of all, you may have noticed a whole lot of commotion about homecoming next week. You can't walk five feet without running into posters and banners and ticket sales booths and tables where you can order your mums. Anyone in here nominated for homecoming king?"

Zach Ellis and a couple others raised their hands.

"Why didn't I guess?" Andy shook his head while laughter rippled through the locker room. "Well, good luck to all of you, but what I want to drill into your heads is that all that extra stuff stays out there. The only event of the entire weekend, the *only* event—and that goes for everything from the pep rally, to the bonfire, to the dance—that concerns us takes place at 1:30 Saturday afternoon. And what's that?"

"The game," a few disjointed voices called out.

"The what?"

"The game!" Everyone spoke in unison this time.

"The *what*?"

"THE GAME!" The answer came in a roar.

"And don't you forget it either. Nothing matters but how you play that game. Not the fans, not the homecoming court, not even your girl sitting up there in the stands thinking what a hero you are. Got it?" Andy waited.

"GOT IT!"

"All right, and if that's not enough for you to play the best game you've ever played, you should know that a scout from the University of Arizona will be at the game."

There was silence for a few seconds, then, "Seriously, Coach?"

"Yes, I'm serious. I knew him when I went to U of A, and I let him know that I thought we had a lot of talent here in Last Chance. The timing of our one Saturday game works for us because he has some players he's checking out in Las Cruces Friday night. He'll stop by here on his way back to Tucson. Okay, that's homecoming, but before we get there, we have a game to play this Friday, and it's going to be a tough one; we can't let up a second. So hit the field—we have a lot of work to do, and the sun goes down earlier every day. Hustle!"

As the team ran out onto the field and Andy and Kev brought up the rear, Kev jerked his chin toward Gabe. "I see Quintana suited up."

"Yep. His doctor gave him the all clear. I don't think we'll play him much Friday, though. No need to rush things."

"I've got to admit I was wrong about him last summer when practice started. He just seemed too small and way too busy with other stuff to make much of a difference. Do you remember him skating into practice at the very last second and then sticking his little brothers and sisters up in the stands so he could watch 'em and take practice at the same time? And then he was always the first one gone after practice so he could get to his job. That's crazy."

Andy watched Gabe a minute. "Yeah, crazy pretty much describes everything he was trying to do, all right."

"So, do you think he has a shot at U of A? He has so much going for him. There's no one who can outrun him, and he slides through the defense like a hot knife through butter. But some of those guys weigh more'n twice what he does, and it will only get worse once he hits college. He could be out of commission for good the first game."

"If he plays like he's played all year, and I have no doubt that he will, they can't help but notice him, but I think a football scholarship is a long shot for the very reasons you mention. I'm not sure that's what he's looking for, anyway."

"Hey, Coach." Zach Ellis broke away from practice and trotted over. "Could I talk to you? Maybe later after practice?"

"Sure. I'll be in my office." Zach trotted off again, and Andy turned to his assistant. "Take over, would you? Let them go about an hour; split the time between offense-defense drills and conditioning drills. I have to take care of some things inside."

As Andy headed back to the athletic building, he heard Kev's whistle and "Listen up!" Kev knew what he was doing. He'd make a good head coach one day.

He tried hard to concentrate on the pile of papers and files on his desk, but his mind kept drifting away. Finally he gave up and, pushing them aside, leaned back in his chair and clasped his hands behind his head. Who knew that his dad, who he hadn't given ten minutes thought to for who knows how long, could get such a massive grip on his life just by moving in for a week or two, trying to show Andy that he loved him, and then dying on his living room floor? Andy's mom had cried when he called her, mostly for those good years that they couldn't hang on to, and even Aunt Barb's voice was gentle and sad as she said she prayed Tim finally had peace. What was left of the life Andy's dad had lived? An old pickup that Andy would probably give to Manny Baca over at Otero Gas and Oil for parts and a few clothes that had seen their day long before Tim Ryan wore them back into Last Chance. And of course there was the scrapbook.

The scrapbook. All those years when, as far as Andy knew, his dad had forgotten he even had a family, Tim Ryan had followed him from Last Chance to Tucson to Denver, carefully documenting a career he could only watch from a distance.

Andy squeezed his eyes shut tight for a minute until the burning stopped. *Dang, Dad. You could have let me know. Just one time. Maybe things could have been different.*

He opened his eyes and blew out a gusty sigh as he leaned forward and grabbed his roster and a highlighter pen. *Or not, but we'll never know now, will we, Dad?*

The names on the roster could have been written in Chinese for all the sense they made, and Andy pushed the document away again. "I've got to get out of here."

Glancing at the school clock that hung on the wall of his office, Andy pulled his phone out of his pocket. Only briefly did his finger hover over Jess's number. She had been so warm and concerned last night while he cried like a baby, and she'd stayed with him long past midnight until he was ready to be alone, but that was just Jess being the only doctor she knew how to be. *Face it, Ryan, you burned that bridge when you decided that you and football were a package deal. Move on.*

He dialed another number. "Ray? Hi, it's Andy. Hey, I know it's last minute, but do you think you could go grab a burger or something with me? I just need to get away for a while."

"Hey, Andy. You've been on my mind all day." Ray sounded pleased to hear from him. "I was just going to call to see how you're doing. You want to come over here? Gran always has enough to feed the county."

"Um, well . . ." Andy's voice trailed away. "Another time, maybe? I'm not real good company right now. That's why I called you."

"Got it." Ray's voice was warm with compassion. "Sure. I'd love to go for a burger with you. I'll just tell Lainie and Gran. But you know when I tell Gran you said 'another time,' she's going to set a date, right? Like tomorrow?"

Andy felt the first smile since yesterday touch his face. Yeah, that sounded like Ray's gran, all right. "Tomorrow I should be able to manage that. Thank her for me."

"Great. So I'll see you, when? Would you be ready in an hour if I came by to pick you up?"

"An hour would do it. I'm still at school."

Andy hung up and leaned back in his chair. Ray was the only one, other than his mom, who knew all there was to know about the volatile years with his dad. Andy could talk or not, and it would be okay with Ray.

"Coach?" Zach Ellis stood in his doorway. "Do you have a minute?"

"Sure, come on in. Have a seat." Andy shoved his papers together and stacked them on one side of his desk; they were going to have to wait. He couldn't get them to make sense, anyway. "What's up?"

"Do you mind if I close the door?"

"Suit yourself."

Andy watched Zach close the door and come take the chair in front of his desk. "Got a secret?"

"No, it's not that." Zach cleared his throat and shifted in his chair. "I wanted to ask you about this scout who's coming next Saturday. Do you know him?"

"Yes, as a matter of fact I do. Dave Williams and I played together at U of A. After graduation, he stayed on and went to work for the football program. He's been scouting for them for at least five years and really knows his stuff. Why? What do you want to know?"

"Seriously, Coach, do you think I have a shot? Seriously?"

"You know, if you had asked me that question when you first came out for football last summer, I would have said about as much as a snowball in a furnace. I could tell you'd been a big shot last year and you thought you had it all coming to you on a silver platter. If I could have figured out a way to send you packing, I'd have done it."

Zach ducked his head. "Yeah, I was a real jerk. Everyone in town was all crazy because Andy Ryan was coming back. It was all anyone could talk about, including my dad. I think I was trying to show that I didn't need to be impressed; I was good too. I see how stupid that was now. Thanks for not kicking my tail out of here."

"Well, something happened, Zach. I'm not sure what you did, but it sure worked. I wouldn't have wasted a phone call on that kid I met last summer, but I want Dave Williams to watch you play. If you go all out and give us the game I've seen you play, I know he'll be impressed."

"Thanks. I'll sure give it everything I've got." Zach looked at the floor a moment before looking back at Andy. "There's one thing, though. Could you not let my dad know?"

"Why wouldn't you want your dad to know? He's your biggest fan."

"That's just it. He'd get so nervous, he'd drive me crazy too. Then he'd hunt down Dave Williams like a dog at the game and try to sit with him and all to make sure he didn't miss anything. Ol' Dave'd probably leave before halftime just to get away from him."

"Think you're being a little hard on him? After all, he is your dad. He wants everything for you." Andy folded his arms and leaned back in his chair. He hadn't found his encounters with Rob Ellis particularly to his liking either, but he was Zach's dad, and he deserved better than he was getting. "Here's the thing. I can promise that I won't tell your dad that a scout from U of A is going to be here for the homecoming game, but don't forget, I just told the whole team, and they might well tell *their* dads. So it's not a secret, and he'd probably rather hear it from you than anyone else."

Zach sighed. "Yeah, you're right. Well, thanks again, Coach. It's really awesome what you did."

"You're welcome, Zach." Andy got to his feet. "Just keep doing what you've been doing, and you'll be fine. Oh, and I do have one more piece of advice. Until ol' Dave invites you to do otherwise, I'd call him Mr. Williams."

"Marta, come in and have a seat." Jess sat down behind her desk and kicked off her shoes. "How do you rate your first day?"

"Pretty good, I think. I didn't have any problems. Eva showed me where everything was. I'm familiar with the billing and scheduling programs you use, but I'll have to practice to get really good at them. Altogether, a good first day. How do you think it went?"

"Great. I couldn't be more pleased. I think we're going to be quite a team."

Eva stuck her head in. "Since we don't have any more patients, is it okay if I close up and go home?"

"Come in. Pull up a chair. We were just talking about how Marta's first day went. Put your two cents in."

Eva perched on the edge of her chair as if she were waiting for a starting gun to sound so she could bolt. "I think everything went just like I told you it would. Marta knows what she's doing, and it's not like you have a thousand patients or anything."

Marta reached over and put her hand on Eva's arm. "Eva, I think your mother would be surprised to hear you talk like that to your employer. What do you think?"

"She wouldn't see anything wrong with the way I talk." Eva pulled her arm out of Marta's reach.

"Well, you might want to think about that a little bit." Marta's smile was warm, and Jess saw Eva's scowl soften and a tiny smile tug at the corner of her mouth in response.

"I'll bet you're wondering when you can go back to Dr. Benavides's office." Jess cocked an eyebrow.

"Tomorrow? She really doesn't need me anymore. Ask her."

"I'll tell you what. Come in tomorrow morning, and if all goes well, you can leave after lunch. How would that be?"

"And then I'm done here?"

Jess laughed. "Yes! You're done! My goodness, Eva, if I ever need to have my ego built up, remind me to go somewhere else."

"I'm sorry." Eva relaxed a little. "You really have been good to work for, and if you were in San Ramon all the time, I'd really like to work for you. I just don't like Last Chance, that's all."

"Well, thank you. I guess I can't ask for more than that—except that I want you to come in tomorrow morning and stay till after lunch."

"Okay." Eva seemed resigned to the injustice being inflicted on her. "Can I close up now and leave?"

"Close away. In fact, why don't you go with her, Marta, and make sure you're comfortable with the procedure?"

They left, and Jess pulled out her phone to check for messages. There were several, but nothing that needed immediate attention, and nothing from Andy. She stretched her legs out under her desk and wiggled her toes. And why would there be? Yes, he had turned to her when his dad died, but just because he needed a shoulder then didn't mean he had changed his mind. He had been more than clear about the way things stood between them.

Marta returned after seeing Eva out. "Is there anything more?"

"No, go on home, and I'll see you in the morning. Oh, wait, you'll need a key." Jess opened her desk drawer, and there in the corner, just where she'd left it, was the plain white envelope with the list of child psychologists she had prepared for Sue Anderson. She handed Marta the key and held up the envelope. "Do you know Sue Anderson?"

"Of course. My Marie plays with her Emma sometimes."

"Well, someday she might come in and ask for an envelope I have for her. She hasn't yet, but you never know, someday she might. This is the envelope. As you can see, there's nothing written on it and I keep it right here." Jess tapped the spot in her top drawer where the envelope rested. "If I'm not here, would you give to her?"

"Certainly. So I guess I'll see you tomorrow?

"Tomorrow. I'll bring something for lunch so we can say good-bye properly. Eva was absolutely right that you can manage just fine without her, but I couldn't just let her waltz away without a proper sendoff. Even if it does mean she has to spend an extra morning in Last Chance."

"Well, good night, then." Marta picked up her coat as she headed down the hall to the front office, turning out lights as she went.

"So, where are we going?" Ray glanced over at Andy before pulling out of the parking lot of Last Chance High.

"Think you could pick something? I'm not sure I could come up with my name if someone asked real fast." Andy felt the knot between his shoulders ease a bit. Calling Ray had been a good choice.

"Well, it's the Dip 'n' Dine or San Ramon, unless you want to go way out of town."

"Not the Dip 'n' Dine, that's for sure. I'm looking for someplace I can just be."

"What about El Guapo in San Ramon? The food's good, and there shouldn't be much of a crowd on a Monday night."

"Perfect."

As Ray headed north and Main Street became the Last Chance Highway at the edge of town, a heavy sadness settled on Andy's shoulders and crushed the air from his lungs.

"Man, that was a big sigh. You okay?"

Andy was silent for a long moment before he spoke. "I was remembering yesterday when I drove up this highway to the hospital and back home again. It just hit me all of a sudden, the way I felt, I mean. You know, I've driven this road must be a thousand times or more, and I wonder if from now on, all I'll remember when I'm on this road is driving to the hospital where I knew they were going to tell me that my dad had died."

Ray didn't say anything for a long while. "So what did you used to think about when you drove up this way?"

"Oh, a bunch of different things—riding a school bus with you and the rest of the team on our way to a game when we were in high school, heading out with my truck all packed to take the I-10 into Tucson for college, things like that."

"Yeah, I know what you mean. Me too. We wore a track in this highway, all right."

"Yeah, those were good days. There was that sense of freedom that you feel when you hit the open road. I'd hate to think that was gone for good."

"No, those memories are still yours. As you said, you've been up this road a thousand times. Yesterday was just one of them. It's gonna take some time, but one day it'll be a memory with all the others. Trust me. When my dad was in that nursing home after his stroke, I drove up to see him every morning. And this road still triggers memories, but now they're memories of him, not his stroke. It'll be the same for you." Ray looked over at Andy. "And I'll bet you'll be surprised at how many of those memories are good."

Andy nodded, although Ray had returned his attention to the road ahead. "I hope you're right."

"I'm right. You'll see." Ray leaned over and turned up the radio.

As the soft crooning of an old Eddy Arnold song filled the cab, Andy felt a wave of peace wash over him. Ray was a good man and a good friend, and Andy was glad he had called him. But all things considered, he still wished he hadn't messed things up with Jess. He would have liked to be with her tonight.

# 22

All of Last Chance seemed to be humming with anticipation as homecoming weekend approached. Black and gold was everywhere. Rita had officially proclaimed the Saturday of the game "Puma Pride Saturday," although how exactly that was to be realized was still unclear. Two pretty girls in black-and-gold cheerleader uniforms had even appeared in Jess's office soliciting her support for the big day. For a sum, she could have a congratulatory message printed in the program, and her choice of "Go Pumas," "Get 'em, Pumas," or "Pumas Forever" stenciled on her front window. They even promised to come back and wash the window by Monday afternoon. What could she say? She chose "Get 'em, Pumas," even springing for the optional snarling puma face stenciled under the slogan. The only person she hadn't seen was Andy.

She had seen him a time or two in the last two weeks, but it was only briefly and in passing. Perhaps he was completely occupied with his team, or maybe he was feeling his father's loss more than he thought he would. Or, though she hated to consider this possibility, maybe the things she had said about football had just cut too deep and caused too much damage. At any rate, taking her to any homecoming event had not been mentioned again. Lainie and Ray had invited her to go to the bonfire with them, but even though she was beginning to realize how much she had been looking forward to going with Andy, tagging along like a third wheel with Lainie and Ray was decidedly not an option.

Friday evening, when she would have been getting ready for the bonfire, Jess was padding barefooted around her kitchen in yoga pants and her Beat Stanford T-shirt, looking for something to eat and feeling very sorry for herself. Heading back to her living room with a bowl of cold pasta, Jess stopped as she passed the front window. That was Andy's truck, and it was pulling up to her curb, and while she was considering whether to run for her room to clean up some, or stash her pasta back in the kitchen, or just stand there wondering what was going on, he got out and walked to her front door holding a large plastic box at his side the way he'd carry a football.

"What are you doing here?" Jess opened the door before he could knock. She couldn't help admiring the effect Andy presented standing on her porch in dark jeans and a white shirt with its collar peeking from a black sweatshirt adorned with a gold snarling puma and the words "LCHS Football" embroidered over the heart. Even if it did make her feel even sloppier than she did before.

"I'm here to pick you up. The bonfire starts when it gets dark, remember?"

"The bonfire? But we broke that off, don't you remember?"

He considered. "Nope. Can't say I do. All I remember is you saying you'd go to all the homecoming events with me, and so I've come to fetch you to the bonfire."

Jess stared at him. Was he serious? He could say the most outrageous things with an absolutely straight face. But turning up to take her on a date she had very clearly broken was a stretch, even for him. Finally, he broke the silence.

"Look. I know we got off to a bad start." He stopped and blew out a sigh before starting over. "No, actually, we got off to a really good start. Things just got bad in the middle there, and I take all the blame. You are an amazing, caring, wonderful woman, and I'm so glad you came to Last Chance. And despite everything I claimed, I guess I was kind of bugged that you weren't impressed by me. And that's really hard for me to admit. So can we go back to the beginning? Would you be my homecoming date?"

She just looked up at him for a moment before her smile broke through. "I'd love to go to homecoming with you."

"Then here." He handed her a clear plastic corsage box in which a gold chrysanthemum nestled in a mass of curling black ribbon. It had a black "LC" made of pipe cleaner in the center, and it had to have been the size of a salad plate.

"What's this?" She carefully opened the shell and sniffed at the flower.

"It's a corsage, of course, and a staple of homecomings everywhere. I brought it to you tonight because tomorrow I won't see you until after the game."

"Pretty sure of yourself, weren't you?"

"What can I say? I had to be confident. If you didn't say yes, I was going to look like the biggest fool in Last Chance, getting all dressed up and turning up with my flower." He grinned. "You want me to help you pin it on? With that gold Beat Stanford on your shirt, it ought to go pretty good."

"I'm not wearing this shirt anywhere." Jess backed away. "What are you thinking?"

"No? Well, you'd better go change then. We want to get there well before it gets dark."

Jess hesitated. She had agreed to go to the bonfire, yes, but that didn't mean she was going to jump through hoops to do it. If he could turn up at the last minute that sure that she'd go with him, he could just cool his heels until she was good and ready to go. She opened her mouth to tell him so, but for once an impulsive side she didn't even know she had told the do-it-my-way side to sit down and shut up. She handed the corsage back to Andy.

"Give me five minutes. I'll be right back."

Andy was waiting where she left him when she came back.

"Is this okay?" Jess was wearing black flats, black slacks, and a soft, black V-necked sweater. "I've never been to a bonfire."

He stood back for a better look and smiled as he handed her the corsage again. "You look amazing. I'll be the most envied guy there."

"I wear this? Like on my coat or something?"

"That's the idea. Except at the dance. There you wear it on your dress, of course."

"Oh, the dance. I forgot about the dance. So I wear it on my dress too? Well, thank you." Jess tried to sound enthusiastic. "You know, I don't think I've ever seen a corsage quite this big."

"Oh, this one is small, comparatively speaking. There are places where, what with streamers and other stuff, the corsage pretty much takes over the whole girl. They look like walking Rose Bowl Parade floats."

Jess laughed out loud. "I love it. Who knew so much was going on outside the lab? So I wear it tonight?"

"No, just at the game and the dance. I was just kidding about pinning it to your T-shirt."

"Okay, then I'll go put this in the refrigerator so it stays fresh. Gotta say, though, you sure seem to know a whole lot about this process."

"This isn't my first homecoming, you know." Andy followed her into the kitchen. "I've bought my share of mums."

"I'll just bet you have." Jess had to move some things around in her refrigerator to make room for the enormous box.

"I was even homecoming king."

"Wow!"

"Twice."

"Do they even do that? I mean, let you run for king after you've already won once?" Jess picked up a gold cashmere scarf she had brought with her from her bedroom and knotted it around her throat.

"I didn't run. They wrote me in. It was the first time it had ever happened, and they changed the rules after that: no write-in vote for a former homecoming king or queen will be counted."

"And you caused the rule change? There is just no end to your accomplishments, is there?"

"I'm telling you, you don't even know the half of it."

Jess laughed again and took a black pea coat from her closet. "I think we should go now. If your head gets any bigger, it's not going to fit through the door."

Andy took the coat from her and held it while she slipped her arms into the sleeves, and when she turned around and smiled up at him, the bantering tone completely disappeared from his voice. "You do look amazing." His hand barely brushed against her face as he touched her hair. "You will be, hands down, the most beautiful woman at the bonfire. You'd be the most beautiful woman anywhere we went." He bent down and brushed her lips with a light kiss.

"Okay, be honest." Jess looked up at him, wondering that she felt so unsettled by so gentle a kiss. "What were you thinking when you came by tonight? Did you really forget? Were you winging it? What?"

He opened the door and she walked out before him. "Not really winging it. Just hoping a bluff would work. I remembered on some level that you said you weren't going to come with me, but it wasn't till today that I realized I had never straightened things out with you, so I just decided to proceed as if I had. And just so you'll feel better? I did not know until you told me whether my bluff had a chance."

"Well, now you know." She locked her door and took his arm as they walked to his truck at the curb. "And that was even before I knew you were the only two-term homecoming king in the history of Last Chance High."

The first thing Jess noticed when she got out of the truck Andy parked in a vacant field behind the high school was the aroma of frying onions. The second was all the people. She had thought this a high school event, but clearly it was much more. It was truly Last Chance coming home. Young couples pushing strollers, older folks holding hands as they strolled through the early evening, families more or less keeping track of their kids as they stopped to talk to friends, knowing that wherever their kids wound up and whatever they did, they were in sight of someone who knew them well. And everywhere she looked were the letterman's jackets. The oldest one she saw had a '57 on the sleeve and was worn by a wiry man with a shock of white hair munching on a cupcake, and the newest, with shiny, unscuffed leather sleeves, were on members of this year's team.

"Where's your jacket?" Jess cocked her head and looked up at him. "I think you're about the only guy here without one."

"At home. I don't wear it much anymore, I guess." Andy shrugged. "I played on some great teams here at Last Chance, but it's the playing I like to think about, and the guys who played with me. I don't need to wear the trophy."

Jess looked around. "I think you're a minority of one."

"Maybe." Andy slipped an arm around her shoulders as they made their way through the crowd. "And if I hadn't had the opportunity to play beyond high school, I'd probably never take the jacket off. When they talk about the Glory Days, it's a lot more than winning all those games. It's a time in your life when you're young and the world is in your hand. Putting that jacket on gives you back a little of that feeling, even if it's only for a night."

"Don't you think that's a little sad? Living in the past like that?"

"Nah. They're not living in the past. Look at them." He pointed to a couple men who, judging from the numbers on their sleeves, were probably in their mid-thirties, laughing and talking. One rested his hand on the shoulder of a boy leaning against him. "They've got families, jobs, lives to live. They might not even live in Last Chance anymore. But at homecoming, they're here remembering. And there's nothing wrong with that."

"I guess not. It's just a different way of looking at things than I'm used to. I've always had to make sure I was ready for what came next. I can't think of one thing in my past that I wish I could go relive. It was hard to get here, and I'm just glad I made it."

"You have every right to be, but you know, that's what makes *me* sad. Thinking of all you've missed working toward your future. This is your very first homecoming, for crying out loud. And you just watched your first football game. That's just depressing."

Jess knew Andy was teasing her—sort of—but his comment put her a little out of sorts anyway. Truth be told, she was much more accustomed to being admired for her life choices than pitied. She walked in silence next to Andy until he gave her shoulders a little shake.

"Come on. I know how hard you've worked, and the sacrifices you had to make to get where you are, but admit it. Isn't your life a little richer now that you've enlarged it? Look around! These folks are having a great time, and be honest, aren't you having a great time too?"

Jess did look around, and to be honest, she *was* having a great time, but she didn't particularly feel like telling Andy he was right, so she shrugged. "Maybe."

He laughed. "You are something else, you know that? But I know what will fix you right up."

"Oh, what's that?"

"A foot-long hot dog."

"A what?" That was the last thing Jess expected to hear. "Why would I want that?"

"Because they're great, that's why, and because the Boosters sell them to support the team, and because that's what you eat at the bonfire. Doesn't the smell of those onions just make your mouth water?"

"Um, not so much."

"Well, come on anyway. There's a whole row of food booths out behind the school, and every club and organization in the whole school has one going, except those running the bouncy house or the pony rides. We're bound to find something you like, and besides, it's your civic duty to support your high school. This is everyone's big fund-raiser of the year."

"Since you put it that way, maybe I should see what they've got. What about salads? Do you think I might find a nice fresh salad?"

"Probably not, but I bet I could score you a funnel cake."

"Practically the same thing."

The walk they took across campus was slow and interrupted often by people who had seen Andy play at Last Chance High years ago and wanted to shake his hand, or who had seen him coach and had observations or even advice that they wanted to share. Andy stopped to speak to each as if they were the one person he had hoped to run into, always drawing Jess into the conversation and introducing her to whoever had stopped them. And when they parted, it was always in the same manner: a handshake, a slap on the shoulder, and a question. "So, are we gonna take 'em tomorrow, Coach?"

Andy always responded the same way. "That's the plan. You going to be there to support the team?"

"Wouldn't miss it." And with a wave of the hand and a nod to Jess, another fan of Last Chance football slipped away in the crowd.

"You know, I'm beginning to understand how you managed to be elected homecoming king twice." Jess bumped him with her shoulder as he took her hand. "I bet if they hadn't implemented that term limit rule, you could get it today."

"And you don't think *that* would be sad?" Andy's eyebrow rose as he looked down at her.

Jess laughed. "Maybe just a little. But everyone seems genuinely glad to see you, and when you introduce me and tell them I'm the new doctor, well, they seem glad to see me too. Rita does the exact same thing, and they get this panicky look on their face, like they're afraid she's going to break their leg or something to make sure I have some patients."

"Speaking of whom, mayor incoming at 2:00."

"There you are, Andy. Evening, Jess." Rita tossed a quick greeting and smile Jess's way before focusing her attention on the new coach. "I've been looking for you. I might need for you to talk to someone here in a little bit. Do you have your phone with you, in case I can't find you?"

"Okay, Rita, what's up?" Andy cocked his head. "I know for a fact that this bonfire is a Last Chance High event. Always has been. So who is it that I might have to talk to? And why do I need to talk to them?"

"Oh, well, I contacted a few sports editors—Albuquerque, Las Cruces, and Tucson, of course, since you played there—and told them about homecoming and the fact this is your first homecoming since you came home to Last Chance. I thought it would make a good story, and they seemed to think so too. None of them promised, but they did say they'd see what they could do about getting someone down here to cover it. And I need to find you if they do show up."

Andy opened his mouth and closed it again. "Sure, Rita. I've got my phone on me. Just give me a call."

Rita gave one sharp nod. "Good. I'm going to go wait by the driveway so I can see them when they get here."

Jess watched her head out at a brisk pace. "Do you think the editors will show up?"

"I doubt it. That's a long way to come to interview a high school football coach, especially of a school this size. But that's Rita, bless her, and why I didn't argue with her. She truly believes that Last Chance is the best-kept secret in New Mexico, and all it needs is a little more publicity."

"I have to say I agree with her, though maybe not that it needs more publicity. I happen to think it's a pretty special place just the way it is, and I'm so glad that it's my home now."

"Me too." Andy brushed away a curl that had found its way to her cheek.

"Andy! I haven't seen you since you got home. Glad you're back." A tall man in a blazer, an open-necked shirt and possibly the only salon-styled haircut Jess had seen on a man since she arrived in Last Chance grabbed Andy's shoulder and extended his hand.

"Greg Anderson!" Andy looked truly pleased to see him. "And Sue! This must be your little girl?"

His forehead furrowed as he looked down, because Emma was sobbing inconsolably.

Greg rolled his eyes, and his smile grew tight. "Yes, this is Emma. Sorry about the hysterics, but she put too much catsup on her hot dog, and big surprise, it dripped all over her dress. Come on, Emma, pull it together. Everyone's looking at you. Just don't be so careless next time."

Emma gasped for breath through her sobs. "I'm sorry. I'm trying. I just can't stop."

Sue Anderson pulled her daughter to her and put her arm around Emma's shoulder. Emma still sobbed. "Greg, I think I need to take Emma home, or at least out to the car for a while so she can calm down."

"All right." Greg was visibly annoyed as he looked from his wife to his weeping daughter, and Jess could tell there was so much more he'd like to say. "Just call me when you decide what you're going to do."

"Okay, I will." Sue wore a determined smile as she turned to Andy and Jess. "Andy, I can't tell you how nice it was seeing you this evening. All the best on the game tomorrow. And Dr. MacLeod, nice seeing you too. I'm sure we'll see each other again." She held Jess's gaze a long moment, and Jess mentally pumped a fist. *Yes! Hang in there, Emma. Help is on the way!*

Greg turned back to Andy and Jess with a short laugh after they left. "I'm sorry you got treated to that display. My law practice keeps me in Tucson during the week, and with only females in the house at home, I have a feeling it's all drama, all the time."

Jess didn't say anything, but Andy still looked concerned. "Are you sure she's okay?"

"Oh, I'm sure she'll be fine. Most of the time, Emma's a perfect little princess, but when the slightest thing does go wrong, this is what I deal with." His smile broadened but still looked a little forced to Jess as he reached for Andy's hand again. "Andy, it was great to see you again. So glad you're back in town. Sometime when I'm home, we'll have to get together and relive old times. And nice meeting you too . . ."

"Jess." She gave her name as she took the hand he offered. "Thank you."

Greg adjusted the lapels of his blazer, patted his hair, and moved off. Andy turned back to Jess. "That was one unhappy little girl! Did spilling something on your dress make you that upset when you were little?"

"Um, short answer? No. Of course, that would have entailed me actually wearing a dress, and that didn't happen very often—and never around catsup."

"Come on." Andy put his arm around her shoulders and looked at the sky. "It's nearly dark, and they'll be lighting the bonfire soon. We need to get something to eat. If anyone tries to stop us, we'll just link arms and bowl them over. Agreed?"

"Agreed."

They walked around the corner of the school building and found the food booths. Some, like the Boosters' hot dog stand, looked nearly professional; others, like the German Club bake sale, were nothing more than two card tables pushed together, covered with a length of butcher paper, and stacked with cookies, cupcakes, and brownies.

"This is more like it." Andy looked around in satisfaction. "Wait right here. I'll be right back."

As Jess waited for Andy to return, she looked around. Picnic tables filled the area, most in groups under signs reading "60's," "70's," or "90's." Beyond the tables and beyond the borders of the school property, guarded by a fire truck from the San Ramon Fire Department, rose the mountain of wood and other flotsam and jetsam that would become the bonfire.

"Hey, look who's here." Jess turned to find the Cooley clan—Ray and Lainie, Steven and Kaitlyn with Olivia between them, and Sarah—all coming from the direction of the Boosters' hot dog stand, although only Olivia and Steven had hot dogs.

"Should have known we'd find you here." Steven took a huge bite of his hot dog and had to shift it to the corner of his mouth to continue talking. "I asked Andy if he wanted to come with us, and he gave a pretty evasive answer."

"What's evasive about 'Thanks, but I've got other plans.'" Andy appeared with a funnel cake and handed it to Jess. "Here's your salad."

"Well, you didn't say what your plans were."

"Nope."

"There you go, being evasive again." Steven finished his hot dog in another bite.

"Where's Chris?" The funnel cake, the first Jess had tasted, was really good. It could hold its own against a salad any day.

"Working, of course. The Dip 'n' Dine won't close for another half hour or so. And he didn't really want to come anyway. He said after working for twelve hours, following me around and trying to look interested while I talked to people he'd never met just didn't sound like all that much fun." Sarah grinned. "Who knew?"

Out in the field, a siren sounded once, and people from everywhere began to make their way to the bonfire site.

Ray fell in alongside Andy. "I saw Rob Ellis a little while ago. He told me you had arranged for a scout from U of A to come see Zach play."

"Zach's a good man and an exceptional football player. I'm glad we could work something out. But all I can do is get someone here; the rest is up to him."

"Well, I tell you what, Rob couldn't say enough nice things

about you. He said he was up all night last night putting together a highlight reel of Zach's high school football career. You know he's been filming every game Zach played in since he first put on a uniform."

"Good. I'm sure that'll be helpful."

They arrived at the bonfire site and joined the others who had been gathering there. Steven hoisted Olivia to his shoulders. At first Jess stood at Andy's side, still holding his hand, but as the crowds pressed in, he pulled her around in front of him, one arm around her waist, the other around her shoulders. She leaned against him and felt his breath by her hair.

When someone lit torches and they were buried in the wide base of the pile, Jess could feel the anticipation build around her. As the flames licked their way up through and finally out the top, the crowd seemed to take a deep breath and let it out in a collective sigh.

Jess leaned her head back against Andy's shoulder and, closing her eyes, felt the warmth of his kiss touch her face. Last Chance was a good place to call home, and she was so thankful she was here. She smiled to think of how recently she would have called it a lucky choice, but even now she could hear Elizabeth chiding that luck had nothing to do with it. And Jess finally understood what that meant. She opened her eyes to watch a spark thrown from the flames circle high into the black sky before it finally disappeared.

# Acknowledgments

Many thanks and much love to my daughter, Kate Gordon, for reading over my manuscript with a medical professional's eye to keep me from saying things like, "She blew on her stethoscope to warm it." Doctors don't do that. It spreads germs. Who knew? Also to my husband, Ed, former defensive end for the Alamogordo High Tigers, who answered all my football questions.

**Cathleen Armstrong** lives in Orange County, California, with her husband, Ed, and their corgi. Though she has been in California for many years now, her roots remain deep in New Mexico where she grew up and where much of her family still lives. After she and Ed raised three children, she returned to college and earned a BA in English. Her debut novel, *Welcome to Last Chance*, won the 2009 American Christian Fiction Writers Genesis Award for Women's Fiction. Learn more at www.cathleenarmstrong.com.

Meet

# Cathleen Armstrong

online at

www.cathleenarmstrong.com

AuthorCathleenArmstrong

@cathleen_arm

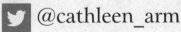

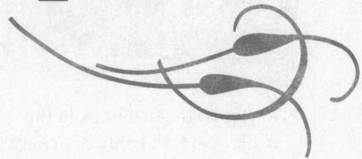

# "A wonderful debut novel."

—*New York Journal of Books*

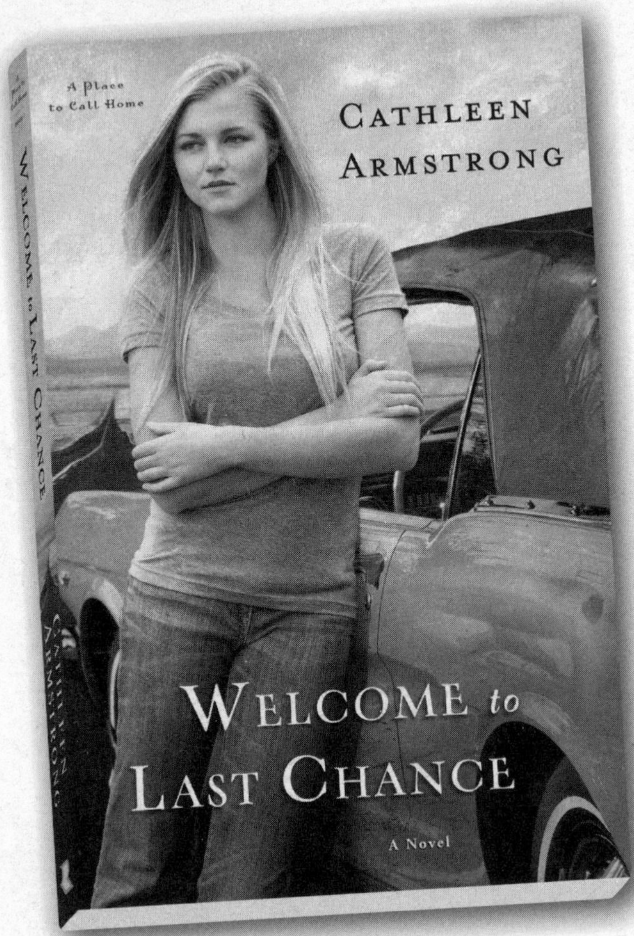


Don't miss the first book in the
A Place to Call Home series!

Revell
*a division of Baker Publishing Group*
www.RevellBooks.com

Available wherever books and ebooks are sold.

"A gentle love story with a cozy feel . . .
[with] well-crafted characters
who feel like old friends."
—*Library Journal*

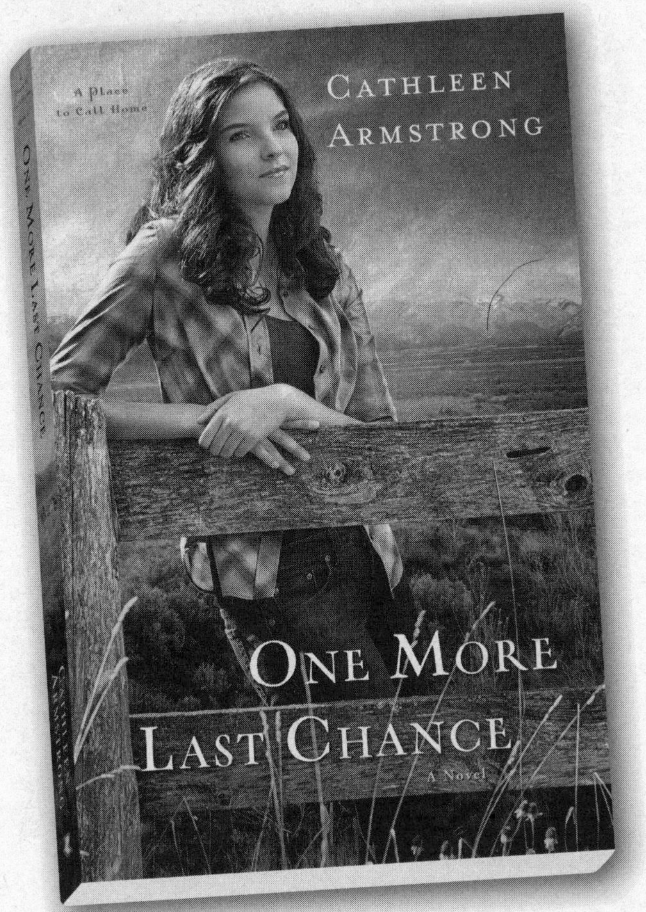


Come home again to Last Chance, New Mexico.

Revell
*a division of Baker Publishing Group*
www.RevellBooks.com

Available wherever books and ebooks are sold.

"Full of adventure, romance, and fun."

—*Library Journal*

Fall in love all over again
with the people of Last Chance.

31901056605639

Revell
*a division of Baker Publishing Group*
www.RevellBooks.com

Available wherever books and ebooks are sold.

42.95

# Psychiatry Mentor

## Your Clerkship & Shelf Exam Companion

SECOND EDITION